BURNING. . .

Lucy tried to bite him again, then felt her hair caught and wrenched painfully backwards, forcing her face up to his. Suddenly his lips closed on hers and his tongue darted around the tip of her own tongue until she found herself responding with a swollen ache in her loins and an urgent need to be fondled, stroked, and pressed even harder against his powerful body.

DESIRE. . .

She hardly knew what was happening to her . . . All she knew was that she didn't want to fight him. . .

Sweet Temptation

CAROLINE STANDISH

ACE BOOKS, NEW YORK

SWEET TEMPTATION
Copyright © 1981 by Lorna Read

An Ace Book
Published by arrangement with Macdonald & Co. (Publishers) Limited

ISBN: 0-441-79124-7

First Ace Printing: September 1982

2 4 6 8 0 9 7 5 3 1

Printed in U.S.A.

Sweet Temptation

CHAPTER ONE

"No . . . *Martin,* not the child, she's just a baby. I don't care what you do to me, but . . . *leave* her, Martin. Oh Martin, *no . . .!*"

Her mother's voice had risen to an agonized scream as a glancing blow from her father's tightly clenched fist caught her on the cheekbone and sent her reeling against the wooden dresser. A sturdy white milk jug teetered and fell, smashing into irregular pieces on the tiled kitchen floor. The moment was frozen forever into Lucy Swift's memory: the blow, the rocking jug, the white explosion on the floor, the sight of her mother on her knees, a crimson mark on her face already turning blue, sobbing as she picked up the sharp shards of pottery, and her father muttering an oath as he swayed unsteadily towards the door.

Looking at him now, hearing him whistle through his teeth as he brushed the bay mare into gleaming splendor with methodical, circular strokes, Lucy could hardly believe that the brutal drunkard and this careful, tender man were one and the same person—her father. Yet her earliest memory was no fantasy. Similar scenes had been repeated time after time during her nineteen years. They had driven her mother, Ann, into premature old age. At thirty-six she was grey-haired and haggard, her body shrunken as if by her efforts to protect herself from her husband's violent words and blows, her face lined and scarred from where he had once, during an exceptional bout of drunkenness, lashed her with a riding whip. Lucy loved her mother with a fervour that had led her, from an early age, to stand up to Martin Swift. Once, at the age of four, she had rained tiny blows on his knees with her childish fists as he sought to knock frail Ann aside, convinced that she was hiding a jug of ale from him. Her hot-blooded defense of her poor, abused mother had often earned her a painful beating, but she knew she also had her father's grudging respect, especially where horses were concerned. Not like her brother, Geoffrey.

As if reading her thoughts, Martin Swift glanced from the fidgeting horse to his daughter.

"Bet Geoffrey wouldn't have made as good a job of it as this, eh?" he inquired, casting an admiring glance at his own handiwork. In the dusty yellow light of the stable, the big mare's hide shone like burnished copper. He didn't expect an answer, but dodged round to the other side of the horse and resumed his hypnotic brush strokes.

Lucy watched him while he worked. At forty years old, in spite of his over-indulgence in ale and spirits, Martin was in his prime, not a tall man, but wiry and strong, with the black hair and blue eyes that betrayed his Irish ancestry although he, and his father before him, had been born in the same tiny Lancashire village where the Swifts still lived. Only his florid, weather-beaten complexion and broken nose bearing its route-map of tiny red veins gave a clue to his outdoor, rough-and-tumble life. Indoors, dressed up, with his body scrubbed clean of the smells of the stable, he could, in a low light, pass for the gentleman he thought himself to be.

Geoffrey was not a bit like his father, reflected Lucy, as she idly chewed on a piece of fresh straw. She missed her brother badly, even though it was three whole years since he left Prebbledale. She had aided his flight and she didn't regret it even though she had, by this risky action, deprived herself of her staunchest supporter and closest confidant, probably for ever. For Geoffrey, dearest, kind, humorous Geoffrey, with his fair curls and poetic nature, was far more like his mother than either Lucy or their sister Helen.

"That mewling little milksop," was his father's usual way of describing him. Born with a deep-seated fear of all large animals, he used to scurry for the nearest hiding place whenever his father came looking for him to take him into the stables and try to invest his son with some of his own horse-lore. Martin Swift was known and respected all over the county and even beyond for his skill in handling, breaking in and training horses. Dukes and earls would send for him and ask his advice before parting with their money for a thoroughbred race horse or a pair of matched carriage horses, knowing that his judgement was sound and unerring.

"No-o-o," he would say slowly, shaking his head as some fine-looking specimen was paraded before him. "Not that one. Weak left hock. 'Twould let ye down over the half-mile." And Lord Highfalutin' would wave the animal away and slip Martin a sovereign for saving him fifty.

The bay mare, Beauty Fayre, stamped a hoof and snorted, breaking Lucy's reverie. Who knew where Geoffrey was now? In the East Indies, maybe, having worked his passage on a trading ship, or even perhaps in the uniform of a naval rating, keeping the look-out while he mentally composed an ode to the heaving sea. Unless he was . . . Lucy couldn't bring herself to consider the worst alternative.

A sound behind her, like the scuffling of a dog in the straw, made her turn her head. One shoulder and half an anxious face were poked round the corner of the cobwebby door-jamb as Ann Swift attempted to catch her daughter's eye without attracting the attention of her husband. Giving an almost imperceptible nod, Lucy took two silent steps backward towards the door and spun quickly round the corner of the building, trying not to catch her skirt on a protruding nail. She had totally forgotten that her sister Helen, with her husband John and twin sons, Toby and Alexander, were paying them a visit that afternoon. Her heart sank at the thought of having to play Auntie to the toddlers, cudgel her brains to think of something to reply to John's barked, banal remarks, and listen to her sister's predictable, boring grumbles about servants, children and the latest London fashions. It was always the same.

"Not married yet, our Lucy?" John would remark in his brusque attempt at a jocular tone. She would wait to see the beads of sweat break out along his forehead as his eyes raked her lasciviously up and down.

"Really, Mother, I just cannot understand how Helen can put up with him. He's a *beast*," Lucy complained to her mother, as she gave last-minute orders to the latest in line of their endless succession of maids, who never stayed long because of Martin Swift's vile temper.

"Shush, girl. He's a good man. She could have done a lot worse," replied her mother, in her quiet, flat voice like a defeated whisper. They'd had this conversation many times before. It was a kind of ritual warm-up to all Helen's visits.

"But she'd *never* have married him, surely, if she hadn't wanted to get away from Father so much," Lucy persisted. "She was only fifteen. Who knows who she might have fallen in love with if only she'd had the chance? She didn't even *know* John Masters, Father fixed it all up. I think it's disgusting—like bringing a stallion to a mare."

"*Lucy!*" Her mother's shocked exclamation held a hint of amusement. She reached out and straightened a roaming lock of Lucy's chestnut hair as the two of them sat side by side on the settle in the window, watching for the arrival of the visitors. How like her father Lucy was, with her straight back, her alert blue eyes, her plump, curving lips and her plain-speaking ways. There was a vividness about Lucy that reminded Ann of her first-ever glimpse of Martin, as he stood in the marketplace of Weynford, her hometown, twenty whole years ago. To her, he had seemed to stand out from his companions as if surrounded by a kind of glow, undetectable to the human eye but nevertheless capable of being picked up by some sixth sense. Even now, in spite of the years of torment and agony she had undergone at his hand, abuse that had caused her ill-health and a permanent nervous trembling, she was still in awe of him, still capable of feeling that same old wonderment whenever he looked at her kindly or gave her one of his special, half-cheeky, half-loving smiles. Whatever he possessed that gave him that unique power over people and animals, Lucy had inherited, and sometimes Ann feared for what Life held in store for her eldest child—particularly now, with Martin so anxious about her unmarried state.

They had discussed it in bed just the previous night.

"Damn that maid!" Martin had expostulated, having sipped at his night-time beverage of warm ale to find it stone cold. "Get rid of her, first thing tomorrow. And what are we going to do about Lucy?"

Ann, used to her husband's abrupt changes of subject, had sighed and withdrawn to the far side of the feather mattress, trying not to incur her husband's further wrath by drawing too many of the coverlets with her.

"Well?" he had snapped, reaching out in the darkness and digging his fingers painfully into her shoulder. "Well? Helen's a year younger and she's got two fine sons already. I'm the laughing stock of the neighborhood, having that strapping lass still on my hands. Why, only yesterday that cur Appleby had the damn' cheek to suggest that maybe nobody would have her because she was soiled goods. Our Lucy! I whipped the blighter to teach him to hold his tongue. Still, an insult's an insult. She's been on our hands long enough, eating our food, taking up room about the place, striding round like a . . . like a great *lad*."

Ann had felt a chuckle inside, knowing full well that Martin did treat his elder daughter almost exactly like a son. She knew, too, that Martin found Lucy a great help with the horses as she had inherited every bit of his own natural talent. Sometimes she wished that Lucy *had* been born a boy, yet her daughter, however strange, was undeniably attractive and it would have been a loss to the male sex if she had been born one of them.

Martin had continued his monologue: "I've seen them looking at her—tradesmen, stable lads, respectable gentlemen. They'd all like to get their hands on her. We could have married her off twenty, thirty times already. If only I hadn't been so soft with her, giving in to her 'No, Father, I won't marry him . . . No, Daddy, I don't like him . . .'

I've had enough. There's a good man I've got in mind for her. None better. She'll marry him and that'll be an end to it, even if I have to take the strap to her."

Somehow Ann, with much nervous clutching and kneading of the bedclothes, had found the breath to whisper, "Who could this be?"

His answer had given her very mixed feelings indeed and caused her to lie awake the best part of the night.

"Old Holy Joe. The Reverend Pritt."

"Here they come!" shrieked Lucy most indecorously as John Masters's coach swept down the lane pulled by a pair of matching greys. Masters was a wealthy grain merchant and Helen, as she stepped from the carriage, was, if not perfectly suited to her middle-aged husband, at least perfectly dressed. The two little boys followed, identically dressed in blue jerkins and knickerbockers, their brown hair combed and twisted neatly into shape.

Binns, the maid, announced them breathlessly at the door: "Mr. and Mrs. Masters and the two Master Masters"—then flushed as if realizing that what she'd said had sounded peculiar.

"Thank you, Binns," said Ann, rising to her feet. "We'll take tea in the drawing-room. And bring some apple cider for the children—*watered,* if you please." Ann was remembering one disastrous previous occasion when the maid before last had failed to water down the cider, resulting in two very dizzy small boys being sick all over the chaise longue.

"Yes, ma'am," said Binns, dropping a brief, awkward curtsy and hastening out of the room as fast as her lumpish country legs could carry her.

"My dear," breathed Ann, embracing Helen, taller than she was, and grazing her cheek on an amber brooch pinned to the shoulder of her daughter's short cape of the most fashionable shade of lavender blue.

Lucy felt her hackles rise as the portly figure of John Masters confronted her and she felt his hot gaze travel up and down her body. The crude sexuality of the man disgusted her. She, who had never kissed a man except in polite greeting, could not conceive of her little sister in the arms of this fat, ugly, lecherous old man, doing all the things you had to do in order to get with child. Lucy's grasp of sexual knowledge was scanty but basic. Living in the country and working with horses as she did, she could hardly have avoided noticing the way they acted at certain times of the year. Her father had always forbidden her to leave the house when a stallion was put to one of his mares. What he didn't know, however, was that Lucy's bedroom was not the stronghold it appeared; an athletic person of either sex could, with a modicum of nimbleness, lower a leg from the windowsill, find a toehold in the crumbling, ivied stone and from there scramble sideways into the old oak tree, from where it was but a short and easy climb to the ground. So, on more than one occasion, Lucy had heard the excited whinnying and snorting of the stallion and seen the mare, hump-backed and docile. Seen, too, the way in which her father and a helper aided the stallion by guiding that huge, terrifying, yet fascinating limb, thick as a man's leg, into the tunnel-like opening of the mare. Watching the frenzied couplings, Lucy had felt hot, breathless, faintly disgusted, yet tingling with strange sensations, much as she felt whenever a man looked at her the way her brother-in-law did.

"I won't ask the usual question," John Masters said by way of greeting.

Lucy was surprised by this change in his usual tactics. Motioning her to sit in one of the two high-backed chairs that stood on either side of the marble fireplace, empty and screened as it was a warm September afternoon, he stood in front of her, swaying to and fro, his fat legs crammed obscenely into his tight, shiny black boots.

"There's no need, is there?" he added, giving her a sly, conspiratorial wink with one corner of a weak, grey, piggy eye.

Lucy sat bolt upright. She took a deep breath, feeling how her tight stays constrained her lungs. "What on earth do you mean, brother John?" she demanded, her words, spoken too loud, cutting across the currents of other people's conversations and stopping them dead. Helen, her mother, her father, even little Toby and Alexander from the privacy of their den beneath a table, were all staring at her, aware of the first rumblings of an emotional storm. Lucy gulped and toyed with a bow on her cream silk dress. She wished she hadn't spoken.

Probably John had only been playing some kind of joke with her. He could not really be privy to some information concerning her future, about which she knew nothing. John Masters's boots creaked as he shifted position uncomfortably.

"Nothing. Um . . . that is . . ." He looked across at Lucy's father beseechingly, and she intercepted his glance.

So there *was* a plan afoot. Of course, she could have taken his remark to mean that there was no need to ask her if she were married yet because she obviously wasn't. But John Masters was a creature of habit, a mortal not blessed with an iota of imagination. He would only have made such a comment, and accompanied it with such a look and a wink, if he knew something which she didn't. After his "There's no need, is there?," there had been a silent, unvoiced "Because it's all been settled."

They were all waiting, her mother brushing crumbs off her lap, her father working his toe into the rug, Helen pretending to straighten her necklace. A muffled giggle from one of the twins broke Lucy's tense trance and gave her back her voice. She directed the full, undiluted power of her iciest blue gaze on her father, who returned it equally coldly.

"Father. If any plans for my future have been made, I think I have a right to know what they are."

"Very well, Lucy, but remember, before you fly into one of your famous tempers—"

Tempers? You're the last person on earth who can

accuse anyone else of having a bad temper, thought Lucy viciously, wishing she were strong enough to pick her father up bodily and shake the truth out of him.

"Remember, I am your father, and head of this household, and as such, my decisions are not to be argued with. You're nineteen years old now, my girl. Nineteen!" He looked triumphantly at everyone in turn and, backed up by their encouraging nods, turned to face Lucy again. "I can't wait for you to choose a suitor for yourself. I don't hold with such liberated notions. Allow a girl to pick for herself and she'll choose some ragamuffin gypsy with a roving eye and no'but two brass farthings to rub together."

"Aye," interjected John Masters approvingly.

His wife glared at him, but Lucy's gaze rested unwaveringly on her father, daring him to be a traitor and bestow her very own birthright of freedom and choice on some man she did not wish to know, and would detest if he were the King himself. *Father,* she willed, trying to project her thoughts behind his eyes and into the farthest recesses of his misguided brain, *Father, I will not be married off. You can't do it. You will not do it.* Her jaw was clenched in a spasm of steely purpose, as she poured her whole being into her gaze. But Martin Swift was untouched by his daughter's silent message.

"I love you, Lucy. I respect you. You are my eldest daughter, my firstborn child, and your mother and I wish to do our very best for you. If you marry the man I have in mind, not only will you live in comfort with a good man, but you will hold a very honorable position in the community, far higher than your mother or I could ever have hoped for. I had no idea that my daughter had been singled out by such an august man as the Reverend Pritt. To be the wife of a man of God, Lucy! When I informed your sister and her husband in the hallway—well, I couldn't keep such a compliment to the family to myself, could I?—they were so pleased for you that . . ."

His voice seemed to be fading into the far distance, like the echo of a stone dropped into a dry well. At the same time, a mist formed in front of Lucy's eyes. She tried to pass her hand in front of her face, on which a cold, clammy perspiration was forming, but her arm was like a lead weight and remained, unmoving, in her lap. Then a great lassitude overcame her and she felt her surroundings dissolve and her chair whirl like a spinning top.

Lucy had never fainted before in her whole life. She came to and found her mother hovering anxiously over her while her sister bathed her forehead in cool water from a basin held by Binns, the young maid.

"Don't you worry 'bout her, ma'am. She be herself right soon enough," said Binns reassuringly, trying to be helpful. Lucy could have embraced her for her honest country forthrightness, but Binns, for all her commonsense, could not smooth the worried furrows from her mother's brow.

"My dear, are you all right? It is very hot today . . . You're not catching a fever, I hope?"

Helen's small, square hand in its cuff of pale blue lace touched Lucy's forehead, then her temples, and finally pulled down the lower lids of her eyes, making Lucy jerk back and blink in alarm.

"The boys had a summer sickness some weeks ago," Helen explained. "They went quite, quite pale under the lids. But there's nothing wrong with you."

"I wish there *was,*" moaned Lucy fervently. "I'd sooner waste away and die than be married to that old . . . *goat!*"

Ann Swift drew a deep breath and bit her lower lip thoughtfully. How she wished her elder daughter were as docile as Helen. She had gone to the altar with John Masters without a murmur and, indeed, the marriage seemed to be working. Helen had her boys and a good allowance and a husband who didn't beat her, even if he did sometimes respond rather over-enthusiastically to attractive members of the opposite sex. At least this philandering tendency kept him from eternally bothering Helen with his attentions. He had done his duty, fathered twin heirs, and now Helen was free to attend to her duties of lady of the house and follower of fashion, something that pleased her far more than her husband's twice-monthly drunken fumblings in her bedroom. Even love-matches couldn't be relied upon to be perfect, as Ann knew to her cost. Yet, for Lucy, that is exactly what she would have wished—the perfect love-match for her beautiful, unruly, head-strong daughter.

"I won't do it," announced Lucy, suddenly and mutinously, waving away Binns's proffered glass of water. "I refuse to allow myself to be incarcerated in that damp prison of a rectory with that revolting, ugly, nasty-minded old man. 'Man of God' indeed! I would never take a young, sensitive child to hear one of our dear vicar's sermons. To hear him ranting about the terrible punishments God has in store for us all if we dare to defy His will or take His holy name in vain makes me think that worshipping the Devil would be the easier option."

"Leave the room, Binns. See how Cook is faring with the roast pork," ordered Ann, terrified lest Lucy's blasphemies be prattled about all over the village.

"Reverend Pritt has a very twisted idea of what God is really like. I think something very terrible must have happened to him in his life to make him turn his good Lord into the kind of enemy he would have us believe God is, someone who isn't kind and just and forgiving at all, but is a wilful tyrant—rather like Father."

Helen clutched her sister's arm in the hope of distracting her from her subject, which was obviously upsetting their mother, who was standing by the window, fanning herself agitatedly. But Lucy was not to be easily deterred.

"I am sorry, Mother," she continued, a softer note creeping into her voice. Lucy loved her mother and the last thing she wanted to do was hurt her, but on the subject of her own life, with her whole future at stake, she felt she had to express her feelings even if it meant coming out with a few home truths. "I know you love Father, still love him in spite of his vile temper and the anguish he's caused all of us. I am his dutiful daughter and have always done my best to obey him, but this is one thing that all the beatings on earth could not force me to do. He can beat me until I'm dead if he likes, but I will *not* be incarcerated with that gospel-twisting, repellent old cadaver Nathaniel Pritt!"

"Oh, Lucy, see sense," put in Helen, stroking her sister's curly hair as if calming one of her toddlers. "He must be about sixty if he's a day. One night with you and he'll probably drop dead of an apoplexy from shock. I bet you he's never touched a woman in his life—"

"And he's certainly not going to touch me!" Lucy exclaimed, brushing aside her sister's hand and swinging her legs off the couch. Her head swam a little as she put her feet to the ground and stood up, but she ignored her lingering weakness. Appalled by the way both her mother and sister were calmly complying with Martin's wishes, as if there were no other possible course of action, Lucy turned to them, appeal in her eyes.

"Can't you see, either of you, can't you understand? I'm of the same blood as you, we're kin— who could be closer? Yet you seem to be made of totally different stuff. Why are you so meek? Why is it that you don't mind having to share a house and your body with an old, fat man whom you don't love?" (to Helen, whose eyes blazed for an instant as Lucy's barb of truth stung home). Then, turning to her mother: "I know you can't stand up to Father. I know that, if you had done, either you'd be dead by now, or he would have turned you out. But you're both trapped—*trapped!*" Her voice was rising on a note of hysteria. The whole room, with its pictures, hangings, heavy, cumbersome furniture and dark-colored floor-coverings seemed to be exuding hostile oppression.

While she had been speaking, she had failed to hear the excited chattering of Toby and Alexander who had been brought back from an interesting tour of the stables by Martin and John and who were, even now, approaching the drawing-room door with their father and grandfather. Martin, his ears as acute as those of the animals he worked with, had heard the sound of his daughter's voice and had noted its excited volubility. He had expected the news of his decision to come as a shock, but he hadn't expected the silly bitch to faint. The sight of his strong, tomboyish daughter collapsing like a pregnant village girl had filled him with disgust, and it was he who had motioned to John to fetch the boys and vacate the room and leave restoring Lucy to her senses to the women of the household.

Martin Swift had one hand on the ornate brass knob of the drawing-room door when he paused and turned to face his son-in-law, one forefinger held to his lips. Far down the hall, the twins were tumbling and sliding on a loose rug while Binns hovered over them to ensure they did not go crashing into a table and upset a vase. He gave John Masters a conspiratorial wink.

All through their outing to the stables, Masters had been playing through a secret fantasy in his head, that of himself alone in a room, with Lucy fainting at his feet. Oh yes, *he* would have revived her all right, with a loosening of her tight-laced gown, to free those sedately confined breasts he admired so much—how different they were to her sister's hard little mounds!—and the warm application of his own throbbing flesh. Lucy never failed to arouse the most ardent male reaction in him. How he would love to have applied his lips to her soft nipples, biting them into nut-like hardness, while his roving hands went searching beneath her petticoats. He licked his lips slowly, feeling a familiar swelling at his groin which he couldn't see beneath his protuberant paunch. He glanced nervously at his father-in-law, to see Martin's face darkening in anger.

Within the room, Lucy was pacing agitatedly up and down. She had to make them *see*. What was wrong with them? Nobody, not even her father, had the right to do this to another human being, to order their life right down to whom they should marry and when. She thought of Reverend Pritt clutching his lectern and rocking back and forth while his congregation's ears were dinned with threats of being visited by plagues even unto the third and fourth generation, his gaunt face grey with stubble, his yellowed teeth spraying the unfortunates in the front pew with holy saliva. She imagined herself spread like a naked sacrifice on a white-sheeted bed surrounded by the mouldering walls and ragged tapestries of the vicarage, with the knobbly, grey, corpse-like body of Nathaniel Pritt kneeling over her, his foetid breath fanning her face, his obscene, maggot-like fingers about to touch her own warm, living flesh.

"No!" she screamed. *"No!* Mother, Helen, you've got to help me! Tell him it's impossible. I don't care that he's the vicar. I don't care about his position in society, I don't want to share it. I'd sooner marry an ostler, a highwayman, *anybody!* But I won't marry that. . . that . . ." Words came to her mind, words she'd heard her father and the grooms use. However, before she could say anything more, the door burst open and in strode her father, his face glowering like a thundercloud.

"Martin!" cried Ann, rushing towards him and catching his elbow in an attempt to halt what she anticipated to be a physical attack on his errant daughter.

"Woman, leave me be," snarled her husband, his face suffused with scarlet. He shook off her restraining hand so violently that Ann lost her balance and fell, dashing her head against the ornately carved leg of a side table.

"Mother—oh, Mother!" wailed Helen, rushing to Ann in a crackle of starched petticoats and kneeling over her prostrate form. "You might have killed her, Father! She's not moving!"

"Serves the cow right. She should know better

by now than to get in my way."

All through this incident Lucy stood unmoving, one hand gripping the high back of the red damask-covered armchair. Her father took two more furious strides towards her, then stopped, and Lucy felt as if her heart had stopped too. How she hated and feared him! Suddenly she was a tiny child again, screaming at him not to hurt her mother. Then she was a young girl being slapped across the face for some minor misdemeanor such as not having bid him a polite enough "good morning." Now, at the age of nineteen, she was almost as tall as him in her high-heeled satin slippers and her will was equally as strong as her father's, if her muscles were not. In many disagreements in the past she had given way, but not on this. It meant far too much to her.

"Well, *madam*," hissed her father, with heavy sarcasm. "So we have a new head of the household, have we? One who sets new rules for herself and all the silly little bints in Christendom?"

Lucy noticed his fists spasmodically clenching and unclenching and steeled herself to expect a blow. Across the room Helen was still kneeling, chafing her mother's temples, and against the tapestry-covered door, a silent observer, John Masters, was nonchalantly leaning, a smug leer on his plump wet lips.

"So Miss High-and-Mighty thinks a vicar isn't good enough for her, is that it? She thinks to stamp her pretty foot and defy her father, who's only a stupid, tyrannical old man? 'Marry an ostler or a highwayman' indeed!"

Lucy's hand flew to her mouth. So he'd over-heard her impassioned, incautious words. There was no escaping a punishment now. Desperately, her eyes flicked round the room, to the door, the windows . . . In her long, full-skirted dress it was impossible to move fast enough to make an escape. Either he—or her brother-in-law—would stretch out a foot and trip her ignominiously, or he would catch at a handful of her dress and tear the delicate fabric. All she wanted to do was ascertain that her mother would recover and then fly out of the room, out of the house, to heaven-knows-where.

Across the room, Ann Swift made a low moan-ing noise and began to stir.

"Thanks be to God!" called Helen, tears stream-ing down her rouged and powdered face. "She's alive!"

For a moment, Martin hovered uncertainly, un-sure as to whether to inspect the damage he had caused his wife, for which he was already feeling repentant, or to continue with his intention to chastise his daughter. Seeing Ann sitting up with her head resting on Helen's shoulder removed one area of anxiety. Instantly, his thoughts flew back to his insolent daughter who was standing there, two bright spots of angry emotion flaming on her cheek-bones, her hair as rumpled as the mane of an ungroomed horse. By God, did she need taking in hand, by a strong, firm man who would bend her to his will and teach her that her place was to orna-ment the drawing-room and his bed rather than the back of a horse or the interior of a stable! Purpose flared in his eyes. Taking two quick steps towards

Lucy, he grabbed her by the wrist and, with one adroit movement, she found herself thrust face-down across the arm of the chair by which she had been standing.

Fury seethed in Lucy's brain. To be beaten by one's father in private was one thing, but here, in front of her sister and her odious brother-in-law . . . She could just imagine how she must look, with her skirts riding up and her chestnut curls fallen round her face. Her father had his hand on her left shoulder and was forcing her painfully down. With a cat-like twist, she jerked her head and sank her sharp teeth into his arm.

"Aaah!"

Her father's cry of pain nearly deafened her as his mouth was so close to her ear. The pressure on her shoulder was suddenly gone but, as she made to spring to her feet, she heard a hated voice drawl laconically, "Whip the bitch."

"John!" replied Helen sharply. "This is none of your business. You keep out of this."

"Hold your tongue, wife, or you'll be getting a beating too. A good flogging never hurt a mare—aye, Martin?"

Lucy caught her breath in a sharp gasp as she saw the object that John was proffering his father-in-law—a small riding switch with a thong made out of tough hide, knotted at the end. Before she could cry out in protest, her father stuck out his left leg and upended her across it. In spite of her vigorous kicking, she felt her silk drawers being tugged roughly down to her knees and her petticoats and skirt hauled up, exposing her naked behind. Lucy had never felt so humiliated in her life, but worse was to come. The leather thong sang through the air and bit into her delicate skin, causing her to shudder in pain. She was determined not to cry out and give her father the pleasure of knowing how much he was hurting her. Down whistled the lash again, cutting across the round cheeks of her bottom, the knot curling round her thigh and stinging it cruelly. The embroidery on the screen in front of the fireplace, of which she had an upside-down view, began to blur as tears misted her eyes. She hated her father. She would never forgive him for this. Her slim body tautened in agony as the lash descended even more viciously than before. She heard her mother's weak voice pleading, "That's enough, Martin," and heard him growl, "Shut up, woman, leave this to me," from somewhere above her head.

Just when she thought she could not bear it any more, the whipping suddenly ceased and the hold on her waist was relaxed. Lucy sank to her knees at her father's feet, her skirts, as they fell back into position, brushing painfully against her smarting skin. But the look she gave him as she raised her flushed face was still defiant, although she knew better than to put her thoughts into words.

"Now I hope we'll have a bit more obedience from you, my girl. I am expecting a visit from Reverend Pritt in about . . ." He paused to consult the French clock on the mantel-shelf. ". . . just over an hour's time. He has already made it known to me that he is coming to ask for your hand in marriage. His own dear wife died many years ago, before he came to this parish, and he is a very lonely man who dearly wants children, which his first wife could not provide for him. Now, go and clean up your face; Helen can help you do your hair in a tidier way than you normally wear it. I don't want the Reverend to think you are a slut. Put your best dress on, the blue one that makes you look like a girl rather than a stable-lad, and come downstairs when I call you. You are to behave to the vicar like a well-brought-up young lady. None of those bold stares, my lass, and no answering back. Just reply politely to any questions he may ask you—and of course you are to accept him. There is no question about that. Understood?"

"Yes, Father," whispered Lucy, frightened of the sarcasm that might creep into her voice if she spoke any louder. His eyes betokened that a curtsy was expected of her. She bowed her head and inclined her knee, then stood up and took stock of the rest of her family: of her mother, crouched on the settle in the window, face in hands, weeping silently; of her sister, pausing in the act of comforting Ann to give her sister a look in which Lucy read, not sympathy, but smugness, a look which said, "I had to go through it and now it's your turn." To her surprise her brother-in-law was nowhere to be seen. She reflected that he had probably gone to check upon the twins who were, no doubt, being plied with buns in the kitchen by Binns and Cook. With the exception of her ill-used mother, Lucy despised the lot of them. Giving Helen a contemptuous glance, she swept out of the room, somewhat hobbled by her drawers which were still at half-mast. She prayed they wouldn't fall down and give her father and sister cause for mirth.

Once in the safety of the dark, panelled landing, she paused, hoisted up her slipping undergarment and made for her room. She had less than an hour in which to devise a plan. Maybe she could think up some way of putting Nathaniel Pritt off her, by saying or doing something so subtle that he, but not her father, would detect it. Maybe she could say something about religion which would show him that she was not in accordance with his own views. He would not want to take for a wife a woman who was not totally committed to his own strong-held beliefs. Yes, that was it. If she could let slip some pagan idea, or some comment that had more in common with the Church of Rome than that of England, maybe he would see at once that she was not the stuff vicar's wives are made of.

There was a knock at her door, and Lucy started guiltily, as if the visitor, whoever it was, had been able to read her thoughts and was coming to assure her that there was no escaping her fate. But it was only Binns, with a basin of warm water which she placed on the marble dresser. Lucy gave her a grateful smile and dismissed her.

Alone again, she sank down onto the gold-embroidered coverlet of her bed and instantly stood up as the pain in her well-beaten buttocks was so severe. On the other side of the room, next to the cupboard where she kept her clothes, was a long mirror in which she could see her image reflected from head to toe. She had grumbled when it was installed, insisting that she didn't mind what she looked like. However, her mother had prophesied that, as she got older, she *would* mind, and so the thing stood there, in its heavy gold-leafed oak frame. Lucy stepped before it and examined her reflection. She saw a tall girl, whose naturally pink and white complexion had no need of rouge, with loose chestnut curls tumbling down to her breasts, wearing a rumpled dress of cream satin and ruffles which she'd always hated because it was feminine in such a silly way. Turning round and craning her head over her shoulder to try and catch her rear reflection, she hoisted up her heavy petticoats, draped them over one arm and stood examining the damage wrought by John Masters's whip in her father's hand. Her white buttocks were criss-crossed with fiery red lines and on one thigh, where the leather knot had caught her, a small bead of blood had formed which had smeared her underclothes. If I were a witch, she thought, I would take some witches' wax and, under a waning moon, I'd make a figurine of John Masters and stab it with a hatpin *there* (she imagined the pleasure of spearing him through the groin) and *there* (now his heart was pierced by a silver barb).

Suddenly Lucy started. Surely her imagination wasn't that strong? For a moment, she thought she had glimpsed the face of John Masters forming clearly in the mirror. Dropping her skirts, she whirled round—and found herself face to face with her hated enemy.

"A pretty sight," he purred, his double chin sinking into his cream-colored waistcoat. "But a few additions from myself would have made it even prettier."

"Get out of my room!" yelled Lucy, furious that her most intimate, private moment had been invaded. She advanced on the interloper, not quite sure what to do, but determined to wreak some damage on him. Like a tigress unsheathing her claws, her fingernails lashed towards his eyes. His arms went up and caught her hands and squeezed them until she squealed. "Let me go, you're hurting!"

"All in good time, little sister." She could feel the disgusting squashiness of his paunch against her waist and the even more distressing lump below it, pressing against her thigh.

"If I scream loud enough, Father, Mother, *someone* will hear," she warned him, and inhaled to fill her lungs for the effort.

"But you won't, will you, Lucy?" he informed her, his small eyes in their puffy surrounds of fat boring into hers. His tongue snaked out and moistened his slack lips. His chest was rising and falling rapidly as he panted in excitement and anticipation. The sight of her exposed bottom and the leather thong thwacking into it had driven him out of his mind with red-hot lust, which he had been forced to satisfy himself by sneaking alone into a closet. But his release had only been temporary; the sight of Lucy raising her skirts on the landing to pull up her slipping drawers had caused his groin to throb anew. How much more voluptuous she was, with her creamy curves and hair of living flame, than her dark, scrawny sister. How often he had regretted having bid for the hand of the wrong one. However, he wasn't a man who would let marriage stand in the way of lust. Giving Lucy's small hands another painful squeeze, he said huskily, "I want you, you little hussy. I may be twice your age but I'll wager I'm a hundred times more experienced between the sheets—or, in your case, in the hayloft."

Lucy looked at him in surprise. She had long thought him to be cunning, but she had no idea what devious scheme he was working on now.

"You can yell all you like, my dear, but I doubt if you'll be heard. Your mother and sister are at the other end of the house, supervising refreshment for your . . . *suitor.*" He hissed the word with obvious enjoyment, reminding Lucy uncomfortably that time was running out for her. "The children have been put to rest in the conservatory," he continued, "and as for your father, he's in the cellar tasting the wine to help him decide which to offer the dear Reverend. So you see, my sweet, we are all alone. I sympathize with you, my dear. Reverend Pitt is an old toad, about as lusty as one of the tombs in his graveyard. It would not be right for your pretty body to go to him without a full-blooded man having enjoyed it first."

"Let go of me!" Lucy demanded again, to no avail. Her brother-in-law pressed his body against her and pushed her relentlessly back towards the bed. With one hand he fumbled at the crotch of his britches, unfastening the buttons, while his other was pushing its way inside Lucy's dress, searching for her breasts. She allowed herself to sag limply onto the bed and then brought her knee up in one swift movement, hoping to catch him on that most hated part of his body, right between the legs. Masters, however, was too quick for her. Anticipating her attack, he skipped sideways so that her knee collided harmlessly with his hip.

"You little whore," he breathed. "You must know how provocative you are, always tossing your curls, with the bold look in your eye and that swaying rump of yours. I've never been able to come near you without feeling my manhood rise to salute you. Look what you've done to me. Go on, feel it!"

He grasped Lucy's hand and thrust it down between his legs. His britches were undone and her hand encountered a slab of hot, hard flesh pushing and prodding against her skirts. It seemed to have a life of its own, like a blind animal. Repelled, she jerked her hand away and most immediately felt his own hand questing beneath her skirts. This way and that she twisted, but his hand moved inexorably upwards. Hot-blooded and easily aroused as she was, Lucy had no intention of losing her virginity to her brother-in-law. She knew she differed from her sister in that Helen felt lovemaking was something to be endured (under attack from John as she was, Lucy fully sympathized with how she must feel), whereas Lucy felt sure that, someday, she would fall in love with a man, probably tall, black haired and brown-eyed for that was the kind of man she dreamt about, to whom she would be only too willing to surrender.

John Masters's attentions were getting too ardent to bear. The squirmings of his body upon hers had worked her skirts up almost to waist level and soon there would be nothing but her tightly clamped thighs to prevent him entering her. She gave a sudden jerk of her hips to try and dislodge him and her reward was a stinging slap across the face from the palm of his hand.

"Give in gracefully, my girl, or I'll tell your father I saw you bare-arsed in the hayloft with one of the stable-lads."

"But I didn't . . . I've never . . ." Lucy began.

"Who d'you think he'll believe?" Masters cut in. "You, who he knows to be a cheeky, devious little bint, or me, his well-intentioned, honorable son-in-law? Do you really think your life would be worth living then? Don't you think he'd treble his attempts to get you married off before your reputation was in question, or your waist started to swell?" His hand moved on her thigh as he tried to insert it between her resisting legs. "Be sensible, Lucy. You're in a tight spot and I . . . well, maybe I'm the only one who can help you. Give yourself to me and I'll put in a good word with your father, try to convince him Pritt isn't the fellow for you, and that maybe I can find someone more suitable amongst my rich friends. I think the mention of money might make him see reason. And I know a lot of young studs who'd be a good match for a lusty young wrench like you."

Sinking his lips wetly on hers, he redoubled his efforts to unclamp Lucy's legs. Just as she felt her resistance weakening, there was a knock on the door and Binns's flat country tones were heard saying, "Your father wants to know if you're ready, miss. The Reverend is expected in fifteen minutes."

"Damn!" cursed Masters, swinging himself off Lucy's prone body. "I never realized the old bastard was expected quite so soon. That doesn't give us time to enjoy each other, does it?" Lucy shook her head numbly, hoping against hope that he was going. With difficulty, he pushed his swollen member back into his britches and buttoned them, pulling his jacket across himself to hide his condition from any observant eyes. "How long will the old boy be here? One hour? Two?"

"I don't know," Lucy whispered, feeling herself trembling all over with relief at being released from her plight.

"Well, I'll stay the evening and come to your room later. Remember what I said. I'll put in a word for you if . . ." Lucy nodded again. Bending towards her, he pressed his lips on hers, causing Lucy a shudder of revulsion; it felt like kissing a slimy, dripping fish. Then he was out of her room, with a wink and a leer, leaving her to collect her scattered feelings.

Where was Helen, who was supposed to be helping her? Where, indeed, was Binns, whom she expected to have been dancing attendance on her, lacing her into her dress, proffering advice about this necklace or that? She had never felt so alone, so abandoned, so confused. As if in a trance, she got up, reached in the cupboard for her blue dress and began, mechanically, to unfasten the cream one she was wearing. Then, struck by a sudden thought, she fastened it again and stepped quickly over to the window.

Outside, dusk was falling and low-flying swallows were dipping over the meadow at the back of the house. She had climbed out of the window before, but never in a dress as full and ornate as the one she was wearing. Still, she had no time to change. Glancing up the hill, her eyes found, and rested on, the clump of sombre pine trees that surrounded the rambling old vicarage. It could have been her imagination, but she thought she spied a moving speck descending the hill path—Nathaniel Pritt on his trusty Welsh cob. There was no time to lose. She unfastened the casement and swung her body out onto the ledge. She clung to the window sill as her feet found the familiar fork in the ivy. Then she was down it, on the tree branch, feeling her skirt snagging on a hundred sharp twigs. She dropped lightly to the ground and glanced nervously all round her. She could hear distant voices from the parlor and the sound of her father shouting, but here, at the far corner of the house, all was quiet.

It grew darker still as she crept towards the high

meadow, wishing fervently that she was dressed in dark clothing instead of the all-too-conspicuous cream dress. Reaching the fence, she lifted a halter off the gatepost and gave a low call to the black horse who was silently cropping the turf.

"Here, Emperor, here boy."

The horse pricked his ears in interest. Martin Swift's prize stallion was always willing to lower his noble pride and answer the call of a human if there was any hope of an apple or a handful of sugar. Obediently, he trotted towards Lucy, a tall shadow in the gathering darkness. Meanwhile, Lucy climbed onto the top of the gate. As soon as the horse was close enough, she held out her hand and, while he was inspecting it for the hoped-for sugar, she slipped the bit into his mouth, the rope over his ears and was on his back before the surprised animal could sense her intentions.

Emperor set off at an indignant gallop over the field and Lucy clung grimly onto his back, thanking God that she'd had the nerve to take those moonlit, bareback rides in the past and accustom herself to doing without a saddle. It always felt strange to be riding astride a horse like a man, especially when wearing skirts of slippery silk and satin, but she jammed her thighs and knees against the horse's polished hide and willed him not to stumble.

The far fence was looming up. Emperor made as if to swerve, but Lucy, by holding him in check with reins and calves, forced him to square up to it. Then, giving him his head, she jabbed his flanks with her heels. He took off like an eagle and soared over, landing in the lane that led upwards, away from the town, towards the moors.

Lucy gave one anxious glance over her shoulder. The Reverend Pritt should be nearing the farm by now. Surely he would hear Emperor's hoofbeats and raise the alarm? Or maybe her disappearance from her room had already been noted.

"Come on, Emperor, boy," she murmured encouragingly, giving his muscular neck a pat. She had no regrets about stealing her father's prize beast. Not after all he'd done to her. She planned to get a safe distance from Prebbledale and then set him free, knowing he could find his own way home by animal instinct. Gripping tight with her knees and crouching low over his neck, she dug him again with her heels. He obligingly set off at a fast canter, tackling the steep hill as if it were nothing but a gentle slope.

As they crested the summit, Lucy stopped her mount and looked round. The moon was out, silvering the trees and fields and revealing the houses and outbuildings of the village in eerie silhouette. Her eyes picked out her own house—and she noticed to her alarm, several dark, ant-like figures darting around: her family, looking for her. Soon they would discover the theft of Emperor, and then the horses would be harnessed and searchers sent out with lanterns to look for her and bring her back.

Ahead stretched the moors, wild, rocky, deserted except for the occasional band of gypsies or robbers. She would take her chance with them, she decided. By tomorrow she'd be far away. She'd disguise herself and maybe find employment in an inn, or perhaps some kind family would take her in. She stirred her spirited horse into a gallop and felt the wind singing through her hair as Emperor's hooves struck sparks from the stony road. The physical exertion of riding stripped her tension from her and she laughed out loud, the wind whipping the sound from her mouth before it could echo among the rocks. They would never find her. On she galloped, into the welcoming darkness.

CHAPTER TWO

Lucy dreamt of snow. She was lying on an endless expanse of it and above her, from an inky sky, soft, white flakes were falling in their millions and settling on her shivering body. Gradually, the shivering stopped and a kind of drowsy numbness took over. She was almost warm now and a deep sleep was overcoming her. She had been told that this was how people died. She didn't mind dying this way, in comfortable, floating numbness. It was as if her body had already left her and only her spirit remained. Yet her senses were still working because she could hear the neighing of a horse. The neighing grew louder, piercing her dream and forcing her awake. She had made her bed under an overhanging rock to protect her from the night dews and had pulled her skirt and top layer of petticoats around her shoulders and arms, to keep herself as warm as possible. Even so, the September night was chilly and the stony ground beneath her uncomfortably hard, and she wished she had brought a warm cloak to snuggle beneath.

She heard the neighing again and, in a sudden fear that Emperor might be under attack from some wild animal, made her way, crouching, from her hiding place, stretched her stiff limbs and set out in her thin slippers across the damp, prickly heather to the place where she'd tethered him to a tree stump. The horse was standing, gazing at her. His ears were pricked and his stance suggested observant attention, but there was no sign of any marauding animal or bird. Nothing, not even a mouse or a hunting owl, stirred on the lonely stretch of high moorland.

Suddenly, without warning, something encircled her waist and gripped her tightly. She thought at first she had accidentally strayed into some kind of animal trap, and screamed out loud, but a man's coarse chuckle behind her told her the "trap" was of human rather than mechanical origin. The moon had tantalizingly hidden behind a cloud and, even if she had been able to twist round sufficiently to face her assailant, Lucy would not have been able to make out his features in the total darkness which now engulfed the moor.

So much had happened to her during the last few hours that now, even at this terrifying moment, she felt numb rather than afraid. Her mind was icy clear and her nerves steady. She knew that, realistically, she did not have the strength to attack and overpower her captor. She doubted if there was anyone within earshot but, with the small chance of their being a poacher or benighted traveller in the vicinity, she opened her mouth and gave vent to a piercing scream, which used the full power of her lungs.

The man holding her seemed unimpressed. "Scream out, me darlin' girl. No one will hear you. There's only miles of hills and the night birds and the dark waters—and me an' me mates."

Lucy's heart sank. So there was a whole band of them. No point, then, in fighting and screaming and risking physical damage to herself. She had nothing to give them apart from Emperor, and they would be foolish to steal him as he was a well-known horse who could be easily traced. Better, she thought, to go with the men willingly and calmly and keep her wits about her. Perhaps these "mates" of his would prove a blessing in disguise, for if they took her along with them she stood less chance of being found by her father.

"What do you want with me?" she asked the man, still unable to see his face.

He remained silent.

She tried again. "Who are you?"

"Me name's Rory McDonnell," he replied in his soft brogue, a mixture of Irish and North Country English.

"Then, Mr. McDonnell, kindly release me. You're holding me so tight that I can hardly breathe. I won't run away, I promise."

How could she run away? Once out of sight of the road, she knew she would only lose herself among the rocks and lakes, and if she didn't have Emperor she would stand little chance of reaching civilization.

"What name are ye havin'?" he asked her. His

voice was soft and sounded young, rather attractive. Lucy wished the clouds would blow away, allowing the moonlight to reveal his features. All she knew was that he was taller than she was.

There seemed no harm in revealing her name to him. "It's Lucy. Lucy Swift."

"Swift as the deer, me little white doe! I won't shoot you, my beauty; you're quite safe with Rory. But I'm afraid I have to do this, although I know you won't like it. It's for your own sake, mavourneen. You don't want to be after dashin' off and breakin' your pretty ankle on the wild moor, where no one will find ye."

Lucy flinched as a length of cord was wound tightly round her wrists. Then her captor stepped to one side, the end of the cord wrapped around his own hand. Once the pressure of his arms was gone, Lucy took several deep, thankful gulps of air, then regarded the man curiously. He was of taller than average height and his face was half covered by a luxuriant beard. In the dimness she would not make out his features clearly, but she guessed he was about thirty. As she stood there regarding him, he tugged on the cord.

"Follow me," he ordered and set off purposefully towards Emperor. He made a clicking noise with his tongue and teeth, then stretched out a hand. To Lucy's amazement, the spirited stallion stepped docilely towards the stranger and allowed his nose to be stroked, whereupon Rory gripped his halter and set off down the hill leading his two prizes.

It was at this moment that the numbness that

had settled on Lucy's emotions lifted and she found herself seized by a surge of pure panic. Where was he leading her? Who were his friends? Were they a band of ragged gypsies who would torment her jealously, strip her of her fine clothes and jewels, maybe rape or even kill her? She hoped there would be women and children among them— she would trust a member of her own sex, especially a mother, to possess some degree of warmth and sympathy, although she had heard of cases where women had actually egged men on to commit terrible atrocities. Not, however, in England. As she stumbled through stones and bracken, feeling sharp stalks and small pebbles working their way painfully into her shoes, Lucy longed for the comfort and safety of her home. She felt a rush of affection for her mother. Maybe she would never see her again! Yet she could never go back to face the things her father had in store for her, especially now that she had stolen his finest horse. No, her home life was now in the past. Yet the future, as it appeared right now, seemed to hold little better: more fear, seemingly, more violence, more threats. She felt totally bewildered by the events that were carrying her along at such a breakneck pace, as an unwilling victim.

As they turned the corner, Lucy still being led by her captor, Emperor still following obediently without so much as a whinny, she noticed that the sky seemed to be getting lighter, lit by an orange glow. They rounded an outcrop of rock and the reason was immediately apparent; Rory's companions, whoever they were, had constructed a sizeable fire and she could make out two or three figures silhouetted against the flames. Rory gave a kind of animal call, like a hunting falcon, and a huge figure uncoiled itself from a sitting position and approached them.

Lucy's heart sank like a stone when the man swam into vision in the flickering orange light. He was a giant, bigger than anyone she'd ever seen before in her life. His cowhide coat was cracked and aged, his hair brindled like a dog's. He, too, sported a flourishing beard and his broad-boned face displayed a mixture of dirt and scars. When he smiled, his teeth were black and brown like the stalks of rotten mushrooms. She had never seen anyone who looked so thoroughly a ruffian.

"We-e-ell," the giant drawled slowly, pushing back his coat to hook his thumbs into his belt and revealing an all-black outfit that made him resemble an executioner. "What 'ave we 'ere, then? Let's see . . . Hmm . . ." He walked in a wide circle round the trio, looking them up and down. "It's been good 'unting for you, Rory me lad. Two fine specimens, a thoroughbred stallion and—" bending his body at the shoulders he brought his massive face down so close to Lucy's that she almost reeled from the force of the liquor on his breath—"a thoroughbred brood mare, too, by the look of it!" Straightening up and towering against the sky, he let out a raucous laugh that caused Emperor to flinch nervously.

"Wouldn't mind doing a bit of breeding with her myself."

The new voice from Lucy's left forced her to turn

her head sharply. A third man had joined them un-
noticed. He was a slight individual, old and
unhealthy-looking, with hollow cheeks and sunken
eye-sockets. From his upper lip sprouted a wispy
moustache. Lucy thought he looked like a sick
weasel. However, he appeared to be an expert on
horseflesh. He ran his hand over Emperor's neck,
across his withers, over his flanks, inspected his
hocks and finally picked up each hoof in turn. At
length, evidently satisfied, he turned to Lucy.

"He yours?" he inquired briefly, almost immediately entering into a spasm of coughing that made
his weak frame tremble like breeze-buffeted reed.

"Yes, he's mine—or rather, my father's," answered Lucy, as sternly and boldly as she could.
These men had to be shown that she was better
than them. Yet in her heart she wondered if she
really was. There, to one side of the fire, was a
group of horses, roped to each other. The men
were obviously horse traders, on their way to a fair.
At worst, they could be thieves. Even this would
make them no worse than herself, for hadn't she
stolen a champion horse from under her own
father's nose?

"Pay a good price to get him back, would he?"
inquired Weasel-face, having recovered from his
coughing fit.

This set Lucy in a quandary. The last thing she
wanted was for the men to drag both her and Emperor back to her father's house, delivering her
back into the clutches of all she was fleeing to
avoid, plus the added horror of her father's un-

mitigated wrath. Yet she couldn't really explain to men of this type that they could take the horse back but not her. That would be inviting them to use her in ways she refused to imagine. Maybe the best way out was to tell them part of the truth.

"No doubt. But, you see, I've already stolen him myself."

Her revelation evinced a shocked silence from all three men. Then, in unison, they broke out into guffaws, Giant slapping Weasel-face on the back with a blow that sent him staggering, and even Rory at her side bellowing fit to burst. Eventually Giant, wiping the tears from his eyes, bent down to Lucy again and chucked her under the chin. She resented such familiar treatment and, huge as he was, she glared at him, her eyes a blaze of blue.

"Pretty little thing. A bit wild and ill-mannered —fancy stealing a horse from your own father!" He started to laugh again, then checked himself. "I'm sure we can teach her a few manners, though, eh, lads?"

"I'll bet," agreed Weasel-face enthusiastically. The pointed tip of his tongue came out and wetted his lips, showing small, yellowed teeth.

Lucy shuddered. These men were bestial. She couldn't bear to be touched by them. But her intuition, sharpened by fear, was as keen as an animal's and she could feel a sensual charge in the air, the kind of electricity that is generated when lusty men, starved of female company, find themselves in the presence of an attractive woman. She stole a glance at Rory, the man who had initially captured her.

He had remained silent. She wondered if it could be that he didn't agree with the sentiments that were being bandied about—or was he, perhaps, worse than either of the others? In the light from the fire, she could make out his features: a strong, well-shaped nose, a broad brow from which his unruly black hair sprang like uncontrollable weeds, and a chin hidden by his beard. He looked younger than she had first thought, maybe only twenty-two or so. He was certainly more agreeable-looking than his ugly, ragged companions.

But she had little time for reflection. Weasel-face began to hum a tune which Lucy recognized as a crude ditty that she had sometimes caught her father's stable lads singing, although they had always fallen into a guilty silence whenever they had noticed she was within earshot. Suddenly she found herself wrenched from Rory's hold by the big man and whirled around in a kind of dance. Within seconds they had drawn close to the fire. Lucy, her hands bound behind her back, lost her balance, staggered and would have tumbled into the flames had not Rory noticed in time and pushed her out of the way.

"Careful!" he yelled. "We don't want the little darlin' to be incinerated, do we?"

Gasping, her lungs roasted by inhaling too close to the flames, Lucy collapsed into an ungainly heap, from which she was hauled to her feet by Weasel-face, twirled round, caught by Rory and flung towards the giant. She was dizzy and in tears, feeling as if she were being used in some perverted game of pass-the-parcel. She closed her eyes. With

Rory so obviously joining in the fun and enjoying it, she was bereft of the one man she hoped would be her ally. She was alone, her wrists bound, at the mercy of these three ruffians who seemed set to torment and abuse her in the worst possible way.

One sleeve of her dress parted at the shoulder seam as she was spun wildly around. Soon she was too dizzy and exhausted to notice whether her clothes were holding together or not. All she knew was that, if her breasts were exposed to their gaze, they would turn into lust-crazed animals—and they certainly seemed determined to tear every shred of clothing from her body.

She felt fingers roughly tugging at her, foul breath on her face, hands fondling her breasts and buttocks. She felt sick. She prayed to faint and wake up hours later alone, with the men having gone. Then, even if they had made use of her body, she would have been unconscious and oblivious of the degrading, obscene experience.

"Smithy—here, catch," called Rory, delivering her with a sharp slap across the rump into the arms of the next man. Opening her eyes briefly, Lucy discovered that "Smithy" was the weasel-faced one. The sight of his grey face and jaundiced eyeballs revolted her, so she closed her own eyes again. She longed to be able to thrust out her hands and save herself from tumbling helplessly into so many pairs of arms. She had no way of warding off the outrages being committed on her body, the fumbling, fondling hands, the wet lips and rank breath, the terrible whirling and pushing.

She found herself briefly in the arms of Rory,

who was grinning down at her, his teeth startlingly white and wholesome in comparison to those of his companions. "Please," she moaned beseechingly, hoping that perhaps she could touch some core of compassion in him. "Please . . . Make them stop."

He didn't answer, just pushed her away from him, calling, "Pat! Your turn!"

So she was lost. She wasn't a person, a human being, to any of them, just an object to be batted like a shuttle-cock from one participant to the next. And when this game was over . . . She was too exhausted to scream or cry. She felt herself crumpling in the giant's arms. He wasn't prepared for her sudden collapse and let her drop onto the ground where she lay, sobbing and bruised, all the breath, spirit and hope battered out of her.

As she lay there, she was aware of a warmth close to her, a body crouching over hers, male smells of sweat and spirits. Her face was turned upwards and a prickly beard scratched her chin. A man, breathing hard, forced his lips down onto hers so hard that her mouth was prised open. A fat tongue probed between her teeth, choking her, almost making her vomit. Her breasts were searched for, found, kneaded by two enormous hands. She didn't need to open her eyes to know who it was molesting her. It was the man from whom she stood the least chance of all of protecting herself, the giant, Pat.

Desperately she moved her head from side to side, seeking refuge from his revolting kiss. Her arms were twisted beneath her, her hands trapped painfully between her body and the stony ground.

She moaned out loud, without being conscious of the fact that she was making any sound at all.

"Stop!"

The word cut through the air like a whiplash. She felt the body above hers tense, the tongue withdrawn from her mouth.

"*I* found the black stallion and the white mare! I know share and share alike is our motto, but that's for the horses, not wenches. I'll do a deal with you. You can have the horse, sell it, split the money. But I saw the girl first, I captured her and brought her here. I've bin telling you for a long time, I need a wife. Well, here she is. My wife, Lucy."

Grumbling, the giant removed his great bulk.

"What's wrong with you?" grumbled Smith. "Couldn't you wait and marry her . . . *afterwards.*"

The bear-like figure of Pat shambled up to him, his eyes small and mean. He gave Smithy a cuff on the side of the head, then turned squarely to face Rory.

"Me Irish friend," he said, his voice heavy with sarcasm. "Pretty boy Rory. Always one for the ladies. I never thought you 'ad it in you to get married."

His face lit up in a cunning smile. He came up to Rory and placed a fist like a joint of beef on his shoulder. Lucy gasped. He could kill Rory with one stroke. Yet all the time, Rory regarded him calmly and coolly, his body unmoving, his demeanor amiable.

"So it's marriage you want now, my *green* little leprechaun."

Lucy saw the corner of Rory's mouth twitch, as

if he were suppressing extreme anger. She had to admire his self-control. She was also impressed by the quick-thinking way in which, by bringing an element of something legal and sanctified like marriage into the midst of an ugly, base scene, he had successfully brought the proceedings to a halt, thus saving her from violation by at least one of his companions. Now she was scared for him. If he were to pick a fight with Pat and be injured or killed, what would become of her then? There would be no one to stop the progress of the hideous man's evil desires and she would sooner die than be forced to submit. But she couldn't understand the course the discussion was now taking. Rory had surely only mentioned marrying her in order to save her. Nobody could force him to carry out his inspired but impossible suggestion. It seemed as if Fate were dogging her with the subject of marriage. Her father, Nathaniel Pritt and now this lunatic situation at the dead of night, on a lonely moor, with three violent, feckless and unscrupulous vagabonds.

The giant was regarding Rory with an ugly glint in his eye. A cunning smile flicked across his begrimed face. "If you're going to be selfish about it and keep 'er all to yourself, then by God, you'll 'ave 'er properly and honestly! Smithy . . ."

The skinny little man scrambled to his feet, left the comfort of the fire and ran to Pat's side.

"You'll be the witness," ordered the giant. "Now fetch me 'oly book."

Lucy looked at them aghast. What on earth was

going on? She shot a puzzled glance at Rory. He looked at her, unsmiling, then, with the same serious expression, took a knife from the pocket of his britches and sawed through the cord that bound her wrists. Her fingers were swollen and painful, her wrists marked with deep, bruised grooves where the twine had bitten into her delicate skin. She rubbed them ruefully, wincing as she accidentally twisted the lacerated flesh.

"Come 'ere," boomed the giant. "Let the service begin."

Lucy took a good look at the black book Smithy had brought, which now rested in Pat's hands. It was, indeed, marked "Holy Bible." An uneasy shiver crawled down her spine. What was this mockery, this charade? The giant had a strange sense of humor. Perhaps it was better simply to let him act out his fantasy rather than risk incurring his fury and the possible resumption of his attack upon her virtue.

Lucy had attended her sister Helen's wedding. To her horror, the giant reeled off exactly the same words. Rory had taken her hand and was clasping it firmly. She gave an experimental tug and his grip immediately tightened, leaving her in no doubt but that it would be impossible for her to break free and run away. She struggled to catch Rory's attention. He was staring at Pat as if mesmerized, but, feeling the power of Lucy's gaze, he inclined his head to face her.

There was so much she needed to say, so much she wanted to ask him. She did her best to whisper without letting her lips move, hoping that Pat wouldn't notice.

". . . any lawful impediment," intoned the giant.

"He can't do this, can he?" Lucy hissed.

A faint nod was her answer.

Lucy felt the blood pound in her temples and her hands went icy cold. It was all a joke; it *had* to be. Let Pat get it over with, let him firmly believe the fantasy that she and Rory were actually married, and then he would not try to molest her again. It was his way of distracting his own lust, of giving himself a reason not to touch her. The words he was speaking were weaving a spell, making her taboo to him and Smithy. But Rory? Surely he didn't believe it too?

She had to make doubly sure, so she caught his eye again and, moving closer to him, whispered out of the corner of her mouth, "He's not a priest, is he?"

Another nod.

Lucy felt her heart hammer in uncontrollable panic. She had to get away, now, before it was too late, before these crazy men tried to make her believe she was married—to a total stranger. Using her free hand, she tried to prise Rory's fingers off her other hand, but he just held onto her even more tightly. Emotions washed over her, each stronger than the one which preceded it; fear, pleading, fury, helplessness, hopelessness.

Suddenly her hand was squeezed. An urgent whisper sounded in her ear. "Go on. You must. He'll kill you if you don't."

She found herself being led forward and forced to kneel before the cracked boots of the "vicar."

Above her head, Pat asked, "What's her full name?"

"Lucy Swift," she heard Rory reply.

"Do you, Lucy Swift, take Rory McDonnell to be your lawful wedded husband, to love and cherish . . ."

There was a roaring in her ears similar to that she'd experienced the previous day just before she'd fainted. She felt herself starting to sway, but a sharp elbow prodded her urgently in the ribs.

"Say 'I do,' " begged Rory. Faint as she felt, she still caught the warning tone in his voice.

She had never before had to struggle with so many emotions all at once. How could she speak these two words, the most momentous words any woman ever speaks during her lifetime? For all she knew, she really was committing herself to something legal and binding. The urgent whisper came again. "Say it."

"I do," murmured Lucy. Seconds later, or so it seemed, she heard Rory repeat the same words.

The huge bulk of the man above her shifted like a tree in a landslip. His stentorian tones barked out, "You may now kiss your bride."

She was pulled to her feet and enveloped in Rory's embrace. She closed her eyes and puckered her lips, bracing herself for a mockery of a husband's kiss. Instead, Rory brushed her lips perfunctorily with his own and murmured, "Well done, girl. Don't worry."

"A drink! A toast to the bride and groom!" Smithy had a bottle of some kind of spirits in his hand, which he offered to Pat, who put it to his lips and took a deep draught.

"Aagh," Pat sighed, wiping his mouth with the back of his filthy hand. " 'Aven't married anyone for a long time."

"Not since you were thrown out of St. Barnabas's, I'll be bound," wheezed Smithy, chuckling catarrhally.

"For squeezing that old girl in the vestry? Oh-ho-ho, that was funny! You should 'ave seen the curate's face when 'e came in and caught me wiv me 'and down 'er front. Oh, the sin of fornication was never one *I* preached against, Smithy me boy!" Pat crashed his hand down between Smithy's shoulderblades, forcing him into another of his terrible, rattling coughing fits. Smithy was doubled up, his cheeks hollowing and puffing as he fought for breath. " 'Ere, 'ave a drop of this." The big man thrust the bottle against Smithy's grey lips and, between spasms, Smith reached out a trembling hand, took the bottle and sucked hard from it. At last, the dreadful, bubbling spasm ceased.

"He's going to die!" observed Lucy worriedly, quite forgetting her own predicament in the face of the old man's desperate state.

"Yes, probably. Aren't we all?" answered Rory.

Lucy, shocked by his callousness, gazed at him open-mouthed. "How can you be so cruel?" she demanded, ready to upbraid him for being so unconcerned about a fellow mortal.

"Smithy's had that cough for years. Never gets any worse, never gets any better. Sure, it's the cross he has to bear."

"And what's yours?"

"Hush up, wife!"

"Wife?" Lucy rounded on him, feeling ready to strike him now that her hands were free again. The fire had died down now and the air was growing cold around them. She could hear the restless shifting and cropping as the horses moved over the ground seeking grassblades among the prickly heather. Pat had guided Smithy to the fireside and was pulling a ragged blanket over him. "I'm no more your wife than you are my—"

"Your husband," interjected Rory, placing an arm round her shoulders which Lucy angrily shrugged off.

"But you're *not* my husband!" Her shrill, carrying tones made Pat look up from his vigil by Smithy and the fire.

"He is, you know. And if you don't stop nagging him, woman, 'e'll take the strap to you!" A guffaw rumbled deep in his chest as he sank down beside the dying embers and pulled a blanket round himself. The sky was still clouded over and, apart from the area near the fire, their whole surroundings were in pitch darkness.

"You stay there. I'll just fetch a blanket," said Rory, and darted off towards a heap of bags and saddlery.

Lucy knew that if ever she was going to get a chance to escape, this was it. Yet something kept her rooted to the spot. She had no idea why she was staying and she examined her mind to see if it could be confusion at not knowing which way to run, or fear of retribution from the fearsome Pat. As she watched Rory delving among the baggage, a realization came to her which she was at first tempted to dismiss as being not worthy of her, but the more she thought about it, the stronger the conviction grew. In the end she knew for certain that the thing which stopped her running was curiosity. She needed to find out the truth about this bizarre ceremony which had just been performed, and the only person who could aid her was Rory. Besides which—and this realization was even worse than the last—there was something about him that prompted her to stay. She needed to talk to him, to thank him for saving her from Pat —and maybe for saving her life, too. After she had spoken to him, after daylight had come and she had got her bearings, then she would look for some means of escape.

Her shoulder ached abominably. Lucy wriggled, seeking a comfortable indentation in her feather mattress. Her pillow, too, was lumpy and hard, unyielding to the butting of her head. She raised a fist to pound it and redistribute the goosedown filling —and felt something stay her arm in its downward swing.

"Wisha, girl, ye'll hurt yourself."

That's not Geoffrey. What's he doing in my bedroom anyway? No, Geoffrey left, he isn't at home any more.

"Father?" Lucy's sleepy, inquiring tones met with silence. She stretched out an arm and encountered not soft, warm coverlets but pebbles and sharp bracken stalks beneath her hand. Her eyelids blinked open. Her bedroom ceiling had lifted off. There was blue sky above her, with wispy white clouds like streaks of spilt milk. What had happened? Where was she? Lucy's heart raced in panic and she sat bolt upright, feeling a breeze around her.

Immediately, her eyes fell on the face of a man lying next to her beneath a ragged blanket. He was staring at her as if she was as much a stranger to him as he was to her. Then her memory came back to her—her flight, her capture, her ordeal round the fire. She remembered Pat holding a bible, Smithy and his coughing fit and her terrible anxiety about whether or not the ceremony she had undergone had resulted in her being married to . . . She looked at Rory again. His long-lashed brown eyes met hers and he gave her a smile and touched her arm familiarly. No, it was all a joke. They were drunk, they had played tricks with her. Now the fun was over and she would be able to explain her position and the true reason for her being alone on the moor. They would take her with them wherever they were going, help her get far away from Prebbledale.

The thought suddenly occurred to her that she had no recollection of falling asleep the previous night. Surely she couldn't have . . . Surely he . . . She scrambled half out of the blanket and drew a deep breath of relief at finding herself still fully dressed and, it seemed, untouched by the man who had shared her resting place. She realized that she must have fallen straight into a deep, exhausted sleep as soon as she had settled her head on the pillow. She felt beneath her and discovered that the "pillow" was, in fact, a folded cloak—Rory's. She had no remembrance of his having placed it there.

He was still regarding her with a warm, quizzical air. Maybe he *had* saved her from a nasty situation the night before but that didn't mean she owed him a place in her life or a share in her body. She pushed the blanket right back and started to get to her feet. Her mouth was dry, her head ached and she felt tired and bruised. As her feet touched the ground, she winced and discovered that the soles of her light slippers were slit in places and her feet lacerated and extremely tender.

"Don't worry, Lucy. We shan't be movin' on to-day. It's the Sabbath and there's no markets or fairs on the holy day. You just take your rest and heal up. I'm sorry about the way me fine friends treated ye last night but ye don't have to bother about them ever again. Not now you're me wife."

The same cold dread that had afflicted Lucy the previous night washed over her again, clouding the fresh blue day with grey uncertainty, as if she'd just woken from a bad dream to find it still continuing in her waking hours.

"Rory McDonnell—if that's your real name . . ." She paused but there was no reaction from the bearded young man who lay, fully dressed, propped on one elbow, grinning at her.

"Tell me, what are you and your ill-mannered friends? Highwaymen? Gypsies? Are you on the run for some crime? You used me last night as some kind of plaything. I'm not used to that kind of treatment." She frowned sternly down at her companion but found it impossible to be angry with someone who was looking so cheerful and friendly, so like a brother. "All right. So maybe you helped me. But it's daybreak now. They—my family, that is—may be searching for me. I remember I told you I had stolen a horse of my father's. It's true. But what you don't understand is why I did it, and . . ."

Lucy's voice trailed off. She wondered why she was bothering to try to explain all this to a man who was a common ruffian and had treated her no better than a slut from some low, bawdy inn. Besides, he was making no attempt to answer any of her burning questions. She stood looking at him indecisively. A glance over her shoulder showed her the ashes of last night's fire, the outlines of two slumbering bodies and a string of horses, some cropping, some standing idly, heads down, dozing in the early morning sun. Emperor was with them, his halter knotted to that of a sway-backed grey cob. If she were just to wander over, give him a pat, untie the rope . . .

A chuckle broke into her thoughts, hauling her back to the moment of her capture the previous evening. A hand sneaked out from beneath the blanket and gripped her ankle, making her squeal in protest.

"I know what you're thinking, me love. But it's no good. Pat wouldn't stand for it after what you deprived him of last night. Don't you remember the vow you gave, Lucy McDonnell?"

She froze. Why did he persist in perpetrating this myth? Couldn't he see she'd had enough? She spat out the words, "What do you mean?"

"Sit down," he commanded, in his soft, persuasive voice.

Maybe he was right about Pat . . . She had better obey. She straightened a corner of the blanket and sat on it, thinking that he had better make his explanation a good one. She could still hardly believe that she was several miles away from home, and that she had spent the night with an uncouth trio of men—and Rory's words did little to make her feel more at ease.

"I'll tell you about me, right? An' then you can begin about you. I'm Rory McDonnell—ye know that already. I'm twenty-two, coming up twenty-three in November, a good age for a man. I've never been much good to no one, especially to meself. Me da' was a tinker; me ma—well, you would have loved her, everyone did. But she's dead. An' as for the old man, I haven't seen him for more than seven year. Last time was at a fairground when he was just about to go into the ring—he was a boxer, you see, and a fair wrestler, too. He winked at me and said, 'Rory, me son, where there's money to be made and you have a talent, you must follow. Gold, that's what matters first, then your immortal soul.' I prayed for him, mavourneen, prayed for him, I did, but they carted him off—"

"Dead?" Lucy whispered. He had no background, no breeding. Most of her father's stable lads could claim better lineage than this Rory. Even her father's family line went back to the great kings of Ireland. Yet, for some reason, she felt as if there was nothing she would rather do in the growing warmth of that autumn morning than sit listening to the vivid reminiscences spilling from the lips of this born storyteller, even if he wasn't directly answering her questions.

"No, bless you," he continued, "not dead. He was carried off to the gallows—or the transport ships, I don't know which."

"But why?"

" 'Twasn't his fault he killed the earl who fought him, but he did. Milord was drunk, did it for a wager. Big hulking fellow he was, an' there's me old da', near on forty, slight and slippery as an elver, and cunning with it. Milord's built like a beef bullock, punching the air, hoping to find a nose in it, and there's Father, calculating his moment and then, oof, a straight left to the point of the jaw. Feller's head snaps back, we all heard it, then down he goes, crack, and everyone fussing and shouting. Then they comes and takes him away. It was a fair fight, but Milord's father insists that because he's a gypsy he's used some magic trick, and so he's accused of murder."

His father—a murderer? Lucy felt herself shiver. How could she be sure Rory was telling the truth? Maybe he was a maniac from a whole line of cutthroats! All she knew of him was what she could see with her own eyes, a young man, with tousled dark hair, talking animatedly, crouching and rocking back and forth on his heels.

"Did you never see him again?" she asked.

"Never. When they came to take him, I ran. Not that I was a coward, Lucy, but it was twenty of them against him and me, and he once said to me, 'Rory, son, if ever the Devil or the Law come, make sure they only take one of us, leaving one to carry on.' "

"And your mother? What happened to her?" Lucy was shocked at her own curiosity. Nobody had ever told her their life story before and she would never have had the boldness to ask. But up here, in the hilltops, with a grouse squawking somewhere in the heather and the breeze ruffling her hair, normal etiquette somehow did not matter.

"My mother, Kathleen . . . Pretty girl, so I'm told. Came over from Wexford to settle in Lancashire with her parents."

"I wonder if she ever knew my father?" burst in Lucy impulsively. "His family did the same thing— came from Ireland, took a boat over the sea to Liverpool. No, that was my great-grandad. It was long before your mother's time."

"Still we might be related. Who knows?" smiled Rory. Lucy found herself smiling back. Rory seemed anxious to complete his story. "Her family didn't approve of her marrying me da'. She gave birth to me, caught a chill and never recovered. Me father nursed her for two whole years after that, while she grew thinner and thinner, until . . . Well, that's the way of the world."

He gazed off into space, then pulled himself swiftly back to the present.

"Us now? Horses is our game. We trade, buy, sell . . . mark a few here and there."

Lucy knew from her father what "marking" was —disguising a stolen horse so that it could be sold as a different and apparently legitimate animal.

"Now take that fine animal of yours—all the dye in the world couln't turn him brown or white. We might manage a sort of piebald, though."

Lucy giggled at the thought of Emperor painted like a circus pony. "It was my plan to turn him loose and send him home," she informed him.

"Maybe that's what we'll have to do, if you don't want your father to come looking for you," he replied.

So he had remembered what she had told him and his companions the night before. Obviously an alert mind was at work behind the casual, nonchalant exterior. What, then, would he have to say on the subject of their mock marriage. Before she could ask this all-important question, he sprang to his feet and offered her a hand.

"A walk? Just over the hill?" he invited.

Lucy didn't need to be asked twice. Her legs were cramped and aching from the dervish whirling of the previous night. Besides, she wanted to see what, if anything, was visible from the highest point. Maybe she was not yet too far from Prebbledale. She had no way of telling how far she and

Emperor had travelled in their wild flight.

The hillside was steep, the bracken turning the crisp, brittle brown of autumn. A curlew gargled its querulous complaint, trying to draw them away from its nest, and once Lucy gasped and jumped as a hare sprang up almost from under her feet and raced, flattened-eared, through a tunnel of undergrowth. As they drew higher and the ridges of rocky ground folded away beneath them, a panorama gradually spread out around them; and as Rory aided her to clamber onto a rocky pinnacle the view below her took Lucy's breath away. In wonderment, she observed miles of wild land, shaded purple, tan and green, rising and falling in irregular patterns, clusters of stunted trees, a sprinkling of white, strayed sheep, a lake grey and opaque in the shadow of an overhanging rockface. As far as she looked, she could see no sign of a rooftop or a distant steeple. Close by them a stream splattered over the rocks, dropping in twin waterfalls to descend into a fern-fringed crevice several feet below. Just before it curled creamily over the sharp drop, its centuries of running had gouged out a hollow in its bed, forming a pool of maybe two feet in depth. Lucy longed to step into it and bathe her dusty, aching body. She mentioned her wish to Rory, who immediately told her to go ahead, promising to stand on the ridge and keep watch to make sure no one trespassed on her privacy.

Gratefully, Lucy lifted the hem of her dress, which was sadly torn from constant snagging on rocks and undergrowth. She glanced up at Rory to check that his back was turned, then gave a small shriek as her legs were enveloped in icy water up to her knees. It was cleansing and revitalizing, reactivating her sluggish blood, clearing her aching head. Lucy bent down and thrust her face into the stinging chill of the pool. Water dripped from her hair, soaking her clothes. It was stupid to be standing fully dressed in a stream when her one desire was to bathe naked. Trusting Rory not to turn around, Lucy quickly discarded her garments and sank into the pool, where she sat on the water-smoothed pebbles and, cupping her hands, sent delicious sprays of water splashing over her shoulders and breasts. Forgetting herself, she began to sing, her head thrown back, her hair streaming in seaweed strands all around her.

Rory, hearing her burst into song, turned his head and was mesmerized by the sight that greeted him. He knew he shouldn't look—but what mortal man, even if threatened with being turned into a pillar of salt, could have resisted letting his eyes dwell on the picture of a naked girl, in all her natural loveliness, relaxing in a rock pool like a sea nymph? When Lucy stood up to attend to her hair, squeezing water out of it and twisting it into a knot behind her, he saw that she was flat-bellied as a lad, but possessed of breasts and hips that swelled out in mature female comeliness. His manhood was powerfully stirred by the sight of this child-woman. He wanted her, he burned to hold her cool, damp, naked body against his own hot, ardent one.

A sudden notion came to him and, with difficulty, he unfastened one of the gold hoop earrings he'd worn since childhood, a legacy of his gypsy blood. Then quietly, so as not to attract Lucy's attention, he stepped out of his own clothes.

It was a small sound, like the snapping of a twig, that made Lucy look up. She had been so absorbed in her task of washing herself and her hair and was now so lost in the sensation of warm sunshine drying her water-beaded body that she had momentarily forgotten the existence of her male sentinel. She cried out in shock and fear as she saw him approaching in all his nakedness, the virile, black curly hair springing from his loins and chest, the powerfully made thighs and shoulders, the soft, dark fur on his arms and legs. She tried to leap out of the pool and make a dash for her clothes but the water dragged at her legs and impeded her progress. With a great splash that sent water cascading anew all over her drying body, he jumped into the pool and landed beside her. She was halfway up the bank when he hauled her back, his hands sliding on her wet skin. Summoning all her strength, Lucy directed a mighty kick at his shins, but the water slowed down the swing of her foot, giving him time to dodge. His arms encircled her, crushing her tight against the uncomfortable reminder of his maleness. Lucy sank her teeth into his shoulder and was pleased to hear him wince in pain. How dare he take advantage of her like this? She had thought she could trust him, he'd given her his word that she could bathe in safety and privacy, and now he was taking advantage of her while she was totally unprotected and completely at his mercy.

She tried to bite him again, then felt her hair caught and wrenched painfully backwards, forcing her face up to his. His lips closed on hers, prising her mouth open so that she couldn't bite him without grinding her teeth horribly against his. His tongue darted round the tip of her own tongue, then against the roof of her mouth, flickering like a snake. Then he slackened the terrible pressure of his mouth and his lips became soft, seeking, exploratory, until she found herself responding with a heavy, drugged sensation in her head, a dragging, swollen ache in her loins and an urgent need to be fondled, stroked and pressed even harder against his powerful body.

She hardly knew what was happening to her. All she knew was that she didn't want to fight him. Her mind screamed, "He's let you down, you trusted him, he's misused you. Kick! Bite! Run!" But her body was reacting without any orders from her mind. She didn't resist as Rory picked her up, carried her to the bank and placed her gently down on a patch of grass beneath a bush of some aromatic herb that tanged spicily in the sun. She was no longer conscious of her unclothed state. She felt her hand being taken and a hard object being firmly pressed down over one finger. She raised her finger to her eyes and saw the sun glinting on gold. She turned it round and saw the break in the metal and, acting on a sudden suspicion, looked at

Rory's ears. One bore an identical ring and in the other was a small hole, empty of the ornament it had once borne.

"One for each of us," he said, smiling at her. "I'll see if I can't get you a better one at Pendleton Fair."

The question sprang to Lucy's lips. "Are we . . . are we really *married?*"

She held her breath, waiting for his reply, aware only of the warmth, both physical and emotional, emanating from the man at her side and of the newly awakened alien sensations deep within her.

His steady gaze never left her eyes. "Yes."

Her eyelids closed and her heart leaped in her chest, pounding like a hammer as she sought to assimilate the import of his words. He began to talk, in the air over her head.

"Patrick trained as a priest many years ago. He's the only one of us who can read and write. He gave it up in favor of the travelling life, booze, women, but he's still qualified to perform marriages, baptisms and officiate at a burial. Those vows we took last night were just as real as any taken in a church. You're me wife, Lucy, in the eyes of God."

Rory's mouth once more engaged her own. His body moved across hers and pressed her down, crushing the life and juice out of the grassblades and wild flowers beneath her. Her nipples tingled as they brushed against the pelt on his chest. His strong hand gently stroked her thighs and parted them.

"Be gentle, *please,*" she murmured, as his stiff

maleness sought entry to her body. There was a sudden sharp pain as he penetrated her, and she cried out, her instinctive reaction being to try and pull away from him.

"There, mavourneen, there," he whispered, caressing her hair. His hands fluttered over her body, pausing here, stroking there, soothing and relaxing her until she felt as if she were floating sleepily on the edge of a dream. Then, in an abrupt change of mood and tempo, his lips rained hard kisses on her face and neck, his teeth nipped her shoulder, bit at her ear, her body was pulled up into his embrace, twisted around, pressed down, as, embedded deep within her, he rode the rhythmic surges of his own fulfilment.

Lucy was caught up and carried along in the urgency of his desire. All pain had gone now and the strange pulsating sensations inside her belly, which forced her to jerk her hips spasmodically upwards, made her groan with delight. Never had she experienced such piercing, poignant ecstasy. Her whole being was overtaken by a series of shuddering ripples which made her shake and tremble. She gave herself to them, tossing her head from side to side, flinging her arms out, crying aloud, and her moans were soon joined by a sighing groan from Rory as he reached his climax and jettisoned his pearls into the seabed of her womb.

Later, Lucy awoke from a refreshing doze and smiled softly to herself as her forefinger traced the outline of her slumbering partner's eyebrow, which resembled a brown furry caterpillar. At last she had an ally, someone who cared for her, someone who pleasured her, a man whose poetic vision and way with words surprised and delighted her. Maybe now her future paths would not have to be travelled alone.

Husband . . . The word was alien to her. She didn't feel like a wife. The perfect marriage she would have planned for herself was to a man who loved and desired her and awoke an answering passion in herself. But, she was forced to admit to herself, that was exactly what Rory had done. Maybe Fate had to move in weird ways to bring about the things that were best for one. Much as Lucy lamented her inability to control her own destiny, she felt like blessing the unseen hand that had brought herself and Rory together. She still felt like Lucy Swift, and not a bit like the Lucy McDonnell the ring on her finger now proclaimed her to be. But she knew it must surely take time to become part of anyone else's life—and, for now, her individuality lay submerged in the afterglow of union and sensual repletion.

CHAPTER THREE

Ever since she was a child, Lucy had loved fairs.
Her father had taken her to many and she had never failed to be fascinated by the clustering throngs
of gaily dressed humanity, the merry-making, the
excitement. Pendleton Fair was only a small, local
occasion, but the populace of many surrounding
villages seemed to have turned out in force. One
had to be on one's guard against the bands of pickpockets who roamed around, looking for a woman
absorbed in gossip or a man the worse for ale who
would not feel the light, dexterous fingers in their
pocket or see the hand creeping into their cloak or
basket.

She had now spent five whole weeks with Rory,
Smithy and Pat. The attitude of Rory's companions towards her had mellowed, especially when
they discovered that she knew every bit as much
about horses as they did, with the exception of
some of the tricks they got up to which enabled
them to pass off an unsound horse as a healthy
specimen, or even, on occasion, to make a fit horse

appear damaged so that they could buy it cheaply.
She did not approve of these sharp practices and
wondered if her father was aware of their existence.

Her father . . . He had caused her endless worry.
Every time they visited a fair, which was two or
three times weekly, as different towns held their
markets on different days, she was constantly on
the watch for him. He would naturally have grav-
itated to the place where the horses were being put
through their paces for prospective buyers. Lucy
could only pray that she would spot him before he
caught sight of her. Yet, she reflected, a market or
fair would probably be the last place he would expect to find his daughter. Doubtless he was happy
to have Emperor back. Pat and Smithy had reluctantly seen the sense in her suggestion that, as he
was an easily recognizable horse, he should be set
free and allowed to wander home, and so they had
led him to the track that wound down from the
moors to the villages in the valley and had left him
to make use of his natural homing instinct.

A group of half-grown lads jostled past her and
Lucy flinched. But she had nothing to fear now
from greedy thieves and pickpockets; she had no
valuables they could want to snatch. At the first
fair they had been to, she had replaced the hated
cream satin gown, with a sensible plain homespun
dress and warm cloak; reluctantly, she had parted
with the gold necklace that she had worn around
her neck ever since her father had given it to her on
her sixteenth birthday. The necklace had fetched a
price well below its worth, but still it had paid for

her other purchases—a pair of strong leather boots for herself and a blue woven shirt for Rory—and there had even been some money left over. But, during the past few weeks, the rain and cold had often obliged her and her companions to seek refuge in a series of inns, and now Lucy had but a few pence left to her name.

She paused as the fragrance of herbs and dried flowers assailed her nostrils. It came from a large straw basket placed on the drying mud; little dried bundles of thyme and rosemary and other species she couldn't name were mingled with sprays of lavender and small muslin pouches containing the withered petals of summer roses which gave off a heady perfume. On impulse, she bent down, picked up one of the fragrant bags and held it to her nostrils, inhaling deeply.

"Two for a farthing, only a farthing," a cracked voice intoned.

Lucy saw that it came from a wizened old woman, who was bobbing behind the basket like a sparrow. She fished in the near-empty pouch beneath her cloak and produced the required sum, selecting a bag of rose petals and a sprig of lavender. She was about to go when the rasping old voice called her back.

"Here, lady . . ."

Lucy ignored her at first, suspecting that the aged crone was about to accuse her of cheating or theft, a common fairground trick to extort more money from an innocent customer. But there was something in the hag's tones that made her obey.

The old woman hopped out from behind her basket and clutched at Lucy with a blackened, shrivelled hand. Lucy drew back in alarm. She had no desire to catch any nasty disease that this crone might be carrying.

"Ye're not married, are you, me dear," said the hag. It was more of a statement than a question. Lucy was about to show her the hand bearing her gold ring, then changed her mind.

"I *am,* mother," she retorted.

"A pretty bride ye'll make, in a silk gown, with your husband. A tall man, and fair. And such a beautiful emerald . . ."

She pronounced beautiful in such a way, giving it four syllables and implying a gloating covetousness, that Lucy thought she must be mad and seeing senile visions. Just as she was wondering how best to detach the scarecrow-like hand from her sleeve, she spied Rory obviously looking for her. She waved with her free hand and called his name.

"That's my husband," she informed the old woman, "that tall young man with the beard."

The old crone bobbed back behind her basket and squatted down, shaking her stringy white locks. She didn't say another word or even look at Lucy, but as Lucy pushed her way through the crowds to join Rory, she heard a laugh like a jackdaw's cackle following her and was glad when she could tuck her arm into his reassuring elbow.

"We've sold the chestnut and—you'll never believe it—we've got rid of the old grey cob at last," he informed her with sparkling eyes and a high color in his cheeks.

Lucy thought that he grew more handsome every day. He certainly grew more loving. He was possessed of a passionate nature, quick to express anger and impatience, quick to forgive and always ready to love. Lucy responded to his sexual demands with alacrity. She had thought their love-making was wonderful that day on the moors, when he had first seduced her, but even this experience had paled into insignificance in the face of the ecstatic occasions since. She felt a little thrill of desire now as she moved her hip against his and let her legs match his stride. She had surprised herself many times since meeting Rory. Hot as he was, she was always ready and burning for him. At first she had worried in case there was something wrong with her: surely it was only men who were supposed to feel this way, not women? Had her mother or her sister ever felt this aching need, this langourous melting which she experienced whenever Rory looked at her or spoke to her a certain way, whenever their bodies accidentally or deliberately touched? Rory said he loved her. Well, maybe this *was* love. She must be the luckiest wife in the world to inhabit such a paradise of mutual feeling and shared happiness.

"You're looking very pretty today," Rory remarked. Lucy wondered if the warm flush on her cheeks was responsible. "Here, me darlin' girl, I bought you a present."

Rory fished in the pocket of his grey britches and

brought out something that flashed golden. Could it be the long-promised wedding ring? Her heart leaped. He placed it in her hand and, to her disappointment, it turned out to be nothing but a trinket, a mock-gold chain bearing a small green stone in a setting shaped like a flower. Lucy reflected ruefully that it wasn't quite the emerald the old woman had spoken of, then thrust the mad witch's words out of her mind. It might not be valuable, it might not be a gold wedding ring, but still it was a pretty trifle, and a present from the man she loved. She thanked him, stood on tiptoe and kissed his cheek, then fastened the necklace around her throat.

"Someday, when I'm rich like your father, I'll buy you a sapphire to match your eyes," Rory promised.

He knew her father, Lucy had discovered, having met him at horse sales in the past. The world of horses was a small one. Lucy found that Rory had a lot of respect for Martin Swift, although at first he hadn't connected him with Lucy. She had never thought of her family as being rich, exactly. To Rory, however, who was used to years of sleeping in the open or in rough inns, a large farmhouse with several acres of land, a collection of good horses and a couple of servants, to say nothing of hired hands and stable boys, must have sounded like luxury indeed.

Lucy didn't like to think of the future, preferring to live from day to day, but she had to admit that it worried her. She certainly did not wish to spend the rest of her life wandering like a gypsy. What way was that to raise a family? She knew full well what lovemaking led to and could only hope that the natural consequences would be delayed, at least until she had persuaded Rory to abandon Pat and Smithy and the roving life and either take a job on a farm, where a tied cottage would be at their disposal or, preferably, save enough to start his own smallholding. Rory had a good eye for a horse and a few wise deals could do it—why share the proceeds with Pat and Smithy? He didn't need them, especially now that he had her, with all her own expertise.

As they passed a stall where a foolish volunteer with his head through a hole in a board was being pelted with rotten fruit, a prize being awarded according to how long he withstood such insulting treatment, Lucy lapsed into a daydream in which she was at a major race gathering, draped in furs, the owner of the best race-horses in the country. As her streamlined thoroughbred sped past the winning post, the name of Lucy Swift was on everybody's lips. Champagne glasses were raised to her, royalty invited her to dine. She would have a fine town house with her own carriage and servants, plus a mansion in the country where her horses would be kept and trained. Her racing colors would be emerald green and kingfisher blue, with her initials LS intertwined, on the sleeve. But she *wasn't* "LS" any more, she was "LM" now! Lucy McDonnell . . . it just didn't have the same ring to it!

She was chiding herself for being a snob as Rory ducked into the doorway of a canvas tent where a cockfight was going on, pulling Lucy in with him. Lucy couldn't bear seeing anybody being hurt, either humans or animals, and she detested the way in which the birds were fitted with cruel spikes on the legs with which to tear their opponent to pieces, but Rory ignored her protests.

All the men in the audience, and the few women present, too, appeared to be drunk. Like a pack of wolves they howled in glee as one unfortunate bird's belly was slit and, slipping in the slime of its own entrails, it was hacked to pieces while still alive by the fierce beak of an evil-looking red-eyed cock whose black feathers dripped blood. Realizing its foe was vanquished, the bird opened its gory beak and crowed, and the whole audience, with the exception of Lucy, stamped on the ground and roared. She felt sick and wanted to leave, but Rory informed her he had a bet on the next fight and promised to go as soon as it was over.

The handsome white fowl on which Rory had unwisely placed his money was soon reduced to raw meat and feathers. Cursing his ill-luck, Rory kept his word and led Lucy thankfully out into the fresh air again. This was one side of her husband she didn't like, the ease with which he gambled and his obvious enjoyment of blood sports. Bear-baiting, bull-baiting, cock-fighting, it was all the same. He'd place a bet and watch the fight with mounting excitement, weaving this way and that as his body followed the movements of the animal his money was on, yelling in delight at the sight of a spurting wound, groaning as his animal fell. After the contest he would turn to Lucy and murmur something ardent in her ear, or give her a caress that would leave her in no doubt that he was feeling stimulated and lusty. And she would pretend to respond although she was feeling sickened and disgusted. But men were like that. Would she be able to respect Rory if he turned pale and ill at the sight of blood, or if he preached sanctimoniously against the evils of drink and gambling? She knew, in her heart, what the answer was.

"Got to get back to Jamieson's Field, darlin', see how we're faring," said Rory, lengthening his stride.

He seemed to have forgotten his gambling disappointment already. His moods changed so rapidly that Lucy was hard pressed to keep up with him. No sooner had she got used to the fact that he was cheerful and whistling than his brow would crease and suddenly he would fly into a rage about the weather, the fact that Smithy had been late getting the horses watered or about his way of life in general. She would immediately adapt her mood to his and be about to say something consoling when, out of the blue, he would be joking and laughing and asking why there was such a worried crease between her brows. Lucy gave up. Rory was Rory and maybe she would never understand him.

"Pat's bidding for a dapple grey that must be three-quarter bred or I'm a blackamoor! Smithy tickled her near hind with me magic potion when

he examined her feet and she should be limping by
now. I've said to Pat, if we don't get rid of that
chestnut mare today we'll all be starvin' men. She
eats so much and bloats herself out with wind so,
that she looks as if she's about to give birth to a
whole herd. I think we could fool anyone that she's
in foal. What say we give it a try, me favorite lass?''

He was in irrepressible spirits and Lucy was
longing for the fair to be over, so that he and she
could be alone together. They were putting up that
night in the Ram's Head, a bustling inn in the market square. They had been lucky to get a room to
themselves, with accommodation on fair days
being always in short supply. Often Lucy had been
forced to lie awake, her ears tormented by the
sound of Smithy's cough and Pat's powerful
snores.

Jamieson's Field was a small fenced patch of
grass where the horse traders always congregated.
The animals were paraded one by one and the asking price given and greeted by guffaws, whereupon
the seller's sights were sensibly lowered and the
bidding started in earnest.

Lucy and Rory reached the spot and had to push
their way through a crowd of coachmen who had
left the vehicles in which their masters had been
conveyed to the sale and were busily and noisily
quaffing quantities of ale from cracked and battered tankards. The bids were emanating from a
solid knot of men, each intent on snaring a bargain. A sale was agreed, a solidly-built hack led
out, and their chestnut mare was led in by Pat. Al-

though a lot of people knew him by sight, his size and appearance still shocked the crowd into silence. Lucy had to admit that the mare certainly looked in foal. Her sides bulged and she walked with the splay-legged gait of an expectant mother, a kind of smug waddle. She was a handsome animal, with strong quarters, a deep chest and a slightly dished nose that spoke of Arab blood. Pat declaimed her falsified ancestry, told of the well-bred foal she was carrying, and asked for twenty guineas. To Lucy's great surprise, a man's voice answered, "Aye."

Rory gave a little jump of amazement and even Pat rolled his eyes, trying not to show how taken aback he was. The confidence of the unknown bidder in the merchandise prompted another man to offer twenty-five. The first man countered with thirty. The bidding rose in rapid leaps to the staggering sum of fifty guineas, whereupon the mare was knocked down to the man who had first spoken. Rory and Lucy rushed up to Smithy, who was standing with the rest of their animals. The old man was wheezing with mirth.

"Heh-heh—to think 'e thought 'e was getting two for the price of one! Oo-oh, that's rich! Some people don't know anything about 'orses, do they? Heh-heh—should 'ave sent 'is ostler!" Smithy doubled up, clutching his thighs.

Rory slapped him on the shoulder. "Ssh, ye fool. Here comes feller-me-lad now!"

Lucy could hear Pat's booming tones and a well-bred voice answering him.

"Yes, I know. Sired by Fleetwood out of Darley Court, eh? I don't believe it, but I'll take your word for it—and if she produces a hairy jackass I'll string you up personally!"

The voice was light, young, refined, and Lucy looked up in interest. The man walking beside Pat was tall, slimmer than Rory and dressed in a magnificent russet coat over a dove-grey waistcoat and velvet britches, all exceedingly well cut. His hair was fair and silky and, whereas Rory's tumbled wild round his shoulders, this man's was tied back neatly. His complexion was pale and his features finely chiselled and there was a haughty set to his bearing that made Lucy feel slightly insulted, as if he were implying that it was beneath him to mix with such riff-raff.

"I have some business to attend to today and won't be back till morning. See that the horse is delivered at eight o'clock sharp tomorrow morning. Darwin Manor—about three miles on the West Road, up on the hill. Ask anyone at the inn where you're staying. They'll give you directions."

"Yes, sir," said Pat, with a bob of his head. It was strange to see the giant deferring to a man a whole head shorter than he was.

"And who shall I deliver her to, sir?"

"Philip Darwin, Lord Darwin's son."

The haughty demeanor, the expensive clothes, the aristocratic tone of voice: Lucy had known he couldn't possibly have belonged to any but the upper classes. As he turned to walk away, he paused and looked directly at Lucy and Rory. Rory was murmuring something to Smithy in a low voice and Lucy thought that maybe the horse's new owner was suspicious, imagining them to be talking about him. She glanced at Rory, then back at the stranger, and suddenly realized that it was at herself that his clear gaze was directed. Embarrassed, she looked down at her feet, then at Rory again, then finally she submitted and returned the stranger's stare. A faint smile curved his lips. Then he gave her a brief nod as if to say he'd looked his fill and seen all he wished to see, and went on his way. Almost immediately Rory rounded on her.

"Little hussy!" he hissed.

"What do you mean?" asked Lucy indignantly, feeling doubly wronged.

"I saw the way that fancy man looked at you, and how you looked back at him—in front of *me*, your own husband!"

Rory had never been angry with her before and Lucy felt desolate. This onslaught was extremely unfair of him; she had done nothing to invite the stranger to look at her other than blush in embarrassment. Maybe Rory had mistaken the pinkness in her cheeks for another kind of flush entirely. His brow was knitted in anger. He looked wild, handsome, an untameable animal. Lucy could hardly believe that he belonged to her, that he loved her. She must find some way of patching up this silly tiff.

But it was not to be. All the way back to the inn he argued and would not see reason. By the time they reached their small attic room with its rickety wooden bed and crudely carpentered table, Lucy felt weary and depressed. What had got into him that had sparked off this totally unfounded jealousy? She had eaten nothing all day, and her stomach rumbled from hunger.

"Rory," she said, covering his hand with hers as it lay across his thigh. They were both sitting on the bed, she on the side nearest the window, he on the end facing the door. "Rory, I love you. I'd never look at another man. There's no one who can match up to you. You've got me, body and soul, for as long as you want me. And if ever you don't want me any more, just tell me and I'll go. I'd never bother you. All I want is for you to be happy."

It cost a lot for her to say these words, angry as she was with his unreasonable behavior, but it was the truth. She couldn't imagine ever making love with another man. Nobody would be able to stir or satisfy her so. And nobody could be more interesting, unpredictable, ever changing, or more loving and caring towards her, apart from at this very moment.

"Rory," she begged, "please believe me, I didn't mean anything. You made it all up. I couldn't help it if he looked at me—"

"Oh, stop whining woman, you're driving me mad. Just be quiet, will you?"

Lucy flinched at his unkind, uncharacteristic words. This wasn't the Rory she knew. There seemed to be some bitterness, some canker inside him that was gnawing and disquieting him and forcing him into irritability. There was nothing she could do to make him reveal his thoughts, but she wished that he trusted her enough to share his worries with her. Was it a gambling debt, maybe?

She shifted uncomfortably on the hard bed and gazed out of the window to distract herself from the uncomfortable silence in the room. She couldn't believe that her marriage could go wrong already, after five short weeks. All those people walking by outside, going to visit friends, family, lovers, or strolling in twos, none of them looked as if they were burdened with as many problems as she. All at once Lucy caught sight of a familiar russet colored coat. Was it . . . ? Yes, it was Philip Darwin, the man who had caused so much trouble. Lucy sent out a silent prayer for Rory not to turn round and spot his imagined rival. She did not dare breathe until the young man was out of sight behind a line of carriages on the other side of the road.

Rory heaved a deep sigh, and the bed creaked as he stood up. He caught her shoulders and turned her round to face him, then placed his lips on hers. Lucy's spirits rebelled. How could he expect her to make love when she was so depressed by his unfair behavior? How could he think of it at a moment like this? Did he have no sensitivity at all? Now, if he were to apologize, beg her forgiveness, tell her he loved her . . . Lucy had never refused Rory before, but now something inside her bridled at the thought of this man who had caused her so much pain satisfying himself inside her body. She felt cold and impatient and knew that his questing lips and fingers would, instead of awakening the usual fiery desire, merely annoy her and grate on her nerves. She desperately needed some time alone, time to think, time to forgive. She pulled back from his lips and twisted away from his fumbling hands.

"No," she remonstrated, in a half-sob. "No, Rory . . ."

She flinched from the look of fury that flashed across his face.

"What do you mean, 'No'? You're me wife, aren't you? Then I'll have my husband's rights! Some men would take the strap to you for this! But I'm not going to force you. All I'm going to do is ask you to see reason, girl, and give yourself to me. Will you? Come on, Lucy."

But Lucy's brain was far too confused to realise that, by complying with her husband's wishes now, she might be avoiding all sorts of future trouble. All she knew was that the husband she loved had changed this day into a man she didn't know, a man who was fired by sudden jealousies, gnawed at by secret worries. If only he could relax, turn it all into a joke as he had done so many times in the past, tell her what was really on his mind. But here he was, one hand on the door latch, stern, enigmatic, staring at her as if he didn't love her at all but saw her merely as an object of pleasure, a pint of ale to be quaffed when desired, then set aside. And if the ale didn't please, then by God he would be angry, berate the landlord, overturn the glass, just as he had overturned Lucy's emotions.

* * *

Rory McDonnell stumbled down the narrow, twisting staircase feeling as if a hundred pins had been stuck into his heart. How could he have left Lucy sobbing on the bed when all he wanted to do was take her in his arms, comfort her, apologize for his bad-tempered behavior and lose himself in her passionate body? Yet how could he explain himself to Lucy when he wasn't even sure himself why he was reacting this way? The sight of her exchanging looks with that damn'fool idiot, that popinjay Darwin, had set something in motion inside him that he'd never felt before in his life. Jealousy was the easiest name to put on it, but there was a lot more to it than that, things Lucy did not know, things he didn't ever want her to know but which, if they were to have any real future together, he must tell her one day.

He loved Lucy. Sometimes the sight of her waking in the morning with that heavy, dreamy look in her eyes and her chestnut curls rumpled, almost brought tears to his eyes. He had always had a streak of poetry in him. Sometimes, in his mind, he likened her to a stately swan; sometimes to a bright, pert robin; sometimes, when she was contemplative, distant, wrapped in her own thoughts, to the veiled moon on a misty autumn evening. If only he could write these thoughts down on paper, polish them, make gifts of them with which to present Lucy. But he couldn't write. He could only express his feelings in spoken words which were gone the moment they were said. He wanted to make her his properly. He loved her far too much to be able to carry on for much longer fooling her, pretending they were truly man and wife. Of course he'd gone along with that ritual on the moor, partly to satisfy Pat's drunken whim, but mainly because, in the depths of his heart, he *did* want to be married to this exceptional girl, with her beauty, intelligence and spirit that called to his very soul.

He had known on first meeting her that Lucy had too much pride and propriety to give herself to a man without the legality of marriage. He had forced her hand, yet he knew she had, in the end, come to him willingly, believing herself inextricably wed. Their love, their need for each other, had built up. She was as necessary to him as the air he breathed. Yet how long would it be before she made a female friend to whom she would talk about their marriage? And how long would it be before that friend questioned the fact that there had been only one witness, Smithy, to their act of wedlock, thus making it illegal, null and void? Never in his life had Rory wanted a woman so much, and never had he been so sure that, sooner or later, he would lose her. Once she found out the truth, she would hate him for certain. Nothing he could do would bring her back and enable her to trust him again. And he wouldn't blame her. Three-quarters of him had believed in that strange marriage ceremony. At first it had been a means to an end, a way of tricking her into giving herself to him. But then love had begun, and grown, and now he was a tormented man with no prospects of extricating himself from the trouble he had landed himself in.

The strong, country-brewed ale went straight to his fevered brain.

"Another, bejasus! More beer for a parched soul!" he ordered, throwing back his head and roaring. When the girl came to refill his glass, he grasped her round the waist and pulled her onto his knee. Later, when he joined her in her dark cupboard of a bedroom under the stair and ran his practiced hands over her plump body, it was Lucy's warm curves he imagined he was touching, and it was Lucy's name he moaned at the moment when his desire spent itself in the soothing, satisfying hollow of a woman's body.

Lucy awoke to find the skin on her face stretched tight with crying. She felt exhausted and emotionally drained. A wave of unaccustomed loneliness surged through her when she scanned the pokey room and found it empty. Her side of the bed was rumpled but the other side was smooth, the sheet and pillow cold to the touch. She felt certain that Rory had not been back. Pulling aside the torn curtain she saw the people were about in the damp street, their collars pulled up around their necks to protect them from the dank, curling fingers of the November mist. She was empty, hollow, numb, with no tears left to cry—and yet, looking back, their argument had seemed so trivial, a mere tiff over an imagined glance, a jealous fancy. Surely he wouldn't *leave* her because of it? It wasn't as if he had caught her in another's arms. Maybe he had gone off gambling somewhere, or had got drunk in some other inn and was even now sprawled on a bench or a pile of straw, sleeping it off. Reason with herself as she might, Lucy still felt a quiver of apprehension as she slid her stiff limbs off the lumpy pallet, splashed some ice cold water over her face from the cracked stone ewer on the table and prepared to go below in search of Pat and Smithy.

She remembered the horse that had to be delivered that morning to the man who was the cause of her marital trouble, and wondered who had taken it. The main room of the inn was empty of guests. A little girl was cleaning out the ashes from the grate and a man was whistling cheerfully as he wiped a pile of pots. Lucy approached him, described her companions and asked if he knew of their whereabouts.

"The big feller? The one with the black outfit to match 'is teeth? Oh aye, I've seen 'im all right, and little old grandad, too—a right candidate for consumption, if I ever saw one."

He paused, put down his cloth, spat into the straw on the floor and ground it underfoot. He was a small, fat, bald man with bright red cheeks and narrow, cunning countryman's eyes. He continued, warming to his subject.

"I remember Samuel Ramsbottom. A good man, Samuel, but never strong, reet poorly 'e always were. Now 'e grew thin and pale and coughed a lot, like that man o' yorn, coughed pink 'e did, froth with blood in it. Went on for 'baht a year, it did . . ."

Lucy was fretting with impatience, but afraid to butt in and annoy this man who was obviously determined to tell his story, in case he refused to give her the information she so badly needed. So she curled her toes tight inside her shoes and steeled herself to look interested.

"One day . . ." His slow, monotonous voice seemed to chew forty times on each word before spitting it out. "One day, 'e was walking down the 'Igh Street, like, when all of a sudden 'e coughed and a great fountain of blood spurted out of 'im, whoosh—all over the white cloak of this fine lady who was walking past. Drenched in blood she was, like a lamb at the slaughterhouse." He paused and chuckled at his own wit. He had obviously related his gory tale many times before and he had Lucy trapped, shuddering, mentally urging him to get to the end and answer her questions. "Oh, ho, ho—it were a reet funny sight, 'er face all green, like, and 'er lovely clothes all covered in . . ." Lucy tried not to listen to his flat tones, his ghastly story. "When we buried 'im 'e was bleached like there weren't a drop of red blood left in 'is veins. All grey and sunken 'e was. 'Orrible."

He looked at Lucy with a satisfied smirk, which promptly dissolved as he realized that she wasn't about to scream or grow pale like other ladies he'd told his tale to. He picked up his cloth again and started banging the pots around. Lucy had to clear her throat to regain his attention.

"My friends . . . where are they?"

He made a vague gesticulation which seemed to indicate that she should go out of the door and turn left. His directions led her to a rough wooden shed round the side of the inn. There was something about the deep rumbling noises coming from within that sounded very familiar to Lucy. Ducking into the doorway, she peered into the gloomy interior and, once her eyes had accustomed themselves to the light, she made out the recumbent forms of several men, sprawled in careless attitudes on the heaps of straw that covered the rough earth floor. One was Pat, without a doubt; his snores led her eyes straight to him. The giant was flat on his back, his cavernous mouth open, an empty beer tankard still in his hand. Curled in a foetal position next to him was Smithy. Was Rory with them? Silently, hardly daring to move in case she wakened anybody and incurred their hungover wrath, she inspected each slumbering figure in turn. One whom she at first thought was Rory on account of his blue shirt and shock of dark hair, sighed and turned over and revealed himself to be a much older man.

Perhaps he had taken the horse. There was only one way to find out. Making her way to the field behind the inn, where they had left the animals in charge of a watchman, stabling being at a premium on a fair day with the winter weather setting in, she took stock of the animals present. They were all there, including the chestnut mare with her falsely bloated stomach. Lucy's heart gave a little lurch. She had no idea what time of day it was and Philip Darwin didn't look like the kind of man who should be kept waiting.

She hurried back inside the inn and inquired the time of the pot-washer.

"Seven, miss," he replied. She knew the use of the word "miss" was a deliberate insult, implying that she wasn't a respectable married woman staying there with her husband, but a whore who had been picked up and passed off as a "wife." However, with so many more important matters on her mind, she couldn't afford to enter into an argument to defend her virtue. She decided to come straight to the point.

"My husband, Rory McDonnell, a young man with a beard and a slightly Irish accent, wearing one gold earring. Have you seen him?"

"Your *husband*," sneered the man. A shifty look passed across his puffy features. "Nay, can't say I have. Must have got up early and gone out for a walk, like, after a night with a hot little lass like you!"

His revolting leer made Lucy feel sick. She found herself briefly cursing Rory for forcing her to lead the kind of life where she was forced to mingle with scum like this man and take the sort of slights he was dishing out. Rory should be beside her, standing up for her, hitting this man in his foul mouth and teaching him how to behave in the presence of ladies.

And then she turned and saw him—and he saw her. They both stood frozen like statues, he in an attitude of guilt, she in one of horror, disappointment and anguish. He was coming out of the slut's tiny room, buttoning his shirt and adjusting his britches, while the naked form of the plump girl, her big, flaccid breasts dangling like lumps of uncooked dough, was clearly visible behind him.

"Rory." Lucy mouthed the word, her vocal chords being momentarily paralysed. She felt a clammy perspiration breaking out on her face and hands and her legs began to tremble uncontrollably. She heard the fat girl gasp and saw her push Rory out of her room so that she could close the door on Lucy's huge, accusing eyes.

Slowly, like a man in a trance, Rory moved towards her, refusing to look at her. Then, without a word, he broke into a stumbling run and bolted out of the door into the street. On an impulse, not knowing what she would do or say, Lucy dashed after him, hearing the snigger of the potman following her. He was running blindly, like a frightened animal, blundering into people and knocking them aside. Curses rang after him, then stopped as the jostled passers-by halted to watch the chase.

"Go on, lass—you'll get him," chuckled one old man as Lucy darted past, her skirts bunched up in her hand to prevent herself from tripping.

But it was no use. Rory was too quick for her. He vanished up a side street and she was left panting, leaning against a wall, wishing she could die right there, on that chill November morning, with nothing left in the whole world worth living for.

Several people peered curiously at the dishevelled young girl leaning against the damp wall, sobbing as though her heart would break, but nobody stopped to say a kind word. It was no business of theirs if a stranger's mother had died or a thief run off with her shopping money. At length, the dampness penetrating her clothes set Lucy shivering uncontrollably and forced her to start walking, although every step seemed useless progress to nowhere.

Suddenly she remembered the horse, and the fifty guineas to be collected from Philip Darwin. *She* would have that money. Rory had cheated her, left her homeless and penniless. Pat and Smithy were all right—they had the other animals which, although they could never fetch such a lofty sum, would at least allow them to carry on eating and travelling. She was the one who was in desperate need, and surely they would forgive her, if ever they found out the true facts. As she made her way back to the inn, her arms wrapped round herself for warmth, she thought of her parents sitting round a roaring log fire—her father who, for all his faults, was a loving, clever man; her faded, adorable mother; her pet cat, Ha'penny; Emperor; the clean, vibrant smell of the stables . . . Her heart reached out in longing for the nostalgic familiarity of all she had left, so many miles behind. Rory's face swam into her mental vision and she made a huge effort and pushed him aside. She had trusted him, loved him, offered him her whole life if he wanted it, and he had chosen to reject her in the vilest way, by preferring the company and body of a grubby, ill-bred alehouse hussy to her own. Oh, if only she wasn't tied to him by the bonds of marriage! He had captured her, forced his will on her. How could she have been so gullible as to believe he wanted her for a life-long companion? Why could he not simply have ravished her and left her to wander on the moors, with her innocence gone, but her body, her mind and heart still free and un-attached to another human being, either legally or emotionally?

Pat's thunderous snores were still echoing round the shed. Lucy opened the gate into the field and nodded to the young lad who stood guard over the animals. He knew she was one of the group who had left them there the previous day and helped her to saddle up the chestnut, stretching the girth with difficulty over her rotund belly.

"Got to ride her gently, eh?" he remarked, with a knowing look.

"Yes, I'll do that," murmured Lucy, scarcely noticing that she spoke, her mind in a turmoil in the midst of which only one thing stood clear—that she must take this horse to Darwin Manor and col-lect fifty guineas. Money and horses. That was all her life seemed to revolve around. It had been that way ever since she was a child, as far back as she could remember. Money and horses—and the un-predictable, unreliable ways of men.

As she took hold of the mare's bridle, she no-ticed the gleam of her makeshift wedding ring. A thick, choking lump of tears gathered in her throat as she looked at the gold hoop which had once adorned Rory's ear. In an instant of wild fury, she snatched it from her finger and hurled it into the field. As she goaded the mare out into the lane, she saw the boy scrabbling among the grass. *Let him sell it if he wants to,* she thought, *it's far more use to him than it is to me.* The gold band had always felt temporary, somehow, and meaningless—like the mockery of a marriage it symbolized. Now she had lost both, but she did not feel in the slightest bit free or light of heart as she set out in the rain to try and find Darwin Manor.

CHAPTER FOUR

The Earl of Darwin raised his head weakly from his pillows when he heard hoofbeats clattering into the courtyard. One yellowed, emaciated hand, bearing a heavy gold ring with the family crest engraved on it, stirred on the sheet, then reached waveringly towards the bellrope. He pulled and a tolling sounded in the servants' quarters but, seeing that Darwin Manor was now reduced to a complement of three, a cook, a general housemaid, and a butler, who were all busy fulfilling the tasks of twelve, nobody answered the old man's call.

"Damnable business," he muttered to himself, "damnable." What made it worse was that he knew it was entirely his fault, and his alone, that the Darwin family were reduced to such penurious straits. The death of his young wife had turned what were formerly pleasurable activities, lightly partaken of, into a way of life. Drink and gambling, the pastimes of many a gentleman of leisure —though few were so over-indulgent as Lord Darwin, who had allowed both his fortune and his health to waste away until now there remained only the merest vestiges of either.

"Eleanor, oh my dear Eleanor," mumbled the old man, allowing his rheumy eyes to fill with tears. "You could have been such a comfort to your dying husband." He was totally forgetting, of course, that, by now, his wife would have been quite middle-aged herself and well past her first sprightliness.

"Nonsense, Father!" rang out a cheerful voice. "You're not dying. Imbibing too much, perhaps, but your guts must be so well pickled by now that they'll find you in your grave two hundred years from now, still in one piece."

The old man's lips tightened in petulance. The one thing he couldn't bear was for anyone to remind him of his own mortality. Why wouldn't they let him do what he wanted to do, slide into the past and live alongside his memories?

"Do something for me, m'boy. Fetch me m'porter."

A deep sigh issued from his son, Philip, who was standing framed in the doorway. He looked at his father with a stern yet indulgent expression, as if about to remonstrate with a mischievous child.

"Now, Father, you heard what your physician said. Not more than two glasses may pass your lips in a day and, to my knowledge, you've had three already. When I heard your bell ring, I thought, 'Has Father found an emerald in the mattress? A store of doubloons in the panelling? Or does he just want a drink?' "

Philip found his father exasperating and foolish;

many was the time he had cursed him for losing the family money by allowing himself to be cheated by bastards like John Hardwicke of Rokely Hall, who, Philip knew for a fact, carried a pack of marked cards always about his person. Yet he was sympathetic towards his father, sorry for the lonely life he had led, grieving so much over his lost Eleanor that he could not bring himself to marry again. Philip had been brought up by a series of tutors until the Earl had decided it was less costly to send him into the army for a spell. Philip had soon become a popular cavalry officer and his good judgement of people had led to several shrewd business deals which brought in enough capital to keep himself in clothes, pay the servants' wages, buy his father's beloved porter and stop the walls of his ancestral seat from crumbling into disrepair—except that it was not his ancestral seat any more. Not since his father's last card game with John Hardwicke, when Lord Darwin had put up his last big stake, Darwin Manor, and lost it to that—that *trickster*, that cheat and swindler. Philip had offered to fight a duel to win back the deeds to his home but Hardwicke—fat, purple-nosed, crude, cowardly Hardwicke—had declined, using a violent attack of indigestion as an excuse. Indigestion! Philip would have liked to have pricked him in the bloated belly with the tip of his sword to relieve the old windbag's internal pressure! And as for horse-faced daughter . . . Philip just hoped he could carry off the wedding successfully. Once she was his and had brought Darwin Manor safely back into his hands again, Philip would soon teach her her place,

the haughty bitch. But, for now, he would play the
charming fiancé, all cooing flattery and honeyed
words. Later on, once he had planted an heir in her
stringy body and gone back to join his regiment,
there would be plenty of time for love.

Then Philip, too, heard the stamp of a hoof on
the cobbles. Peering through a distorted diamond
pane of the mullioned window, he made out a figure on a plump horse. This was the moment he had
been waiting for. There might be a lot of unfair
things in his own life, he reflected, but some of
them he could do something about, and by Jove he
was going to put paid to this one. Rogues and
tricksters of any sort would be better thinking of a
quick escape route rather than coming up against
Philip Darwin. It would give him immense satisfaction to see the hangman's noose biting into their
necks.

Lucy thought she had never seen a place that
looked so devoid of life. Yet it could have been a
beautiful, graceful house, with flowered creepers
twining up the walls, rich tapestries in the windows
and smiling servants at the door. There should
have been children's laughter, constant visitations
of titled ladies and gentlemen in smart carriages,
instead of this brooding air of silence and neglect.

Perhaps she was too early and the occupants of
the Manor were still abed. As the young man had
said the previous day, the great house was easy
enough to find. Indeed, it would have been hard to
miss, with its grey turrets sticking like jagged teeth
out of the clump of trees that surrounded it, a

patch of mystery and majesty set in the fair pastureland of the Pendleton Hills.

It had taken the lazy chestnut mare at least an hour to toil up the long slope to the Manor. Lucy had expected some kind of welcome, even if it had been only the head stableman. Surely they were waiting for her? Or had Philip Darwin regretted his purchase already and gone into hiding in the far recesses of his grand house? But maybe his "business" had kept him away longer than he had expected. After her recent experience, Lucy had grave doubts about the nature of any man's absence from home.

She had no intention of leaving the horse without collecting the payment for it. The nobility, Lucy knew only too well, could cheat as much as any common man, and think less of it. No, she would wait—all day, if necessary. It was a cold, dank morning and the dawn drizzle was giving way to steady, soaking rain. The mare disliked it as much as Lucy did, and stood with her head drooping and her tail clamped to her hocks. A vivid memory of Philip Darwin came back to Lucy now, as she sat shivering in her saturated cloak. Those grey eyes, so haughty and aloof, had held a twinkling warmth when they met Lucy's, a kind of intimacy which had hinted at a kind of kinship, as if he had realized that Lucy was different from her companions, maybe a cut above them, and was curious and interested. Behind his aristocratic, commanding façade, Lucy had sensed gentleness and humor. Maybe it was intuition, or perhaps she was totally fooling herself, but she had felt there

were a lot of admirable qualities about the young
man, which was why she was feeling so guilty now
about bringing him a horse with no pedigree, a
mere mongrel, who was not even in foal. She would
not try to take his money under false pretences if
she did not need it so much herself. She would
come to him now, apologize, explain and refuse to
sell the animal to him, and face the fury of the others when she got back. Yet, if this were just an ordinary day, she would not be sitting here now, wet,
cold and confused. Pat, Smithy or Rory would
have taken the horse and she would be back at the
inn, making preparations to move on to their next
destination. Maybe there would be no sales or markets for a few weeks, if the bad weather settled in;
they would eke out their money by eating sparing-
ly, the men drinking the cheapest ale, and she
would be able to spend many warm, loving hours
in Rory's arms.

Lucy felt a pang of emotion drive through her
like a rapier. There would be no more intimate
hours of laughter and love with her husband. Rory
had gone. He had let her down in the worst way a
man could ever betray a woman, through another
woman. That slut! Lucy thought of her now, the
tousled brown hair, probably lousy, the blubbery,
sensual lips, the lard-like skin and big, drooping
breasts. A slow-witted, bovine animal, sensate only
when brought to life by a glass of wine, a gold coin
and a man's organ between her floppy thighs. Ugh!
Lucy wished she could have marked that dull, common face with her fingernails, torn her hair out,
bruised her body, sent her naked out into the rain

and fog for daring to seduce her beloved Rory. Yet, she thought, deliberately calming her thoughts, perhaps it was not totally the girl's fault. Maybe—no, it couldn't be true, surely he wouldn't . . . ? But maybe Rory had been attracted to the grubby drudge. If that were so, then Lucy could only be glad that he was gone, for how could she ever bear to let him near her own body again? And the strain of always having to watch him when he was in the company of other women, whether fine ladies or common wenches . . .

The anger raised by her reminiscences fired her to dismount from the chestnut mare, place the reins around a mounting block to prevent the animal from wandering and walk round the side of the house to the great oak main door. Grasping the heavy iron knocker, she raised it, then let it fall with a ringing thud on the studded door. Almost immediately, as if someone had been lying in wait for her, the huge oaken structure creaked open to reveal a familiar fair-haired figure standing inside. Clad in a ruffled white shirt, a lovat jacket and matching britches, Philip Darwin was a spectacle to set any maiden's heart fluttering, but Lucy, in her overwrought state, was in no mood to be impressed. Uncomfortably aware of her wet, bedraggled state, she hoped he might at least invite her in to dry her sopping clothes by the fire and take a warm drink. But there was no friendliness or invitation in his face, just fathomless coldness which she didn't understand, and when he spoke, his voice was like splinters of glass.

"I suppose you were too ashamed to come

straight to the door. I watched you from the window, sitting on that wretched nag, trying to pluck up courage to rob me."

"I . . . I d-don't understand," stammered Lucy. The trouble was, she *did* understand. So Darwin wasn't a fool after all. He *did* know horseflesh— and now she was to suffer for his knowledge.

Philip cursed the fact that one of the men hadn't come with the horse. Dealing with a man would have been easy. But this girl, with her wet locks plastered to her white face, and that big-eyed, forlorn expression—the hussy! Fancy sending a girl with that dud nag. It must have been a deliberate move. He was willing to bet that they used her like this all the time to attract men's eyes away from the steed they were buying, so that their minds would be too occupied to notice the ewe-necks, the spavins, the scars from over-reaching, the wheeze and hack from damaged equine lungs. And then she would deliver the wretched animal, too, and distract the lascivious fools all over again, and probably con them into driving her home in their own carriage! Jove! To be cheated by a fellow man was bad enough, but to be taken in and maneuvered by this chit of a girl!

Lucy watched the cold light in his eyes change and become purposeful, and she started to back away, hoping she could scramble onto the mare and be gone before he could pursue her. She turned, made a sudden dash and a spring and was across the chestnut's back, but Philip Darwin was right on her heels. Winding his hand in the sodden material of her skirt, he tugged hard, unbalancing

Lucy and sending her tumbling towards him. She kicked furiously with her feet, sending the mare shying away from beneath her. For a second she felt as if she were suspended in the air, then, with a painful thud, she landed on her hip and elbow on the hard, slippery cobbles.

Before she could scramble to her feet, Philip Darwin had bundled her up and was dragging her towards the open door of the stables.

"Let me go, d'you hear? Take your hands off me, you—"

All the breath was knocked out of her as he caught his foot behind her ankle and sent her spinning into a large bale of straw at the back of the shadowy stable. Panting for breath, Lucy raised her arms to protect herself as Philip, his eyes narrowed and cruel, stretched out a hand towards her. In that instant, the memory of the beating she had received from her father the night she ran away from home came back to her in discomfiting detail. Then she had fought, bitten, scratched and kicked, yet still she had been overpowered. Perhaps there was another way of dealing with this kind of tight situation—with calm reason and cool logic. Philip didn't look like the kind of man to be swayed by a woman's pleas or tears. But perhaps if she could stand up to him, win his respect . . .

Trying not to open her eyes too wide he thought she was trying some feminine wile, she gazed at him and caught his attention so that his movement towards her was arrested in mid air.

"I understand why you are angry," she said. She meant it; so would she have been in his position. But wait a minute; if he already knew that his mare "in foal" was a swindle, he must have known at the very moment when he was bidding for the horse . . . Or had somebody informed him later, Pat or Smithy perhaps, in return for a financial gift from Philip for exposing their trick? No, they would never do that. It would be the end of their livelihood if they did. They had to be careful, especially when so many of the horses they had handled were stolen property. A man could be hanged for less than that . . . *Hanged!* A sudden shudder possessed Lucy as she gazed into Philip's steely eyes. He was coming towards her again. He had her tight by the arm, twisting her flesh, making her cry out in pain.

Her face must have shown how much he was hurting her, because he suddenly smiled coldly and said, "Go on, you little bitch, cry! There'll be time enough for tears when the hangman is marching you to the gallows!"

Lucy's mouth dropped open in disbelief. What had she done? She was innocent of everything. It hadn't been her idea to pass off the mare as being well-bred and in foal. It had unfortunately fallen to her to deliver it, that was all. Yet even as she thought this she blushed, remembering her plan to keep Philip's fifty guineas for herself.

He held her down on the prickly straw, his fingers digging cruelly into her upper arm. Lucy remained still. There seemed no point in crying out or struggling. No, her first idea was the best, to reason with him.

He started speaking, slowly, as if talking to himself.

"Thieves, crooks, swindlers. They've taken so much from me." Then, fixing Lucy with a glare that frightened her, he spoke directly to her, venom in his words. "I've been watching you lot. I've been following your progress, you know. Oh yes, you might have thought you'd got away with disguising Silver Maiden, that grey that went missing from Lady Pettigrew's orchard last June—"

"But I was nothing to do with it," Lucy pointed out quietly, though her heart was thumping in her chest. "I didn't even know them then. If you'd just let me explain—"

"You've no need to explain anything," snapped Philip, shaking her and making her bite her tongue painfully. "You've fallen in with them, and so as far as I'm concerned you're all as bad as each other. You know what the penalty is for stealing horses and cheating honest citizens. I've got you in my hands now, and you're going to lead me to the others. And then . . ." He paused. Lucy's heart was pounding so loudly that she could hardly hear his final words, which he spoke softly and sibilantly, with an air of smug triumph. "And then it will give me great satisfaction to watch you all hang together."

"*No!*" The word tore itself from Lucy's lips before she could check it. Suddenly her calmness left her and she twisted herself violently round in order to try and escape from Philip's determined clutches. At the same time she calculated how far away his leg was, and landed a mighty kick in the center of his left shin.

But Philip was wearing leather riding boots of excellent quality, and he reacted no more than he would have done had a butterfly landed on him.

"You heard what I said, didn't you?" he inquired, moving so close to Lucy that she no longer had enough room to take a swing at him with her foot. "People like you are the scum of the earth. They don't deserve to live."

He drove his knee hard up against her thighs, attempting to prise them apart. Lucy felt that his bullying ways had gone far enough.

"Son of an earl you may be, but your manners are no better than a butcher boy's," she announced, in her coolest, haughtiest tones, fixing him with her most glacial stare. "I demand that you release me right now and, what's more, give me the apology that's due to me for your unforgiveable behavior."

Philip laughed out loud. Down the far end of the stable, there was a sudden flutter of wings and a huge brown barn owl swooped low over their heads and glided out of the door, causing Lucy to squeal in terror as she felt the wind of its flight brushing her hair.

"Pretending to be a lady now, are we, now that the shadow of the noose is round your neck? You're going to recant, are you? Call a churchman and confess your sins? Well, maybe God will forgive you, but I'm not God and I have no intention of letting you get away with your theft and fraud one moment longer. I've been trying to track down your particular little group for a long time, that huge oaf who pretends he's of the church—"

"But he *is!*" interjected Lucy vehemently. Philip ignored her.

"—that shrivelled little rat with the consumptive cough, and that bearded lady's man."

Lucy's first instinct was to spring hotly to Rory's defense and tell him he was her husband and an honorable man. Then the events of earlier that morning came back to her and she held her tongue.

"Not to speak of *you*, my pretty one." He rolled his upper lip back from his teeth in a dog-like snarl.

Lucy shrank back from him. Was he going to have a fit? She had heard that the aristocracy frequently had fits; something to do with inbreeding, she'd been told. Or was he going to strangle her there and then, to save her the public agony and humiliation of hanging?

It soon became obvious to her that he was going to do neither. Pinning her arms behind her back in a vice-like grip, he nonchalantly reached for the clasp of her cloak and unhooked it. The sodden garment fell from her shoulders and Lucy felt suddenly vulnerable, knowing there was nothing but her woollen dress between his eyes and her bare skin. It felt horribly like the situation she'd been in with Rory and his companions, but on that occasion she'd been saved by Rory's intervention—although, she reflected, it hadn't exactly done her a lot of good. She was beginning to learn about men, to discover what motivated them: money and sex.

With both, their instincts were acquisitive and urgent. She was no longer a virgin, it was true, but she still had no desire to be taken and ravaged by a cruel, sadistic man, who refused to let her explain her circumstances and seemed intent on taking not only her body, but her very life.

"Philip Darwin." She had to try talking to him again. If rape was indeed what he had in mind, he was certainly taking his time, toying as he was with the laces that held the front of her dress together. "If you are a gentleman and an intelligent, just human being, then at least let me put my case before condemning me to be handed over to the authorities. I was not with that group of men of my own free will. I—"

Her words were cut short as Philip's cold lips closed on hers. He had been toying with her, like a cat plays with a mouse; now the game was over and the prey was to be devoured. The prickly straw scratched at Lucy's back as he seized the neckline of her dress and tore it at the side seam so that one of Lucy's marble-white shoulders was exposed. At the sight, his lust was up and now he wrenched at the front, pulling until the homespun material stretched and frayed. He saw the gleam of Lucy's breasts in the gloom and, inclining his head, sank his teeth into the fleshy curve of Lucy's cleavage, leaving two semicircles of bright red. She winced, writhed, but it was no good. His hand was maneuvering her skirts out of the way and she could feel, with sinking heart, his hardness rubbing against her thigh.

Suddenly, without any prior warning, there was

a piercing scream from the direction of the doorway.

"*Philip!*" The voice was female and sounded agonized and tearful. Then there was the sound of running footsteps across the yard.

"Rachel! Oh no—*Rachel!* Rachel, *wait!*" All at once Lucy was free, as Philip released his grip on her and tore off in pursuit of the unknown interloper.

Trembling from cold and shock, Lucy sank into the straw bale, trying desperately to find some way of securing her torn dress over her bruised and smarting flesh. The miracle had happened after all. She could go now. Her mother had always said she had a guardian angel and, for the first time ever, Lucy thought she must have been right. Grimacing at the feel of her wet cloak, she draped it once more around her shoulders and fastened it. She was just about to tiptoe out of the door when she heard voices, raised in argument, one pleading and apologetic, the other adamant and tearful.

"No, Philip, I *won't* forgive you! How could you do this to me, you—you heartless *traitor?* Two months before our wedding, and I catch you with . . . with . . ." The voice tailed off into sobs and Philip's took over.

"Rachel, my dearest love, it's not how it seems, I promise you. There's a good reason. I'll tell you if only you'll listen. It's nothing to do with you, with love . . . It wasn't even a passing fancy. It's nothing. That girl—she cheated me, stole from me. She had to be punished, so—"

"A fine way of punishing her!" Rachel's voice

was cutting and bitter. Lucy felt a stirring of sympathy for the unknown, unhappy girl. She knew exactly how she must be feeling.

"My darling, this was an unfortunate, isolated incident." Philip's voice was wheedling and persuasive and Lucy hated him for his attempts to extricate himself from his dilemma. She almost felt like stumbling out in her ragged, bruised state and showing the girl how her precious sweetheart had abused a total stranger, thus making her loathe him even more.

But Rachel's next words, spoken in chilly, arrogant tones, sent her mind and sympathies spinning in quite the opposite direction.

"Like father, like son," she sneered. "Your father is fool enough to lose your family money, your fine house, to my father, on the turn of a card. And now his equally foolish son, you, Philip Darwin—" Lucy, from her hiding place in the stable, could imagine Rachel pointing an elegant finger at him. "—has thrown away his only chance to get some part of his inheritance back. I realize now that you never loved me, although I once stupidly imagined that you did."

"But Rachel—"

"No, no excuses. Do you think that I, Rachel Hardwicke, wish to be married to a ne'er-do-well who courts sluts every moment my back is turned? Why, I'd be a laughing stock in my own house! I don't wish to hear your . . . *explanation*. There will be no forgiveness, either from myself or from my father. I'm totally disgusted with what I've just been forced to witness. I don't want your title, I don't want you. And I hope never to set eyes on you again. As soon as your father passes away, Darwin Manor becomes mine. As for what happens to you, well, doubtless you can find some little serving maid with an accommodating body who will be only too pleased to take you in. Goodbye, Philip."

Lucy heard the sound of a horse's hooves and risked a glance out of the stable doorway. She saw a stiff back, clad in tawny velvet, and a long skein of blonde hair tied back with a brown ribbon, vanishing down the drive atop a roan mount. Philip was standing, gazing after her, unmoving. She could hardly believe what she had just heard. It explained so much about Philip, particularly about his attitude towards her. No wonder he felt so bitterly about people being cheated. Although Lucy knew nothing whatsoever about Philip's father—or the mysterious Rachel's father either, for that matter—she felt in her bones that the Darwin money and property had not been won honorably.

As soon as Philip turned once more in the direction of the stables, Lucy realized that she had missed a golden opportunity. Or had she? The only ways to leave Darwin Manor were by the driveway, and she could hardly have walked straight past Philip and his fiancée, or else over open fields where, once again, she would surely have been spotted. She darted back inside the dark stable, trying to blend with the shadows. At once, her dilemma came back to her. She was in terrible danger, not only from Philip but from Pat and Smithy, too. Maybe, right at this moment, they were discovering the theft of the horse and the disappearance of herself and Rory. They would jump to the wrong conclusion, of course; they would assume that she and Rory had stolen the mare and run off together. If they came looking for her, Rory or the horse at Darwin Manor, they would be walking straight into a trap. Yet there was no way she could warn them, and no way she could explain her actions to them.

Now Philip expected her to lead him straight to the remaining members of the party. If they had noticed anything the previous day, that look which Philip had given her, for instance, or if Rory had informed them of his jealous suspicions, they might think, quite naturally, that she was siding with Philip against them. Yet if she refused to obey Philip, the situation was just as bad for her. Whichever way she looked, the outlook was equally bleak.

She saw him silhouetted in the doorway and drew in her breath. He turned his head this way and that, looking for her.

"I know you're in there. Must I take a lantern and find you, or will you be a good girl and come here?"

Was she imagining things, or was his voice really not so stern as earlier, before his encounter with Rachel? The tone of icy accusation seemed to have gone. He appeared to be making an effort to sound commanding and authoritative. A quick glance round assured Lucy that there was no other way out of the stable building. She was at a dead end, with nothing but a row of loose boxes between herself and Philip.

Taking a step forward, she said softly, "I'm here."

He made no move to approach her, so Lucy walked up to him, still clutching her cloak tightly around her to hide her torn dress. She had an intuitive feeling that she should be reasonable with him, in spite of the way he had abused her.

"I . . . I couldn't help hearing what happened. I'm sorry. But if you'll let a woman you don't even know give her opinion, I'd say it was for the best. She doesn't sound like the sort of girl who'd make a man very happy." There—she'd tried her hardest to be consoling. Now would he soften his feelings towards her?

To her amazement, Philip raised one fist and brought it smashing down against the doorframe. Beads of blood sprang out along his grazed knuckles but he made no attempt to rub or suck them, simply left his damaged hand dangling at his side. There seemed to be some kind of inner battle going on inside him. Patiently, Lucy waited for a reaction or an order.

"What's your name?" His voice seemed to come from far away, as if he were speaking in a trance.

"Lucy Swi- er, McDonnell, Lucy McDonnell."

He made no comment about her hesitation. Dully, he inquired, "I suppose you heard what passed between my betrothed and me?"

"Yes," Lucy murmured, as solicitously as she knew how.

"It's terrible. If I've lost her, I've lost everything."

Lucy felt compelled to point out that it was

largely his fault; it he had only consented to the kind of reasonable discussion she had wanted, none of this would have happened. Somehow, she managed to hold her tongue and merely remarked, "I gathered there was more than simply love at stake."

Philip raised his head and looked at her, as if seeing her clearly for the first time.

"Look, I . . . That is . . ." he stumbled, "I . . . I want to say I'm sorry for what I did." His words started coming out in a rush, tumbling over one another. A faint flush rose in his pale cheeks. "I was very angry. It was true that I had set out to put a stop to the horse thieving and crooked trading that has been going on, but I shouldn't have treated you like that. I saw you only as a thief, not as a woman."

"I suppose if I had been a man, you would have given me a good hiding?"

"Yes, of course, although I don't know what chance I would have stood against that giant of yours."

"And would you really have turned us over to the authorities, seen that we all hanged?"

He fell silent, biting his lower lip thoughtfully. Then he raised his chin defiantly and said, "I can't lie about it. Yes, that was my intention."

Feeling that the perfect moment had arrived, Lucy spoke up boldly: "I'd like you to know that I didn't fall in with the bunch of thieves, tricksters, horse traders, or whatever you like to call them, entirely of my own free will. I was out alone, I was set upon at an isolated spot and captured. For various reasons, I could not get away from them. I was as much their victim as, now, I am yours."

She faced him as defiantly as he faced her. She tried hard not to blink or let her gaze waver as his grey, inscrutable eyes held hers.

Finally, he broke off the contest, looked away and said, "I think I believe you."

Lucy felt weak with relief. So there was some hope for her. Maybe if he'd let her tell the full story, then perhaps there was some way in which he could help her.

He seemed suddenly to remember that it was raining, and stepped into the shelter of the stable, next to Lucy. He stayed a little apart from her, as if trying to retain some shreds of dignity. Taking his silence as encouragement to carry on, Lucy found herself explaining the events that had led up to her capture on the moor, then the weird ritual she had been forced to undergo with Rory. The only thing she omitted to mention was her feelings towards Rory, giving him the impression instead that she was held as Rory's unwilling consort and that it was relief, not jealousy, that she had felt that morning on discovering him with the girl in the inn. She even told him of her plan to steal his fifty guineas and at that he let out a peal of laughter.

"You poor girl," he chuckled, then, recovering himself, looked at her rather sadly and said, "Do you think I would really have given it to you? Did I really seem that much of an ass to you all yesterday?"

Lucy couldn't say "Yes," so contented herself with the tactful, yet enigmatic, "I had my doubts."

As if he felt he were getting too friendly with somebody who was, in spite of everything, his prisoner, Philip Darwin's face underwent a rapid change of expression, causing Lucy's ray of hope to vanish. The warmth and compassion vanished and in their place was an unwelcome resemblance to his earlier hard approach.

"I can see that you are in considerable distress and that your life is in a mess, my girl. Still, although I must admit that your plight touches me, I feel I cannot go back on the solemn promise I made myself to put an end to all this crooked horse dealing. It is still within my power to end not just the livelihood but the lives of you and your cronies. However, I do believe, after what you have just said, that you are an innocent victim of circumstance."

Lucy felt a huge relief. Yet instinctively she knew that there would be a price to pay. Philip Darwin was obviously no spineless, effete upper-class wastrel. She had an idea that he was about to strike some kind of bargain with her. Would it mean giving her body to him? Would she be forced to betray Pat, Smithy and, worse, Rory? What was she going to have to do in return for his sparing her life?

But Lucy's curiosity was not to be assuaged. Philip Darwin was apparently unwilling to explain what was in his mind. Instead, he smiled at her, a cold, grim smile.

"Come with me, my girl," he said, propelling her out of the stables and across the courtyard. "You're going to stay a while at Darwin Manor."

CHAPTER FIVE

The room was almost bare. The carpet must have
been at least a hundred years old, Lucy felt, and the
floorboards beneath it could be glimpsed through
the holes. The bed and the giant oak cabinet in one
corner were ornately carved with a matching leaf
pattern and the same family crest Lucy had noticed
above the front doorway of the Manor. The whole
house spoke not of austerity but of grandeur faded
to a genteel poverty. A maid—perhaps their only
maid—had brought in some logs and lit a roaring
fire and Lucy felt her convulsive shivering starting
to ease. The window was set into two feet of solid
grey stone and opened onto a balcony overlooking
a stretch of parkland. Once it must have been beautiful, for the trees outside were set in rows flanking
a wide avenue, now a wilderness of fallen branches
and tangled undergrowth. Through the driving
rain, Lucy spied a glitter of water beyond the trees
and some remnants of ancient statuary—or were
they just tree stumps covered in ivy? Once, she
thought, fine lords and ladies must have strolled,
laughing, arm in arm, down that avenue, to dawdle

by the fountains while musicians played on the flat
lawn outside the orangery. In her mind she cleared
the tangled weeds and dead branches, plucked the
fallen leaves and coarse, alien grasses from the
lawn, restored the fallen masonry at the foot of the
walls and revitalized the heart of the crumbling
mansion, covering the naked walls with paintings
and tapestries, placing an ornamental table here, a
vase there, adding carpets, cushions and brocades
in rich, glowing colors. Then she peopled it, imagining the conversations, the intrigues and romances, the fine clothes, sweet music and rich
food.

So lost was she in her imaginative exercise that
she did not hear the maid enter the room and
jumped when she felt the touch on her elbow.

"Sorry, miss. The young master said I was to
bring you dry clothes. I'm afraid it's not very fashionable, but then, you see, it's one of my own.
Made it myself, miss."

Lucy stared at her, and at the simple brown dress
lying over her arm. The woman was prematurely
old, grey-haired, round-shouldered and hollow-
faced. She looked as if she had seen hungry days,
but there was an air of contented resignation about
her and her lined mouth was smiling with pride as
she proffered the dress. Lucy took it, examined it.
Although the material was simple homespun wool,
the stitching was so fine as to be almost invisible,
the sleeves perfectly set into the armholes and the
waist gathered into soft pleats that fell the full
length of the skirt.

"It's beautiful," smiled Lucy and the woman glowed with pleasure. "I shall be proud to wear it."

"The young master said that, after you were dressed, you should join him for luncheon in the banqueting hall. I will show you the way."

Lucy could not resist asking a question. "You said 'the *young* master' . . . Is Mr. Darwin's father still alive?"

"Yes, miss, although he's failing. These days he seldom leaves his bed. Matthew—that's my husband—sees to him. He won't have a woman near him since the mistress passed away."

Her eyes darkened for a second as though she was reliving a sad memory, when she resumed her composure and began assisting Lucy to remove her damp garments. When Lucy took off her cloak, revealing the ragged tears in the dress, the woman tut-tutted and asked Lucy's permission to mend the damage, which Lucy gladly gave.

"Will you be staying long, miss?" she inquired. "I'll try and finish the sewing tonight, but if Matthew insists we must spare the candle, I'll have to carry on tomorrow. I'll rise before dawn and—"

Lucy butted in on her eager promises. "I think I shall be here for a while, a few days at least. You will have plenty of time to finish the work. I'm very grateful."

The dress was a little large, but at least it was warm, and Lucy had grown quite used over the last few weeks to the slightly itchy sensation of wool next to her skin. She remembered that she was still wearing the trinket that Rory had bought her at the fair. She was about to lift it from inside the dress and let it rest on the brown wool, to give her neckline a touch of decoration, when something stopped her. She was in an Earl's house. Even if he and his son were now living in reduced circumstances, there had been a time, remembering Philip's argument with his betrothed, when they had known real gold and real jewels. She didn't want to stand before them wearing the kind of bauble a scullery maid might have sported. Although she couldn't match the Darwins in lineage, her father was wealthier than they, and Lucy had a well-developed sense of good taste. So the necklace stayed inside her bodice.

Now the maid was brushing her hair, trying to smooth out the wet tangles. Lucy bore with her patiently as she tackled each knot in turn, knowing full well that she could do it much quicker herself. But the maid was a good woman and Lucy had no desire to hurt her or rob her of her pride in her handiwork. As her chestnut ringlets were tugged this way and that, Lucy asked curiously, "What happened to Mr. Darwin's mother?"

"It was when the baby was born, miss. She lost too much blood and wasted away. The master never got over it." There was an odd restraint in her voice. Lucy wondered at it, but dismissed it as imagination.

"And Mr. Darwin—who brought him up?"

"At first there was the Countess of Harringford, the Earl's sister. The Earl was overseas on a long campaign and she took Philip for two whole years, until the Earl came back and she found herself with child. Then the young master was brought back here and Matthew and myself did our best for him. When he grew older he had tutors, but he still looked on myself as his mother, until the Earl over-heard him calling me Mama one day and forbade it.

"He had a governess and a nurse then, until the Earl started to lose his money and they had to leave. But I'm talking too much—" Her hand flew to her mouth and she looked at Lucy as if begging her forgiveness. "I always used to be a terrible chatterbox when I was young. Matthew could nev-er get me to stop talking. And now, apart from Cook, it's so rare that I get the chance to talk to another woman—" The shocked expression came back into her face. "I do beg your pardon, miss. For all I know, you might be a lady yourself. Mas-ter Philip didn't tell me . . ."

"Don't worry, er . . ." Lucy looked at her inquir-ingly, inviting her to give her name.

The greying-haired maid quickly provided the information: "It's Martha, ma'am."

"Oh, really Martha, you can go on calling me 'miss'—or Lucy, if you prefer." Lucy had warmed to the woman, who could obviously be both friend and ally to her. "Regrettably, I'm not a lady, a countess or even a duchess—I'm just plain Lucy Swift."

What on earth had possessed her to say *Swift*? She had already told Philip that her surname was McDonnell. Still, it would be too awkward to change things now. She did not want to have to go through the ordeal of explaining. Not yet, anyhow.

The fire had dried her hair swiftly. Martha

brought her a glass and Lucy was pleased to see the pinkness that the heat had brought to her cheeks and the gleam on her clean, rain-washed hair. The shade of the dress was maybe a little drab, but her own vivid natural coloring overcame it. She now felt ready to face Philip and asked Martha to lead the way.

The corridor was uncarpeted and Lucy's footsteps echoed round the panelled walls until she felt she sounded like a whole army on the march. She told Martha and they both giggled, until the maid put a finger to her lips and intimated that they were drawing near the banqueting hall. Martha went ahead and opened a door. Lucy walked past her and found herself standing at the top of a flight of wooden steps leading down to the scantily carpeted floor of a huge rectangular room. Tattered remnants of flags, along with the mounted heads of magnificently antlered deer, adorned the dark panelled walls and at one end of the room was a long stained-glass window bearing the now familiar family crest. Below it, a collection of ancient lances were criss-crossed in an orderly pattern.

As she gazed round her, fascinated, she felt her eyes being drawn to the centre of the room, where an enormous wooden table bearing two branched candlesticks, lit because of the dimness of the day, dominated the floorspace. Two places were set at the table, but no one was seated there. In the great hearth a towering log fire roared and crackled, sending skeins of red sparks shooting up into the dark chimney. Lucy was surprised that there was no scent of dampness or mustiness in the vast hall and said as much to Martha, who informed her that keeping a fire burning in the hall throughout the winter was one of her master's few extravagances.

A scraping noise, as of a door being pushed open, sent Lucy's eyes searching keenly across the room. She sensed a movement and found it. The tall figure of Philip was silently poised in a doorway at the far end of the hall, just to one side of the wall bearing the ornamental window. As she watched, he descended a flight of stairs similar to the ones on which she was standing, stood by one of the set places at the table and beckoned to her. Feeling unaccountably nervous, Lucy began to descend the stairs.

Then Philip's voice rang out: "Stop!"

Lucy felt a hot blush mounting to her cheeks as she sensed his eyes inspecting her. His next words made her redden still more.

"That dress—terrible. It just doesn't suit you. *Martha . . .*"

The hunched woman scurried to Lucy's side.

"You know where Mother's things are. Find her something better. She looks like a peasant in that rag of yours."

"Sorry," whispered Lucy in Martha's ear as they retraced their earlier journey down the corridor. She was furious with Philip, not only for the way in which he had made her feel insulted, as if she were an object, an article of furniture maybe, which had to be draped to suit him, but also for hurting

Martha. She saw the stricken look on Martha's
face and smarted for her. Why did Philip have to
be so cruel? A stirring of fear revisited her. If he
could be this unkind to the woman who had
brought him up from a small child, what could he
have in mind for her? The memory of his behavior
in the stable came back to her and she shuddered,
but then recalled how different he had been in
those moments when he had dropped his guard. He
was an enigma, a completely unpredictable man,
and she was, unfortunately, absolutely at his
mercy.

Back in her room, Lucy gave in to a bleak wave
of loneliness, the first emotion of this sort she had
experienced since leaving home. She missed the
cheery and loving company of Rory. Doubtless he
was in some other inn by now, revelling in the company of some new woman. Lucy winced and thrust
aside the thought. She was not going to think of
him impressing another with his stories, pressing
another with his body. An excruciating, infuriating
pang of desire stabbed her at the thought of Rory's
naked, virile body. Luckily, at that moment there
was a light tap at the door and Martha entered,
carrying a swathe of pink material that brushed the
floor. As she lifted it and shook it out, Lucy gasped
at the magnificence of an old-fashioned but exquisite dress made of gleaming, light-catching silk
draped with lace of a paler shade, and worked with
beads and ruffles on the low-cut bodice.

"I can't wear that!" exclaimed Lucy worriedly.
Not only was it too grand and too old for her,

being more suited to a titled lady of at least twenty-five, but Lucy feared for the effect on Philip of seeing her clad in a gown which had once graced his dead mother.

"But Master Philip said I was to take away that one and give you—"

"I don't care what *Master* Philip says. I am not wearing that gown. Take it away. If he insists on lending me something that belonged to his mother, then please find me something simpler and more suitable. I may be dining in a grand house, but I'm just an ordinary young girl, not a dowager duchess! And anyway—" she lowered her tone confidingly —"I'd much rather wear that dress of yours than all this finery."

Martha looked pained and anxious. "Cook has the food all ready and the young master has a fine temper when he's aroused. You've no need to take my advice but I'm giving it with the best of intentions. Give me my dress back, wear this one and keep Master Philip happy."

"Oh, all right, if I must," sighed Lucy wearily. She felt very hungry after all and if it meant gliding to the luncheon table in a thirty-year-old ballgown, then glide she would, although she would feel utterly ridiculous.

Philip stared—and kept on staring as she walked down the staircase towards him. Although she didn't know it, the soft pink shade of the dress picked up the copper lights in her hair and enhanced the whiteness of her throat. In her old rags she could have been a gypsy girl, but now her descent from the kings of Ireland was apparent in the set of her jaw and cheekbones and the vivid blue of her eyes. Martha had found some powder from somewhere and had applied it to the bruises on her neck so that they no longer showed. Lucy knew she was curious as to how the injuries came about, but she felt that, at this stage in their short acquaintanceship, she could hardly tell her that they had been inflicted by Martha's "young master."

A guarded look came over Philip's face and he moved his eyes from the dazzling figure that confronted him, swallowing hard once or twice as he offered Lucy a platter of meat. Lucy had noted the effect she had had on him and was pleased. *Let* him want her! She had escaped his lecherous hands once and she would do so again, although she still felt worried about his intentions.

As Lucy was placing a slice of meat on her plate, a man suddenly materialized at her side, having entered the room on silent feet.

"Allow me, miss." He took the serving dish from her and, with impeccable manners, proceeded to serve the rest of the meal to both Philip and Lucy.

Bowing his head to his master, he apologized for not having been there earlier, having been out chopping wood. Lucy realized that he must be Martha's husband Matthew, a pleasant-looking man of perhaps fifty, with silver hair and an engaging smile. Philip forgave him and explained to Lucy that servants were in rather poor supply in their household.

"I gathered that," she replied, "from what I overheard of the conversation between yourself and, er, Rachel." She felt embarrassed about speaking the name in case she upset Philip—yet why should she care? She couldn't allow her feelings to slip like this, and let herself sympathize with him in the way she would sympathize with any other human being who hadn't put her through the ordeal Philip forced on her in the stable.

She sent a sideways glance across the table. Philip's corn-colored hair was glinting in the firelight. He caught her eye and remarked, rather bitterly, "Yes. Rachel . . . the girl I was to marry." He sighed heavily. "That's where you're going to help me."

Lucy pricked up her ears and sat with a forkful of meat poised halfway to her mouth. Perhaps he wanted her to act as a go-between, passing messages and apologies to Rachel and negotiating between them. Alas, she was not destined to play Cupid, as Philip's explanation revealed.

"If you heard much of that conversation, you will probably have gathered what has happened. My father was, as Rachel so rightly pointed out, extremely foolish. He had no talent with cards and he could easily be tricked by unscrupulous people like Rachel's father. I begged him to stop gambling, but he wouldn't listen. He said gaming was his only pleasure in life now that my mother was gone."

"Why did he never marry again?" asked Lucy, thinking that a man with a title and a manor house and all the accoutrements the Earl of Darwin must once have had would have been a pretty catch for any young lady.

"He was devoted to my mother, Lady Eleanor. She was very beautiful and, I hear, gentle, kind and accomplished, too. Everyone loved her, as Martha will tell you. My father wrapped himself in a solitary world after my mother died. He didn't think of the future. Even now, his mind dwells in the past. I've heard him talking to my mother as if she is there with him in the room. That's why losing the money and the house didn't mean anything to him. He was an old man, destined to die soon. He didn't think about his son being left with nothing to inherit. The one thing I cannot understand is why he gambled my mother's jewels. I would have thought they would have been more precious to him than either money or property."

"Do you love Rachel?"

Philip froze in the act of helping himself to another dish, Matthew having left the room to fetch more wood.

He sat in silence for a few moments, as if battling with his conscience, then answered finally, "No. I admire her, I respect her, but I don't love her. She's cold—" *as you are cold,* thought Lucy—"and she has a cruel, callous streak in her like her father has. I've seen him whip a dog to death with his riding crop just because it had chewed one of his boots.

"No, as a marriage, it would have been one purely of convenience. Hardwicke desperately wants a title for his daughter. I will inherit my father's on his death—but that is when Hardwicke will own Darwin Manor. I want to keep this house. It's been in my family for three hundred years, although it's been rebuilt several times, and bits added here and there." His eyes sparkled as he talked about his home, bringing a warmth to his expression which softened his angular features and made him look younger and slightly vulnerable. Lucy found herself reminded of her brother Geoffrey, who had possessed the same color of hair and eyes, and slightly similar features.

"So by marrying Rachel, you would be able to carry on living here and she would have gained a title, thus pleasing everybody." Lucy's words were a statement of fact and Philip nodded. "By losing Rachel, you've lost Darwin Manor. I can see your problem."

She pushed her plate aside, feeling replete. Philip had also stopped eating and was looking at Lucy as if trying to make up his mind whether or not to say something. Her stomach tensed as she remembered that she was not just his luncheon guest but his prisoner. Briefly, she wondered where Rory was, and whether Pat and Smithy had moved on to the next town. If only she could get a message to them, to warn them. Maybe Martha . . .

Philip made up his mind and started to speak.

"Lucy McDonnell, you have impressed me as a girl of courage and spirit."

Lucy looked at him, startled. What could this be leading up to?

"After my father played his last game of cards

with Hardwicke, in which he lost Darwin Manor and handed over the deed to that obscene old ale-sack, I went into the study where they had been playing and I found—" he fished around in a pocket and brought out an object that looked like a playing card—"this."

He handed it to Lucy. In the gloomy room, it looked just like an ordinary ace of clubs with a pattern on the back. She handed it back to Philip with a puzzled expression.

"I can't see anything odd about it."

He leapt from his seat and came round the table to Lucy's side.

"Here," he said, turning the card over. "You'll have to look extremely closely, but just by this red design in the corner—"

His index finger pointed to the place and Lucy bent her head to examine it. There, to one side of the swirling pattern, was a tiny marking in a slightly different shade of red. She looked up at Philip, sudden comprehension in her eyes. "You mean . . . ?"

"Yes. Every single one of his cards is marked in some way. I have visited his house since and stolen a good look at each of his packs of cards. If you didn't know what you were looking for, you'd miss it, but I knew what to expect—and this is what I found. I'm surprised the old cheat has got away with it for so long. Yet he boxes clever and makes sure his phenomenal wins are sprinkled with a few losses, so that his success, could, by a slight stretch of the imagination, be attributed to luck."

"Isn't there anything you can do? I mean, is there no one to whom you could expose this trickery?"

Philip shook his head. Striding to and fro in front of the fire, his hands clasped behind his back, he seemed to be considering how to reply.

"This is a private matter," he said at length. "Hardwicke has many influential friends. All I want is to recover what is rightfully mine. And I want you to help me do it."

"How?" Lucy half rose in her chair, gripping the edge of the table. At last she was going to find out what Philip wanted to do with her.

He paused in his stride. "It won't be easy," he said, looking at her warningly.

"Easier than the alternative," muttered Lucy drily.

"I want the deed to the house back," he announced abruptly. His chin came up and he stared at Lucy almost defiantly, as if challenging her to play the weak woman and gasp, "No—I can't possibly!"

He looked surprised when she inquired quite calmly, "And how do you propose I do that?"

Philip fetched a wine decanter from a side table and filled the two glasses that were standing by their plates. Lucy's hand stretched halfway towards her glass, then she removed it as she saw that Philip was not drinking.

"In answer to your question," he replied, his face resuming its usual stern expression which reminded Lucy once more of her position in his household, "what I propose is this: that you take up the position of personal maid to Rachel Hardwicke."

If a battalion of mounted cavalry had, at that moment, ridden their horses right through the wall and into the banqueting hall, Lucy could not have been more thunderstruck. To steal into somebody's house and take something was one thing. That quite appealed to her sense of daring. But what he was proposing was, quite frankly, incredible and, she felt, way beyond her powers to carry out.

"I—a maid?" she said wonderingly, her pride pricking her.

"Don't forget, it's that or your life," reminded Philip. At once, Lucy's strength and courage came back to her and when she next spoke to him, she was in total command of her senses.

"Have you thought that maybe she saw enough in the stable to be able to recognize me?"

"It was very dark, and besides, you were struggling and your hair was all over your face. The only thing she got a good view of was my back."

"Is she in need of a maid, then?"

Philip flung back his head and laughed, showing small, even white teeth. "Rachel is always in need of a maid. It's no sinecure working for Rachel Hardwicke; the duties are, to say the least, arduous. But you shouldn't have to stay for long. If you leave after two weeks or so, you'll be just another in a long succession of girls who, unable to stand working for Rachel, have done precisely the same thing. Rachel's mother is a good woman; she always gives them a reference. She knows only too well what her daughter is like."

"But I've never been a maid before. How am *I* supposed to get a reference saying I'm a good, honest, trustworthy lady's maid?"

The more Lucy thought about it, and the more she recalled Rachel's imperious tones, the less she liked the idea. As for stealing . . . Suddenly she remembered Emperor and was forced to admit to herself that she was capable of a large degree of skulduggery so long as her conscience was clear.

"Leave that to me," said Philip. "I am quite sure my aunt in London, Lady Clarence, will oblige. She is quite au fait with the situation."

"Just supposing for a minute that I *do* get the job, which I think is highly unlikely—"

"Nonsense, they're desperate for someone," put in Philip.

"As I was saying," continued Lucy. "Suppose that they do take me on. What then? I have no idea of what this deed looks like or where it is kept. How am I supposed to get it back?"

Phillip pulled his chair out from the table and carried it round, placing it down beside Lucy's. He pushed aside the dishes and cleared a space and then, dipping his finger in his untouched wine, began to draw on the table top the interior layout of Rokely Hall, the Hardwicke's home.

"Here is the entrance, and the corridors leading to the drawing-room here, the dining-room there; here's the study, and here, to the right of the study door, is the main staircase."

Lucy nodded. He shifted his seat a bit closer to her own.

"Now, this is the plan of the upstairs rooms. The servants' quarters are all at the back, over here." He placed a knife to the right of his fast-drying map. "This fork represents the main corridor on the first floor. Rachel's bedroom is here." He picked up a silver salt cellar and placed it close to the edge of the table. Lucy wondered how many times he had entered that room himself—if the frosty-sounding Rachel had permitted him, which Lucy doubted very much.

"There is an empty guest room here, next to Rachel's. There is Rachel's mother's dressing-room and bedroom, and interconnecting with them —here—is the master bedroom where John Hardwicke sleeps. His dressing-room connects with his wife's."

He was sitting so close to Lucy that his sleeve was brushing hers. She gave a slight shiver and didn't know why. Philip had taken a handkerchief and was mopping up his wine-tracings. Dipping his finger in the glass once more, he began a fresh drawing.

"This is Hardwicke's bedroom. Bed here, dresser there, bureau, chest, door leading to dressing-room here. He keeps the key to the bureau in the oak chest over here by the window. There is a small ledge inside and the key is on it."

"How do you know that?" asked Lucy wonderingly. Philip just smiled and continued.

"Inside the bureau on the right-hand side there is a small drawer with a brass handle. That's where he keeps the deeds not only to his own house but to some farm cottages he owns, a property in London and . . ." He paused. ". . . Darwin Manor."

"And does he keep this drawer locked?" inquired Lucy, thinking how very complicated it all seemed.

"Unfortunately, yes. He always carried the key about his person, usually in a pocket inside his jacket."

"How am I supposed to get it?" Stealing a key out of a chest was one thing, but having to be a pickpocket required a sleight of hand which Lucy felt she simply didn't possess.

"That, my dear, is a problem you will have to solve. All I can do is get you into the house. Once you are there, you will have to think up your own plan for acquiring the key and the deed."

"And when I have the deed, will you let me walk out of this house a free person? If I am to go to so much trouble for you, I don't wish to think that you are likely to change your mind and hand me over to be hanged!" Lucy's eyes were wide with alarm. This awful thought had only just occurred to her, together with the remembrance of that cold side of Philip's personality which she hated. Perhaps he was not to be trusted at all. Then she felt a sudden soft touch on her hair; Philip had put out his hand and was stroking one long ringlet. She flinched in shock and he immediately pulled his hand away as if from a scorching candle flame.

"Forgive me," he muttered. "That hair of yours is so tempting, especially with the firelight shining on it."

"And I suppose my body was tempting to you there in the stable this morning!" snapped Lucy. She regretted her words immediately she saw the expression that came over Philip's face, that closed, cold look she was getting to know so well. He got to his feet.

"This is a business transaction. You fulfill your side of the bargain and I shall fulfill mine. And if you fail . . ."

Leaving these fateful words hanging in empty air, he bounded up the staircase, slammed the door and was gone, leaving Lucy sitting there alone, in her borrowed finery, wondering what she should do now.

Her solitude lasted a mere few seconds. Matthew appeared, silently as ever, and began to clear away the dishes. Lucy suddenly remembered the mare she had brought with her that morning and asked Matthew if he knew anything about it.

"She's been stabled, miss. Saw to it myself. She in foal?"

His honest brown eyes gazed searchingly at Lucy, making her wonder just how much he knew. Deciding that honesty was the best policy, she shook her head.

"Didn't think so. Way she bolts her food, she be just filled up with air, like. Had 'un like that myself —oh, near twenty years ago now. Used to bloat out like a nine-month-gone woman. Ye'd tighten the girth, like, then be reet sorry ye did, for half an hour later, ye'd find your saddle slipping round her belly and yourself on the floor!"

Lucy joined in his chuckles. She had witnessed

the mare play precisely that trick on Rory once. He had landed with a crash on his backside in a patch of nettles, amidst guffaws from Pat and Smithy. She wondered if Philip really was going to try and find them and expose their trickery. Maybe he was riding down to Pendleton at that very moment. Part of her, the bitter, hurt side, wanted to see Rory wiped off the face of the earth. How did any man deserve to live after what he had done? But not hanging—no, that was too slow and too cruel. Death in a duel, now that was honorable. Even death by natural causes was acceptable. Yet she feared Rory would end up dying at the hand of some jealous woman and she knew in her heart that she was neither vindictive enough nor hard-hearted enough for the death-dealer to be her.

Matthew cleared his throat. He had finished tidying the table and was asking Lucy if she wished to be escorted to her room. She accepted gratefully. It was only late afternoon, but she felt heavy-headed and sleepy, although neither she nor Philip had drunk their wine. Had he poured it out intending to toast the success of her mission? If so, her hasty words had spoiled the moment. She hoped her flash of temperament had not persuaded him to change his mind. She would sooner act the part of a maid and a thief than lose her life, even if that life hardly seemed worth the living any more.

Lucy awoke to find Martha tending the fire. She had dozed off lying on top of the bed and her beautiful dress was crushed out of shape. Martha glanced at it disapprovingly.

"If you were planning a rest, you should have told Matthew to ask me for a nightgown," she said.

"I'm sorry," Lucy replied. "I didn't mean to. It's just that . . . well, I had a rather bad experience earlier today, which upset me a lot and I think I must have been quite exhausted."

Martha shot her a sharp look. "Is that how you came by those bruises on your neck and shoulders?"

"No. Well, actually I had *two* unfortunate experiences this morning . . ."

Lucy suddenly wondered what Martha must think of her. She had come into the house a total stranger, ragged as a gypsy, bruised like a slut—and, for all Martha knew, that was precisely what she was. Perhaps she should explain.

"I'm not what you think I am, Martha. I come from a good family—"

"I never doubted it, miss," interrupted the woman in a kindly tone of voice. She reached out and patted Lucy's hand and said consolingly, "You're young enough to be my daughter, you know. You don't have to tell me anything, but if you want to, you'll find I have a sympathetic ear."

Lucy gestured to her to come and sit beside her on the bed. Martha obeyed and soon Lucy found herself confiding everything about her home life, about how she had come to run away and be captured by the horse traders, and Martha listened spellbound. The only thing she found herself unable to tell Martha about was her moorland marriage to Rory. She felt the woman would be unable to understand how she had accepted it so willingly, or how attracted to Rory she had really been. Better to let her think him a vagabond who had abducted her and then betrayed her with another woman. Let the sacred ritual remain her own secret.

As she expected, Martha's eyes flashed with fury when Lucy described how she had seen Rory coming out of the tavern whore's room.

"Did you go for him? Is that how you came by those marks?" she asked eagerly.

Lucy shook her head.

Suddenly, a look of understanding dawned in Martha's eyes. "Master Philip was angry about the mare."

Lucy nodded gratefully. So they *did* know. This would save her a lot of awkward explaining. "It wasn't my idea to sell him that horse. It shouldn't have been my job to deliver it, but there was nobody else."

"Yet you knew the horse was not in foal?" Martha's inquiring glance was keen.

"Yes," Lucy said gently, "I knew. But there was nothing I could do—and besides, with no home to go back to and Rory gone, I—I needed the money."

"I see." For a moment Lucy thought the older woman was about to censure her. She was relieved when Martha put a hand on her arm and said, "You poor lamb."

Something broke inside Lucy then. Maybe it was Martha's slight similarity to her mother, or her warm, kindly tone of voice. Whatever it was, she suddenly found herself sobbing her heart out and turning blindly to Martha for comfort. The motherly woman wrapped her arms around Lucy and rocked her while all the grief and shock she had suffered welled up and poured out of her in a series of racking sobs and flooding tears. When she could cry no more, Martha offered her a handkerchief and Lucy blew her nose hard and mumbled her thanks.

"You just stay there and rest," ordered Martha. "I'll fetch you up a nice refreshing drink from the kitchen." Lucy smiled weakly at her and lay back against the pillows. "I'll get you that nightgown, too."

"And would it be too much if I asked to borrow that dress again, the one you made?"

The delight in Martha's face made asking the question truly worthwhile.

Martha was gone a long time. When she returned, bearing the clothing she had promised, she informed Lucy that the "young master" had gone out and that she would be dining alone that evening.

"Couldn't I eat with you and Matthew? I'd like that," Lucy asked.

But Martha immediately rejected this idea, telling her that if Philip were to find out, he would be angry. "Walls have ears," she added darkly and Lucy felt it best not to press the subject, while wondering what she meant.

So, clad in the warm, homely dress, she ate a modest repast of chicken, vegetables and fruit, worrying all the while about Philip. She knew she shouldn't care about the fate of her erstwhile companions, but they had been quite kind to her and she wished them no harm, even Rory. She asked Martha for something to read to pass the time and Martha confessed that, as she herself couldn't read, she didn't know one book from another.

"Just fetch me anything," Lucy informed her and Martha reappeared after a short while with a leatherbound volume which turned out to be most interesting, as it dealt with local myth and folklore and even contained a chapter about witches, which interested Lucy greatly.

She had no idea how much time had elapsed, but the candles in her room had burned low by the time Lucy heard voices coming from somewhere near her door. She recognized them as Philip's and Matthew's, but, strain her ears as she might, she could not make out what they were saying. Shortly after that, she blew out all but one candle, donned her nightgown and prepared herself for bed.

No sooner had she snuggled down beneath the warm covers than she was roused by a tapping at her door. She held her breath, frightened to utter a sound. Martha's phrase about walls having ears came back to her. Did this mean that there was some other inhabitant of the hall, perhaps a mad person, about whom she had not been informed? She checked the whereabouts of the nearest candlestick, with which she planned to beat the intruder about the head.

The tapping sounded again and then, to her horror, the door slowly began to creak open. Lucy felt a scream rising in her throat. A faint, spectral glow shone through the increasing gap in the doorway and the scream was just about to burst from her when she heard a voice calling in a low tone, "Lucy?" and saw the tall figure of Philip hovering in the doorway, a lantern in his hand. "Are you awake?" he added, in the same understone.

"Yes," stated Lucy, louder and more firmly than she had intended, causing Philip to jump slightly so that his lantern swung wildly and sent shadows flickering across the ceiling.

"I just wanted to inform you that a messenger is at this moment on his way to my aunt in London. He should return with the reference within ten days."

Why had he disturbed her at night to tell her this? It could have waited until the morning. Lucy felt the flesh on the back of her neck begin to crawl with unease. He must have something else to tell her, something unpleasant. People were only roused from their beds at night for the delivery of bad news.

Her presentiment proved correct.

"I also think you should know," announced Philip formally, "that Rory McDonnell is dead."

CHAPTER SIX

They were all being so kind to her, Martha, Matthew, even Philip. For three days Lucy could not get up at all and when she rose on the fourth day, Martha fussed round her, making sure she wrapped up warmly and drank a bowl of nourishing broth.

Philip had called in to see her several times on that dreadful first day but she had been so lost in grief that she could not speak to him and, after several vain attempts at cheering her up, he had left, feeling helpless in the face of a woman's tears. It wasn't until the third day that Lucy had felt sufficiently in command of herself to ask him to describe the circumstances of Rory's death. She had wondered if Philip himself had killed him as part of his campaign to stamp out crooked dealing of all kinds, but when Philip unfolded his tale she felt that she believed him.

"I was down in Dudcott, doing some business there, when I heard a terrible commotion coming from an inn. All the townsfolk flocked to see what the fuss was, and I went along with them. I could hear a woman screaming, "Murder, murder!" Then out rushed that giant of yours, blood all down his coat. Three men were hanging onto him, trying to restrain him.

"I called to a couple of soldiers, who were shopping for supplies, to help halt the giant and they put down their bags and brought him to a stop, not without having to draw their swords. Once he was secured, I pushed through the crowd and went into the inn."

Lucy wasn't sure if she could bear to hear the next part of the story. To think of the man she had once loved so dearly lying dead, even his friends not having been able to protect him!

"The innkeeper was bending over the figure of a man lying on the floor," Philip continued. "It was the bearded young man I saw you with that day at Pendleton, without a doubt. Do you really want the details? They're not very pleasant."

"I want to hear everything—*everything,*" pressed Lucy. "After all, he was my husband."

"Your . . . Yes. Well, he was sprawled on the floor like I said, and a knife was sticking from his back, an unusual-looking knife with a carved wooden handle."

"That's Pat's!" Lucy exclaimed. She had seen that knife very often during the weeks she had spent with the group. He took it everywhere with him, not just for protection but to use for cutting rope for halters, working stones out of the horses' hooves, even for spearing his food and eating it.

But surely Pat would not have . . . ? Philip answered her question for her.

"The innkeeper told me that there was a fight between Rory McDonnell and the big man—"

"That would be Pat," Lucy interrupted. "But why were they fighting?"

"If you'll just let me continue . . . It seems the disagreement concerned a horse—and from what I gather it was about that old nag you brought me. Pat accused Rory of having delivered the mare as arranged, and pocketing the money for himself."

"But the lad who was looking after the horses knows it was me who took the horse! Surely he would have told them?" Suddenly a terrible thought occurred to Lucy. Suppose the boy *had* told Rory; Rory might have been feeling guilty about his earlier behavior, he might have tried to protect Lucy by pretending to Pat that it was he who had taken the horse . . .

Rory must have died trying to protect her! She had as good as killed him with her own two hands!

"Lucy? Lucy, are you all right?" Philip's eyes rested anxiously on the ashen face of the girl before him. "Are you all right?" he repeated.

"I . . . I'm all right," she replied woodenly. How could this cold arrogant man understand the way she felt? Rory had been so full of life and laughter —and now he was dead. All because of her.

"What will happen now?"

"Pat will be hanged for murder, I expect. He has been taken off to prison in Liverpool already. As for his accomplice, Smithy . . . Well, he has the remaining horses, I suppose, and could carry on the business, if it could be called that, on his own, or else join forces with some other dealers. Though, from what I've witnessed, he isn't in the best of health."

"No," agreed Lucy, wondering if the frail little man would survive the winter.

Philip tactfully left her at this point, and once alone Lucy sank into a dull torpor of misery, her hand clutching the little necklace Rory had given her as if it were a talisman which could protect her from the happenings of the present.

By the fifth day, Lucy felt well enough to accept Philip's invitation to a ride round his estate. Martha produced a faded green riding habit, another item from the wardrobe of the late Lady Eleanor, and lent her her own warm cloak and, thus attired, Lucy mounted a chestnut hunter belonging to Philip and they set out to ride the boundary.

The horse gave Lucy a spirited ride, bucking and skittering in the freezing air, shying every time a bird or small rodent rustled in the bushes. Several times Philip complimented her on her riding skill, and the exercise and chill, windy weather brought a glow to her face which she knew became her. She thoroughly enjoyed the ride. Philip pointed out the local landmarks which could be viewed from the hill and talked about everything he would do with the grounds if he had enough money.

Finally, they paused by the ornamental lake and

Lucy saw that her surmise of the first day had been correct—there *were* statues around the lake, badly in need of cleaning and repairing. She would have loved to tackle the job herself and mentioned this to Philip, who just laughed and said it was a job for a workman who didn't mind getting filthy. Lucy, not wishing to appear unfeminine, dropped the subject.

The next few days were spent in similar fashion, riding, talking and dining together in the evening. Gradually, her mourning for Rory lessened and she found herself enjoying Philip's company now that he had dropped his guard of icy formality. On several occasions she caught herself looking at him admiringly. He was a good-looking man in a clean-cut, very English way which was totally unlike Rory's unruly image and ruddy, outdoor complexion. He was an amusing, witty companion and his stories about London society and his cavalry experiences had her convulsed with mirth and almost forgetting both her recent tragedy and Philip's cruel treatment of her on their first meeting.

It was at night, when she was alone in bed, that the sorrow and loneliness would steal over her. She would thresh round in what seemed like acres of empty space, longing for Rory's warm, strong arms to take her and hold her. Sometimes she would imagine him lying next to her in the darkness. Her hand would trace his outline, her lips move towards the place where his lips should be—and find nothing except unconsoling emptiness. Then the tears would come again; she would

cry herself to sleep and next morning Martha
would tut at the dampness of the pillow and the
blotchiness of Lucy's face, and bring her warm water to which she had added a few drops of essence
of rosemary, to soothe and clear Lucy's skin.

One morning she awoke to find a strange, cold,
white light in the room. Pulling back the curtains
she found the whole world covered in crisp snow.
A blackbird was trilling on the tree outside her
window, the only sound in a muffled, dead uni-
verse. Then, with a harsh, warning chak-chak, the
blackbird flew off and Lucy heard men's voices
downstairs.

Dressing quickly, in case the disturbance concerned her, she lingered in her room until Martha
knocked to bring her some breakfast—new-laid
eggs, lightly scrambled, fresh-baked bread and a
glass of warm milk, which Lucy demolished
ravenously. She always seemed to have more of an
appetite in the winter. After finishing her meal, she
wandered round the house, always avoiding the
upper floors in case she encountered Philip's
father. All thoughts of running away had left her
now, although she could easily have done so. But
that would have meant stealing another horse and
heading who-knows-where, for Liverpool maybe,
with no money in her pocket and snow on the
ground. Darwin Manor was beginning to feel
almost like home to her now and every day she was
relying more on Martha's friendship and Philip's
company.

She paused by the door of the library, which was

where the voices were coming from, and was about to walk by when the door was suddenly flung open. Lucy flattened herself against the wall, half hidden by a large cupboard. Through the gap between the back of the cupboard and the panelled wall she could see Philip escorting another man in the direction of the front door. The library door had been left open and she could see a sheet of paper lying on the table. Calculating that it would be several minutes before Philip returned, she darted into the room and snatched up the paper.

The beautiful script that covered the page in swirls of black ink was signed with the seal of the House of Clarence—it was her reference from Philip's aunt. With the shock of Rory's death and her depression of the last few days, plus her growing, grudging liking for Philip and their rides together, Lucy had completely forgotten about the purpose for which she was being kept at Darwin Manor, and she found she didn't at all like being reminded.

Passing her eye quickly down the page, she noted that she was supposed to have been in Lady Clarence's employ for two years as a general housemaid, but had been trained to take over the duties of Lady Clarence's personal maid should she fall ill. The reason for her leaving was given as an inability to settle down in London, Lucy being country-born and bred. However, Lady Clarence had added, she was honest and dutiful, clean and trustworthy and could be relied upon to perform her tasks with speed and industry. The reference was such a skillful lie that Lucy found herself admiring the lady's artistry and regretting that she could not meet her as she sounded a pleasant person with a lively sense of humor.

Replacing the letter in the exact position wherein she had found it, Lucy left the library and wandered on down the corridor, through the banqueting hall and into the long-neglected ballroom with its faded, cob-webbed hangings. Filled with spectral light reflected from the snowy ground outside, the ballroom was a haunted place of half-glimpsed figures, unfinished romances and a tingle in the air like the vibration from unheard violins. Lucy knew it was only her imagination at work, but she loved to linger in the ballroom, looking out at the park from the huge windows which ran the whole length of one wall and opened onto a long, covered balcony from which one could descend, by way of stone steps, to the sloping lawn below.

As she stood dreaming by the window, shivering slightly in air that was so cold that she could see her breath in it, the sound of the imaginary violins in her head grew louder. Humming to herself, she began to move her body, letting her feet carry her in a waltz tempo out into the middle of the dusty floor. Closing her eyes, she imagined a partner guiding her, and she dipped and swayed and twirled until she had made a complete circuit of the room and found herself by the windows once more, whereupon she halted, panting and chiding herself for being silly. She could still hear the echoing strings playing the dreamy, slightly wistful waltz

melody and she shook her head to wake herself up
—but the sound carried on.

It was only one violin, not many, and she had no
idea where the music was coming from, but it filled
her with terror. Lucy had never seen a ghost but
she believed in them all the same; and now it
looked as if she was having a personal experience
of a shade from the past. She couldn't see anything
but at any moment she expected a man from another century to materialize, wearing strange, old-
fashioned garb. Perhaps it was the Devil himself!
The book she had read several nights earlier had
mentioned that the Devil sometimes prefaced his
appearance with the sound of a violin. She began
to shake and feel faint. What would she do if she
were suddenly faced with a satanic vision? Make
the sign of the cross? Recite the Lord's Prayer?

Speaking aloud, with all the conviction she could
muster, Lucy began the first few words: "Our
Father, which art in Heaven . . ." She had got as
far as "Thy will be done . . .", her voice growing
shakier with every syllable, when peals of demonic-
sounding laughter rang out and echoed around the
empty room. He was here! Any second now she
would see him, red-eyed and fork-tailed, and he
would drag her off to his sulphurous underground
pit to wreak terrible tortures on her!

No—he would not get her! Mobility suddenly
returned to her limbs and, with a piercing shriek,
Lucy flung herself towards the door, tearing her
fingernails painfully back in her effort to wrench
open the unyielding barrier between terror and

safety. With all her strength she scrabbled, pushed and pulled, but it was jammed, or else locked from the other side, or perhaps held fast by some supernatural power.

When she realized she was trapped, she sank to the floor, her eyes wide and staring, willing whatever was in the room to go away and leave her alone. There was no sound at all now save that of the spasmodic rattling as the windows were buffeted by gusts of snow-bearing wind, but still Lucy remained there, tense and alert. And then she heard it, a slow, muffled creak, followed by another, slightly louder. Footsteps—but where were they coming from? A grey mist of terror formed in front of Lucy's eyes and the room seemed to recede and then return in waves of dimness and clarity. Still she could see no one and yet she felt as if she were being watched, an uncomfortable sensation which made her scalp crawl and the tiny hairs along her arms bristle like the fur of an angry cat. The footsteps stopped, and the sensation of being observed grew stronger. Lucy's heart was thudding so hard that she could see the tiny, rhythmic movements of its palpitation in the fluttering material stretched across her breast. Out of the corner of her eye she glimpsed a movement. One of the frayed wallcoverings was wafting as if in a draught—and a dark-clad man was standing in the center of the ballroom floor, surveying her.

All she glimpsed before the rushing noise in her ears overwhelmed her like a dark tide was his vague outline and the violin he held in one hand.

The next thing her senses reported to her brain was a feeling of warm pressure against her lips and forehead. Then she heard her name being repeated over and over again: "Lucy, wake up. Lucy Swift, are you all right? Please wake up, Lucy."

She wasn't conscious of having signalled her eyelids to open, but they did and she found she was gazing directly into the concerned grey eyes of Philip Darwin. As soon as he saw she had recovered consciousness, a look of relief came over him and he placed an arm under hers to help her to her feet.

"I'm so sorry," he said. "I really do beg your pardon. I had no idea you would wander into this particular room when you did and I had no intention of scaring you."

"I—I thought you were a g-ghost," stammered Lucy, shivering with a mixture of fright and cold.

"Here, let me help you to the drawing-room. Matthew or Martha can fetch you a drink to warm you up and steady those nerves of yours."

The Darwin Manor drawing-room had once been elegant and attractive. The room, of noble proportions like the rest of the house, was at the rear and looked out over an exquisitely laid-out rose garden, now, like the rest of Lancashire, hidden beneath a blanket of snow. A warm fire was crackling in the hearth and the heat of the mulled wine which Matthew had brought sent threads of fire burning through her right down to her toes.

She thanked Philip gratefully, then asked, out of sheer curiosity, "Do you often spend time in the ballroom?"

"Yes, as a matter of fact I do. I love the atmosphere there. Years ago, when my father still had some money, we used to have some glorious times. Apparently, when my mother was still alive, the Darwin Manor balls were talked about all over the county. Relatives would come all the way from London specially to attend. My father carried on the tradition for a while after my mother's death, because everyone hoped it would help take his mind off his grief—and I think some hoped he might even find himself a second wife from among the guests—but when I was about four or five years old, entertaining in our house gradually dwindled, partly through lack of money and partly because my father grew tired of the endless matchmaking that was being done on his account. However, I think my love of music dates back to those happy times."

"You play the violin very well," Lucy informed him, privately thinking that he could express his feelings far better through the well-tuned strings of the instrument than he could through his own vocal chords. "I couldn't see you when you were playing. Where were you?"

"Next time you enter the room, look way up towards the ceiling at the far end of the room. You'll find a small gallery there—'the kissing gallery,' we used to call it, because couples would stray there from the dance floor and conduct their courting high up over the heads of their mothers and fathers and sometimes even their wives and husbands. There's a narrow staircase leading up to it which starts behind the tapestry next to the big mirror with the gold surround. It's not a place you would find by accident. I, of course, have always known of it."

"I suppose there are a lot of hidden ways and secret hidey-holes in an old house like this?" Ever since childhood Lucy had nourished a secret dream in which she would discover such a passage and find hidden treasure at the end; but alas, the Swifts' farmhouse, being a mere sixty years old, held no such surprises.

"Yes, there are some," replied Philip, smiling at her sudden enthusiasm. "However, I hardly think you'll have time to explore them. I received the reference from Lady Clarence this very morning."

Did that mean he wanted her to leave immediately? She wasn't in the least bit prepared and she felt sad at having to terminate what was fast becoming a very pleasant existence. Everything seemed to be happening far too quickly.

Philip must have informed Martha already of Lucy's imminent departure, because the maid was waiting in her room with the dress in which Lucy had arrived, now neatly mended. It was wrapped up in a small bundle, from which protruded a scrap of brown material that Lucy recognized—it was the homespun garment which Martha had made herself, the one Lucy had so admired.

"Martha! I can't take that, I mustn't. You've put so much work into it, so much love," Lucy exclaimed.

"That's why I want you to have it, lovey. You'll

need it over at Rokely Hall. It's a cold house, so they say."

The maid's raised eyebrow indicated that her words held more than one meaning.

Feeling a rush of gratitude, Lucy hugged her. "Oh Martha, dear Martha, you've been so good to me all the time I've been here. I really don't want to leave in the slightest!"

"Then why must you? It's bitter weather. It must be something really important to force you out on such a day." The maid's flat statement held an un-spoken question.

"It is," Lucy told her. "It's something I have to do for Phi—for the young master."

"I see. Well, I hope some good comes of it, for it's a reet bad day for a journey."

Martha resumed her bustling about and resisted Lucy's offer to change back into her old dress and return the velvet gown of Lady Eleanor's which she was wearing.

"The young master said as how you were to take it. We don't want that Miss Rachel looking down that snooty nose of hers too much, do we?"

Martha hardly needed to spell out her obvious dislike of Philip's former betrothed. As Martha had met Rachel, Lucy ventured to ask, "What's she like?"

"Your face and figure would beat hers into a cocked hat. She's cold—cold as that snow outside and hard as an iron horse-shoe. The young master would have had full hands and an empty heart if he'd married that girl. I've not time for any of that

Hardwicke crew, nor has my Matthew. They're mean and devious, sneaky as foxes in a thicket. Have as little to do with them as possible, that's my advice."

Lucy longed to be able to tell Martha what she was actually going to be at Rokely Hall, but she refrained, partly from fear in case Philip found out she'd been prattling his secrets to the maid, and partly because she knew the warm-hearted woman would be horrified and upset at the thought of her having to work in close proximity to Rachel Hardwicke.

When at length she stepped into the small carriage driven by Matthew which was to take her down the snow-covered lanes to Rokely Hall, Lucy felt like a martyr going to the stake. Her final vision of Darwin Manor was of a towering grey building, with Philip standing, dwarfed by the huge doorway, and Martha's anxious face peering from the library window.

"You little cat. You did that deliberately!"

Rachel's face was close to Lucy's and there was a mad yellowish glint in her narrowed eyes. Suddenly her hand lashed out and struck Lucy on the cheek. The force of the blow was, in itself, not so painful but the large emerald ring Rachel was wearing caught her on the cheekbone, drawing blood which trickled in crimson beads down Lucy's face.

The girl was of an age with Lucy and, if it hadn't been for the mission she had given her word to fulfill (how could she forget Philip's dark words, "It's that or your life"?) Lucy would have struck her back. The girl was so coldly, deliberately spiteful and cruel that Lucy wondered if she were possessed by an evil spirit. She had been there only three days and already they had been the longest, most unpleasant three days in her whole life. Nothing she could do was right in Rachel's eyes. No sooner had Lucy brushed her hair into shining golden splendor and twined it into ringlets with heated irons, than Rachel would twist her wrist painfully, as if trying to make her burn herself on the hot tongs, then rake her fingers through her locks, undoing all Lucy's careful work and insisting it was exactly the opposite to what she wanted.

She was the same over her clothes. "Fetch me my green dress," she would order imperiously. Lucy would go dutifully to the closet and bring Rachel the required garment, whereupon she would tear the dress from Lucy's hands, throw it on the floor like a child in a tantrum and fume, "Not that one, stupid, the peacock blue one."

"But you said . . ." Lucy had soon learned not to use these words or, indeed, to argue with Rachel in any way. For disagreeing with the pale-eyed girl would bring an instant tongue-lashing down on Lucy's head, or even painful physical punishment; Rachel was not above picking up a riding whip and slashing at Lucy in fury for a slight misdemeanour.

Lucy put up her hand to feel the wetness on her cheek, and brought her fingers down bloodied. She did not have the temperament to bear much of this

kind of treatment, but . . . "It's that or your life!"
Biting back words of acrimony and reproof, Lucy
picked up the hairbrush which she had dropped
when Rachel hit her and recommenced dressing
her hated mistress's heavy, straight locks. How she
hated her! The closer Christmas loomed, the more
irritable Rachel appeared to become. Christmas
Eve was in three days' time and on that night a
major ball was due to be held at Rokely Hall, to
which the gentry of many surrounding towns and
villages had been invited. As far as Lucy could
ascertain, the main thing that was preying on
Rachel's selfish mind was the weather, which was
preventing any young beaux or dandies from coming up from London and spending the festive sea-
son at Rokely Hall. She had done nothing but
moan ever since the snow had set in and Lucy
dreaded the thought of having to spend that most
precious time of year, Christmas, in her dis-
agreeable company.

As she brushed—as gently as possible so that
Rachel couldn't accuse her again of pulling her
hair—Lucy thought about her mother, all alone
with nobody except Lucy's father to prepare the
Christmas goose for. Even he would probably be
drunk and unappreciative. For the first time since
leaving home three months earlier, Lucy felt a
sharp pang of homesickness and Rachel's golden
hair blurred into a haze before her eyes as she
thought of the sorrow and loneliness which must
be eating at her mother's heart. First her brother
Geoffrey, and now herself. How could her mother

bear it? Maybe she was ill, pining for her two miss-ing children. Lucy longed with all her heart to be able to knock on that familiar door on Christmas Day and bring a glow of happiness to her mother's careworn features.

"Bitch! I've told you not to do that!" Rachel's elbow shot out and dug Lucy sharply in the mid-riff.

She felt she would reach forward and strangle the girl if she kept on at her this way. No wonder all Rachel's other maids had handed in their notice, or else run away. Lucy hoped they had found better positions with kinder mistresses. At least they were properly trained maids. What was she to do, with no home to go to and nothing but a forged refer-ence to her name?

By the time she slumped onto her hard, narrow bed that evening, Lucy felt weak and dizzy from exhaustion. Not content merely with striking and insulting her, Rachel had, in a fit of pique, hurled a small glass vase across the room. It had hit the wall, smashed to smithereens and Lucy had been required to get down on her hands and knees and pick up every sliver of glass so that Rachel would not cut her feet when walking about her room. Lucy, however, cut her finger painfully, whereupon Rachel had laughed and taunted her. She longed to be able to lay her hands on Philip's precious deed so that she could walk away from Rachel's tyranny into freedom, but John Hardwicke had been away on business in Manchester and was not expected home until Christmas Eve.

Lucy had not yet set eyes on Rachel's father but she had spoken briefly to her mother, meeting her first of all when she was interviewed for the position and several times after that. Lucy had been impressed by her. She was a tiny, dark-haired woman, as delicately made as a doll, totally different to her rangy, blonde daughter who, Lucy guessed, must surely take after her father. Harriet Hardwicke spoke in a thin, silvery voice which was in perfect keeping with her dainty appearance.

"So you are Lucy. Lady Clarence speaks very highly of you. She sent me a letter to say she was giving you a good reference, and her recommendation is certainly good enough for me. I hope you will settle in well with us, and join in the Christmas festivities we always provide for the servants. Maud will show you to your room, which you will share with Daisy, the head housekeeper." She had given Lucy a charming smile and passed her over to the stout Maud.

In turn, Maud had introduced Lucy to her roommate, Daisy, who turned out to be fat and possessed of a snore every bit the equal of Pat's. So Lucy could only snatch brief moments of sleep before being awoken by yet another gargantuan rumbling. Daisy was fussy, and a grumbler—and she also, Lucy discovered, had a liking for the bottle which no doubt accounted for her surplus weight and the fumes of ale that hung heavily on the bedroom's air each night.

It was while she was lying exhausted yet sleepless on that third night, occupying her mind by mulling over the activities of the past few weeks and trying not to dwell too much on thoughts of Rory, that a fact emerged which Lucy couldn't explain. She was haunted by a memory of Philip's voice, the voice she had heard while emerging from her faint in the ballroom, repeating the name "Lucy Swift." Why should he have done that? He knew quite well that her surname—Rory's name—was McDonnell. Then she recalled having told Martha that her surname was Swift, rather than McDonnell. Perhaps Martha had passed that information on to Philip . . . Yet it still did not make sense. Her reference from Lady Clarence, too, had been made out for "Lucy Swift." The speculation disturbed Lucy. It was almost as if Philip was trying to discredit her marriage to Rory. Yet he had been sympathetic enough over the subject of her husband's death.

Lucy was suddenly exposed to the freezing cold night air as Daisy turned over in bed with a great lurch, taking all the covers with her. She sighed resignedly. The woman was nothing but a big, fat, selfish, slovenly pink pig. Her one redeeming feature was the fact that she, like Maud, was kind-hearted, a characteristic in very short supply in the Hardwicke household. Lucy filched the counterpane which was lying loosely on the top of Daisy's heap of blankets and wound herself tightly in it. Before she fell into a dreamless sleep she sent out a silent prayer that over the festive period an opportunity would present itself to acquire the deed and free herself both from her slavery to Rachel and her obligation to Philip.

* * *

The following day Maud fell ill with a streaming cold and a fever. Harriet Hardwicke declared that she could not bear to have her near her, not only because of her unsightly red eyes and streaming nose but also because she had a dread of catching it, too. So Lucy was summoned at dawn to attend her.

When Rachel discovered that Lucy was not free to receive her orders and tormentings that day, she flounced into her mother's room and complained, "Really, Mother, I think this is very selfish of you. *I* need Lucy more than you do." Then, apparently realizing that her mother was not at all impressed with her show of temperament, her sly personality at once underwent an astonishing change from the spoilt child to the honey-voiced wheedler. "I *do* want to find myself another beau soon. Dear Mother, I *know* you want me to make a good marriage. Father told me that he might be bringing Lord Emmett back from London with him. You know how much I liked him when he visited us last Christmas, only he was betrothed to that dreadful woman Cecilia Monotony, or whatever her name was."

"Countess Monatova," put in her mother gently. "A very charming girl, as I recall, even if her English was not perfect."

"I didn't like her," continued Rachel, an angry glint entering her eyes.

Had Lucy known Mrs. Hardwicke better she would have shot her a sympathetic glance because she felt sure Rachel's mother found her only daughter a trial at times. However, feeling unsure of her ground, she kept her eyes modestly applied to her task of hunting for a missing garnet earring in one of Harriet's overflowing jewellery cases.

"I never cared a fig for Philip Darwin anyway." Rachel's attempt to worm her way round her mother by sweet talk had obviously been abandoned. "He's got no money, and what use is an empty title? I never wanted to live in that crumbling mausoleum Darwin Manor, either. It's like a . . . a . . ." Rachel's feeble imagination groped for a simile and failed to find one. Warming to the subject of Philip, Rachel proceeded to express her feelings on the way Philip Darwin had treated her. "Finding him in the stable with that—that *slut!*" Her tongue spat venom like a snake's.

Lucy felt her face beginning to burn. How much had Rachel seen? If she put her mind to it, would she find something familiar about Lucy, something which would connect her with that particular incident?

"I have never been treated so grossly," Rachel continued. "It was not just the mere fact that he was being unfaithful to me, but she wasn't even a woman of quality! I could see that from her dress and from the broken-down nag she had for a mount."

Lucy burned still more, hatred in her heart.

"But Rachel dear, he wasn't expecting you. Men will be men, after all," protested her mother mildly, giving Lucy the impression that she had liked and sided with Philip.

"That's not the sort of man *I* want!" Rachel retorted, tossing her head.

Lucy had found the earring but was refraining from announcing the fact in order to catch anything else Rachel had to say about Philip. Not that she cared, she told herself, but it was, after all, quite fascinating to hear somebody one knew being gossiped about, apart from the fact that Rachel's remarks added more fuel to her loathing of the girl.

"I want a man who worships me, who will dote on me and give me everything, *everything*. I want him to be completely satisfied with me so that he will have no need to seek another woman. That's the only reason they do it, you know, Mother," Rachel announced, fixing Harriet with gimlet stare. "Look at Father, for instance—"

"Rachel! Mind your tongue." For a tiny, fragile-looking person, Harriet could, when aroused, produce a sharp tone of voice.

"It's what I think, so I'm going to say it. If you had not stopped sharing Father's bed all those years ago, he would have had no need to go galloping off to London and Manchester and all those other places he goes to."

"It's business, Rachel, purely business."

"That's what he tells you!" retorted Rachel impudently, not letting her mother insert another word into the conversation. "I know all about Susan in Liverpool, Carrie in St. Albans, Ettie in Covent Garden . . ."

Lucy watched Harriet's face pale to a waxen shade and then flush with a crimson tide of anger and outrage.

"Rachel! Cease this poisonous, lying talk at once. If you were younger, I'd send you to your father for a whipping! I would be pleased if you kept your fantastic ideas to yourself and refrained from speaking of them in front of either myself or my servants."

Lucy wondered if she ought to offer to leave, but it seemed that, the instant Harriet remembered Lucy was there, she forgot again as Rachel caught her up once more in the tangled, emotionally charged situation of a mother-daughter relationship in which neither participant had much patience or sympathy for the other, and no respect whatsoever.

"Go to your room." Harriet's bird-like frame was quivering with rage and nervous shock.

"I've seen the letters, the gifts, the bills, they're all among his papers. You can go and look too, Mother. 'To my dear Carrie, one hundred pounds in payment for the generosity of her warm heart.' I saw that written down in his ledger, and lots more besides. Go and look, go and *look!*"

Rachel's strident voice rose to a crescendo and she danced triumphantly round her mother's room while the small woman darted after her, ineffectually flailing her arms. At the doorway, Rachel paused, looked expectantly at Lucy and commanded, "You. Come with me and do my hair."

"I'm sorry, I am under Mistress Hardwicke's orders today. I am not free to serve you unless she bids me," said Lucy, politely but firmly, hoping her tone of voice would give Harriet courage and let her know she had an ally. Her words seemed to work, for Harriet withdrew to her toilet table, took the earring which Lucy was proffering and informed her daughter that this was quite correct and that she would send Lucy to her later if she could spare her. Rachel shot Lucy such a look that she almost flinched. Had Rachel been one of the Pendle witches, Lucy was convinced that she would have died on the spot from such a dagger-thrust of a glance. She ignored her, however, and proceeded to affix the earrings to Harriet's tiny, almost translucent ears that resembled fine porcelain rather than human flesh. When she next looked up, Rachel had gone.

"Thank you, Lucy," said Harriet.

The remark could have been related to the finding of the missing jewel, yet Lucy thought she detected something extra—perhaps gratitude for helping give her the strength to stand up to her willful, spiteful offspring. Not another word was spoken as Lucy powdered and rouged the woman's delicate face and arranged the lace at her collar and cuffs. When she had finished, she stepped back, regarded her handiwork and announced, with a certain amount of pride in her voice, "You look just like a princess, ma'am."

Harriet, obviously pleased with her appearance, smiled kindly at Lucy and replied. "You do your job very well, child. Lady Clarence must have been sorry to lose you."

Lucy smiled deferentially back. She could understand now why so many girls from lower stations in life aspired to a position such as this. Attending a grateful, pleasant person made earning one's keep seem worthwhile and, if one's mistress was attractive, as Harriet undoubtedly was despite her age, also gave one a good deal of creative satisfaction. Lucy herself had picked out the dress from among Harriet's sizeable collection as being one that would greatly suit her. Harriet had admitted that she had never worn it, thinking that the deep wine shade of the expensive brocade was unbecoming to her pale complexion, but now she could see in the glass which Lucy held in front of her that her complexion gained from the color. Her lips and cheeks looked redder, her teeth whiter and Lucy had arranged her hair in a younger, prettier style than the way she normally wore it. As Lucy watched her gazing dreamily and fascinatedly at her reflection, she could see five, ten years slipping from the tense, bustling little woman. With her doll-like looks, she was almost a young girl again and Lucy thrilled for her. Maybe, when her husband next saw her, he would realize what his bed had been lacking all these years; maybe their marriage would start afresh, revitalized by this new, attractive change in his wife.

When Lucy actually laid eyes on John Hardwicke, she wished such thoughts had never crossed her mind. She would not have visited the attentions of this ugly, loud-mouthed, porcine bore on any woman. He strode into Rokely Hall, flinging doors open on all sides, letting great clods of mud and melting snow from his boots fall all over the carpets instead of scraping them off at the door as any civilized man would have done. He bawled for his family and his servants and when the latter appeared he immediately had them busy dancing attendance on him, bringing him dry clothes, pouring him mulled wine, removing his boots, offering him food and giving his companion—an effete-looking young man in foppish clothes—the same treatment.

Lucy lingered on the landing which this commotion was going on. So that weak, dandified youth was the beau on whom the fiery Rachel had set her heart! Lucy felt sorry for him. Doubtless, if John Hardwicke could buy Philip and his title for Rachel, he could buy this pretentious popinjay, too, with his ruffles and jewels and affected lisp.

"I've caught you slacking! Come here at once and I'll give you plenty to do!" The imperious tones cut through Lucy's thoughts and she turned to face her hated enemy who was beckoning triumphantly from the doorway of her bedroom.

"Yes, miss," said Lucy dully, wondering what kind of tortures and baitings this female fiend had in store for her now.

"That man in the hall with Father is Lord Emmett, the man I intend to marry. You will dress me in a way that will appeal to him. I want to look like one of the court ladies, fashionable and alluring. I know you're only a country bumpkin with no taste, but do try to find something among that awful, outdated collection of mine that will be suitable for the occasion."

"And that will get you whipped by your father,"

Lucy added silently, thinking of the habit among court ladies of leaving certain appendages hanging almost out of their clothes which, to Lucy, seemed no more seductive than a cow strolling through a field with its udders swinging.

Dress after dress was brought and refused, with mounting impatience, by Rachel. Finally, she slapped Lucy's arm, called her "a stupid numskull," and sailed to the capacious wardrobe herself, whereupon she pulled furiously at a dress and suffered a near smothering as a heap of heavy costumes descended onto her and knocked her to the floor. Lucy could hardly hold back a loud laugh as Rachel kicked and writhed beneath the heap of dresses.

"Help me, you oaf! Get them off me!" Rachel screamed. She delivered an extra hard kick to Lucy's shins for her pains, as if the avalanche of silks and satins had been caused by her maid's carelessness rather than her own.

Rachel finally settled on a dress of yellow silk with an overskirt of palest primrose lace. Lucy thought privately that it caused her to resemble a milkmaid rather than the great lady she imagined herself to be. The shade drained the gold sheen from her hair, leaving it looking like a hayfield after the harvest. It also added an unhealthy liverishness to her complexion but Lucy knew that it was definitely not her place to point out, no matter how tactfully, that perhaps the dress wasn't such a good choice after all. At least Rachel seemed reasonably satisfied, although she grumbled about the neckline not being revealing enough.

"Shall I alter it for you, miss?" offered Lucy.

"What? Allow you to lay your clumsy fingers on one of my best gowns? Thank you, no. I'll wear it as it is. Maybe Lord Emmett will appreciate a girl who is rather more demure than the ladies he's been used to. He may find me a trifle refreshing, don't you think?"

With a flaunt of her petticoats, Rachel simpered at Lucy who had no intention of pandering to her colossal vanity and merely nodded. Instantly, a dark cloud crossed Rachel's features and she reached towards her dressing table as if about to hurl something at Lucy's head.

"I can hear Mistress Hardwicke, your mother, calling me. If that will be all, miss . . . ?"

Lucy ducked out of the door and was convinced she could hear Rachel swearing like a trooper behind her. Where could she have picked up such foul phrases? As she passed the door of the library wherein John Hardwicke was engaging Lord Emmett in some kind of guessing game involving the names of women and horses, she learned the answer to her question. She didn't linger, however, for now it was her turn to don her best dress and try to prettify herself in order to attend the Christmas party which the Hardwickes provided annually for their servants.

CHAPTER SEVEN

"Well now, you're a pretty little thing, aren't you, m'dear? C'mon, your master won't bite you. Come over here, where I can see you in the light."

Obediently, Lucy edged forward towards the pool of light cast by the oil lamp which was placed in the center of the library table. She had been quite looking forward to relaxing in the company of Daisy, Maud and the other staff of Rokely Hall, many of whom she hadn't even met yet, and it was just her bad luck to be passing the library door as John Hardwicke lurched unsteadily out in search of a fresh supply of liquor. The lamplight illuminated the dress borrowed from the late Lady Eleanor so that Lucy looked as if she were clad from shoulder to foot in drapes of shimmering gold.

"Parfait!"

The affected voice made her turn her head, to see Lord Emmett draped languorously across a chaise longue, peeling a grape with a bored expression.

"Happen she's new. Haven't seen her before myself."

"Your wife made a good choice." Emmett's lips curled sardonically.

"C-can I go now, sir?" Lucy bobbed a quick curtsey and scuttled for the door, but her exit was barred by Hardwicke's foot.

"Not so fast, not so fast. Stay a little and sup some wine with us." His crimson-veined nose spoke of much imbibing over many years and, to her disgust, he simultaneously winked lecherously and let out a loud belch. Lucy had been wrong in her summing-up of Daisy. Compared to this John Hardwicke, the woman was, perhaps, a plump cow. Only Hardwicke deserved the epithet of pig, in both looks and manners. As she looked at him she was reminded, rather horribly, of the incident that had taken place what seemed like years previously but that was, in fact, only a few months in the past, between herself and her brother-in-law, that other John. It would always be a name associated with boorishness and lechery in her mind. Her quick brain sought a way out of her dilemma.

"But—the party. They're expecting me."

"Party—humph!" Hardwicke snorted and turned to his companion. "Little minx thinks a servants' party more important than being invited to join her betters!"

"Don't aspire to the court, do you, Hetti?" The bored aristocrat seemed to speak without moving his lips.

"Beg pardon, sir, my name's Lucy."

"Hettie. They're all called Hettie," remarked Emmett woodenly, addressing his cluster of grapes.

"Come here, Lucy," ordered Hardwicke, patting his fleshy lap, while Lucy tried her best to suppress a shudder. "Here, I said," exclaimed Hardwicke, a slight edge entering his voice.

She had to escape somehow. Why did these things always happen to her? What was it about her that made men, particularly old, ugly ones, feel they had to entice and seduce her?

"Here, puss, puss, puss!" mocked Emmett, rubbing his thumb and index finger together.

"But sir, the party . . ." Lucy faltered.

"Do as your master tells you!" thundered Hardwicke, his bushy eyebrows meeting across his bulbous brow.

"Like animals. Have to show 'em who's master," simpered Emmett.

With dragging footsteps, Lucy approached Hardwicke who was sitting in a deep armchair by the fire. As soon as she was within reach, he grabbed her around the waist and pulled her roughly onto his knee.

"Give her a good frigging I say, John. Let's have a bit of Christmas sport around here." Emmett's face showed its first sign of animation as Harwicke's hand pushed at Lucy's bodice, seeking the warm mounds of her breasts. "Wouldn't mind giving the fire a poke myself."

"Seems she's my property so I claim first go," announced Hardwicke, his wet, blubbery lips seeking Lucy's. Instinctively she shrank away from his kiss and was rewarded with a sharp rap across the cheek from the back of his hand.

"Naughty, naughty. Must do what your master says," intoned Emmett, then added, "What say you we play forfeits?"

"How do you mean?" grunted Hardwicke. His fingers had entered Lucy's bodice and were now probing beneath her shift. The touch of his clumsy, podgy fingers made her flesh crawl. How could she escape without infuriating him?

"Sirs, I beg of you . . ." she pleaded, her sweeping glance meeting the eyes of both men. "I'm only new here, I came but four days ago. I want to do a good job as Miss Rachel's maid. I don't want to get mixed up in anything that might affect my position in this household . . ."

Both men burst out laughing, Hardwicke wheezing until the tears ran down his bloated red cheeks.

"Position—humph! Haw, haw! The only position for you, m'dear, is on your back with your legs spread!"

"Oh no—round your neck, John, your *neck!* Have you no imagination?"

It was then Lucy realized that, with both men egging each other on and neither wishing to lose face in the estimation of the other, her chances of excape were slim.

Hardwicke, still wheezing and puffing, squeezed one of Lucy's nipples painfully, then, with enough strength to tear the throat from a threatening mastiff, wrenched the lace that fastened Lucy's bodice together clean in two.

Emmett applauded his feat with slow handclaps. "You've opened the chest, now let's see the treasure!" he quipped.

"No! How dare you?" protested Lucy as her breasts were unceremoniously heaved out of her shift.

"Mmm, mmm . . ." murmured Emmett, making a loud sucking noise on his grape.

"Put those away, these are sweeter," joked Hardwicke, pressing his lips to Lucy's breast and attacking one of her nipples like a starving baby.

"Please, sir, you're hurting me!" Lucy's cry of pain was genuine.

"Please, sir, you're hurting me," mimicked the odious Emmett, in a falsetto voice. " 'Please, sir, *hurt me'*—that's what you'll be begging in a minute! You love it, you little bitch. Look at you, giving him suck like a wet nurse! I've got something I'd like you to suck . . ."

Lucy wished she could stop her ears to protect herself from his crude words. Hardwicke was worrying her breast with his teeth, scraping the tender skin. She dared not try to pull away from him in case he bit her even harder. Emmett, still reclining on the damask-covered chaise-longue, was languidly stroking his fingers up the inside of his thigh, caressing himself, although his features betrayed not one trace of arousal.

As Hardwicke fumbled with his britches in an attempt to encourage Lucy to manipulate his semi-aroused manhood, Lucy discovered that she possessed an ability of which she had not previously been aware. The only way she could describe it to herself was as a feeling of being far away from what was happening to her, as if her body were doing things but she herself were not conscious of feeling anything. It was like the sensation she experienced just before falling asleep or collapsing in a faint, a dream-like feeling, as if it were all happening to somebody else and some small part of her was somehow tuned to it.

"There, my little maid. Be a good girl and—"

Lucy had guessed what he was about to say, but before she could react there was a knocking at the door.

"Quick—it might be my wife! In the cupboard with you!" Hardwicke bundled her behind a screen and out of sight and Lucy could hear men's voices and a clinking of glasses as a servant obviously provided fresh victuals. The door clicked shut again.

While she had been in hiding, Lucy had thrust her lace together anyhow and fastened up her dress. The "cupboard" Hardwicke had pushed her into so unceremoniously was, in fact, a recess to one side of the fireplace, which was screened off and held a pile of logs for the fire. It was dark. Lucy hit her toe against a log and stumbled, groping for the wall behind her to regain her balance. As she touched the oak panelling, she heard a whirring sound and suddenly, to her horror, found herself tumbling backwards into what felt like empty space.

Stifling a scream, she flung out her arms and found she was in some kind of narrow passageway. In the dim glow from the fire and the library lamp and candles, Lucy's eyes, accustoming themselves rapidly to the lack of light, made out the first two in a flight of stone steps leading up and away from the library.

Without a second's hesitation, Lucy began to climb, knowing she had no time to lose, for Hardwicke would soon come to haul her back into his clutches. She prayed that he would be too drunk to mount the steep steps in pursuit. She could imagined Emmett's affected drawl informing Hardwicke that there were "plenty more Hetties."

The shaft of light from the library was soon far behind her. She had no idea how many steps she had climbed, fumbling for each one with her foot to make sure she didn't fall into some yawning chasm or come up against a blank wall. At least the passageway was dry, although the stone walls were freezing cold and the ceiling, in some places, so low that it brushed her hair. Suddenly she heard the sound she feared—Hardwicke's inebriated bellowing.

"Lucy? Lucy! Come back here. Confound the girl. *Lucy!*"

She heard a mumbled conversation ensue between Hardwicke and Emmett, then the sounds dwindled as she climbed even higher, her hands on the walls on either side of her guiding her ever upwards. She wished there had been some way of securing the panelling behind her so as not to have given away the secret of her escape route. Wherever the stairway may lead, it would be of no help to her in future now that Hardwicke had discovered it. She raised her foot mechanicallly to take the next step and found that the regularity of the treads had ceased. She prodded the darkness with her toe and examined the walls with both hands, her fingers encountering a thick cobweb which made her shudder. The whole passageway was taking a turn to the right. Fumbling her way round the curve, she readjusted her steps as the staircase began to climb regularly once more.

Panting with exertion and fear, having tripped over her trailing skirts many times as she made her ascent, Lucy at last reached the very top step. An expanse of panelling faced her. Somewhere, she knew, there had to be a release mechanism which would open a door for her if only she could press or twist the right spot. She felt a growing apprehension as to where she was about to emerge. Maybe she would find herself in some deserted room, long boarded up, the only exit from which would be back down the passageway and straight into the triumphant arms of the men she sought to escape. And it would be most embarrassing if she found herself in, say, Rachel's bedroom or that of one of the servants, particularly if the inhabitant was male. Then she remembered that they would all be attending the party. By now, her absence was bound to have been noticed. Wherever she found herself—that was, if she could ever manage to make the unresponsive panelling yield—she would have to go straight to the party with some trumped-up excuse about a headache or suchlike, or else the rest of the staff would think she considered herself above them and the function not important enough for her to attend. It was vital that she did not draw attention to herself in any

way. Let them all think her a London-trained
lady's maid for as long as it took to steal the document. Afterwards, once she had gone and the theft
had been discovered, let them think what they
liked. For, with Philip's help, she would be far
away.

Starting at the top left-hand corner, her fingers
systematically examined every panel. In ' the
darkness she felt a bit like a slow snail exploring
with its long, probing eyestalks. It must have taken
her ten minutes to reach the very last panel on the
right and still she had encountered no welcome
click or sliding aside of the heavy wood. Feeling in
great need of a rest, she let herself slump down
onto the top step—and, as she did so, her hip
caught against a lever of some sort which was sticking out of the wall. With a great slithering and
creaking, as of an old door which has not been
opened for generations and is almost sealed into its
surround by rust and rubble, a complete section of
the panelling slid away, leaving an opening large
enough to admit a man if he bent double.

Thankfully, Lucy crawled out of the square hole.
Her feet landed on thick carpet and she was aware
of the dull glimmer of a window somewhere to her
right. No abandoned room, this! It was obviously
in frequent, if not daily use. She stood poised for a
moment, listening. No voice or footfall came to
her, but she noticed a shaft of light gleaming from
beneath a door and realized she must be somewhere in the main part of the house. If this was so,
she had no time to lose. At any moment the occupant of the room might return and she would be

discovered. Wishing that she had a candle to see
by, Lucy sought for some means of closing the entrance to her secret tunnel. As she prodded and
pushed, she remembered the conversation she had
had with Philip on that very subject. Now her
childhood dream had come true; she *had* stumbled
on a secret passageway, but there had been no leisure to seek for treasure, no time to feel thrilled
and excited. She pressed something which looked
like a knot in the wood and, to her relief, the panel
slid shut with another protesting creak. Now all
that remained was for her to leave the room as un-
noticed as she had entered it.

She took several bold strides in the direction of
the door and had almost reached it when something made her turn back. There was something
nagging at the back of her brain, something she
had remembered, or else noticed about the room
she was in. She traced her thoughts back. The first
thing she had seen had been the window. She
turned her eyes towards it. There, below it, was the
bulky outline of a large wooden chest. An oak
chest, by a window. Why should that seem familiar
to her? None of the rooms at home had contained
a chest in such a position, apart from the settle in
the window of the drawing-room. Perhaps that was
what she was thinking of. Her hand reached for the
door handle, yet still the uneasy memory was
plaguing her. She was standing by a carved wooden
bureau. Behind her was a four-poster bed with a
dresser next to it, bearing a water bowl and jug.
The positioning of all these objects seemed so . . .

Lucy's hand flew to her mouth. Of *course* they seemed familiar! She had seen them before in her mind's eye, their shapes and positions having been suggested by a diagram drawn in wine on a table-top. She was in the bedroom of the very man whose attentions she had fled, John Hardwicke!

Lucy's heart thumped in panic. Did he know where the secret staircase ended? Was he, right now, waiting on the landing to pounce on her as she emerged from his bedroom door, thinking herself safe? Was he—and here a pang of horror stabbed shudderingly through her—was he already in the room, smiling sardonically to himself as he watched her blunder around in the gloom? She steeled herself to probe every shadowy corner with her eyes. No, there was nobody there. She did not have that prickling sensation of being watched that she had had in the Darwin Manor ballroom. Tak-ing courage from the knowledge that here, at least, she was alone, she walked over to the oak chest and lifted the lid. There, just as Philip had predicted, was the ledge and on it a single key. Should she pocket it now? No, Hardwicke might miss it and raise an outcry before she had had a chance to se-cure the other key, the one which opened the drawer inside the bureau. Closing the heavy lid, she glided soundlessly to the door. Opening it care-fully, just enough to allow herself a quick survey of the corridor, she prepared to make a dash up to the next landing, from which it was an easy journey to the servants' staircase at the back of the house. There was nobody around. Breathing a sigh of relief she stepped out into the corridor, closing Hardwicke's door behind her.

She had almost reached the bottom of the flight of stairs leading up to the top floor when she thought she heard a woman's voice call her name. Composing her face so as to show no traces of anxiety or guilt, Lucy looked over the banister. There, standing in the entrance hall, was Maud.

"Where on earth 'ave you been? I've searched everywhere. We've all started without you, I'm afraid, but, if you come quick, there'll still be some left."

Lucy smiled at her gladly. "I was on my way when the master called me and then I had a duty to perform for Miss Rachel." That would explain what she was doing on the first floor.

Maud looked at her suspiciously. "But Miss Rachel has gone over to visit the Squire, accompanied by Lord Emmett."

"I know," Lucy lied glibly. "But she had spilt some powder in her room and wanted me to clear up the mess."

Maud accepted this explanation and rolled her eyes up in sympathy. She, too, had borne the vituperative force of Rachel's tongue in the past and didn't in the least envy Lucy her position as Rachel's personal maid.

"Come along with me now. You won't escape this time! There are several nice young men all dyin' to meet you." She sneezed and mopped at her nose.

"Bless you!" exclaimed Lucy. Although she'd

only known the older girl for a few days, she was already quite fond of her. At twenty-three, Maud was a born spinster. Broad-faced and plain, she loved her work in the big house and, while allowing herself to exchange badinage and gibes with the male servants, readily admitted that she preferred to keep her own company, having, in her own words, "twice the nous" of any of the males who had ever paid her court. The day Lucy arrived, Maud had declared her "a lost lamb" and taken her under her wing.

As Lucy allowed herself to be led into the servants' dining-room, a wave of heat and a cheerful hubbub hit her and she felt herself begin to perspire beneath the heavy stuff of her gown. She had had no idea Rokely Hall employed so many servants. There seemed to be scores of them, although a rough count which she carried out later made it nearer eighteen, including coachmen, gardeners and stableboys. She already knew several of them by sight—including the cook, a huge woman even larger than Daisy, Mrs. Ramsbottom; the butler, Hawkins; the little scullion, Teresa, or "Tree" as she was nicknamed; and Hardwicke's personal manservant, Jamieson, whom Lucy had hated on sight almost as much as his master, owing to his dark, rather devilish looks and his manner of looking down his nose sarcastically at her.

Maud, snuffling and coughing from her cold, introduced her to the head groom, who was named, most inappropriately, Adam Redhead, in spite of his mop of fair curls; the two stable boys, Davey

and Jim; Dickon the gardener, a grizzle-haired,
aged man, and his young assistant Tom, a lad of
about Lucy's own age; and the coachmen, two
brothers similar enough to be taken for identical
twins, separated by only eleven months between
them, named Nat and Josiah. They had brought
their wives to the party, and a group of young children, some belonging to them and others who were
the younger brothers and sisters of some of the other servants, were chasing round screeching and gig-
gling and getting under everyone's feet.

A great deal of ale had already been consumed
and Lucy felt far too stiff and sober to be able to
enter into the spirit of the occasion. She lingered
with Maud and Daisy, until the latter slumped into
a snoring heap across the table, to the great amusement of all. The food which Mrs. Ramsbottom had
provided on the thoughtful instructions of Harriet
Hardwicke was plentiful and delicious. Lucy ate
her fill of slices of pheasant and venison and dainty
pieces of spiced pie, and sipped at a tankard of ale
which Maud thrust into her hand. She could sense
the eyes of the other women on her gown. No
doubt they were wondering how she came to be in
possession of such a grand, if old-fashioned,
garment. Let them think what they wished. She
would not be here much longer and their tongues
would wag all they liked once she was safely back
at Darwin Manor.

Gnarled old Dickon produced a pipe from his
pocket and proceeded to play a merry air to which
some of the servants started to dance. Maud, in

spite of her cold, was pulled to her feet by Nat, the elder of the two coachmen, and found herself whirled round the table in a fast jig. Lucy sat there dreamily in the steamy room, idly drumming her fingers to the rhythm. Was this what Christmas used to be like for the servants of Darwin Manor, in the days when Lady Eleanor was alive and Philip still unborn? She tried to picture Philip in his father's place, as the Earl and head of the household. Somehow she couldn't see him as a benevolent master or even as a gentle, loving husband who would grieve over the loss of his wife to the point of driving himself demented, as the old Earl had obviously done. Leaving aside the incident in the stable which perhaps, by a slight stretch of the imagination, had been justified—wouldn't she, too, have been furious if she had been cheated and knew it?—her subsequent knowledge of Philip had only strengthened the first impression she'd gained of him at Pendleton Fair, as arrogant, self-opinionated, intelligent and cold.

She gazed vacantly at the gyrating figures, who were laughing, tripping, seizing mugs of ale and taking quick gulps as they passed the table, and listened with half an ear to the reedy pipe music. If Rory had been here, he would have transformed the whole room with his larger-than-life personality, his singing, his joking, his ability to hold a group of people spellbound. She would not have had to return to her room lonely and uncomforted, for he would have held her close, murmured compliments to her beauty, assured her that she was loved and desired. To have been married for so short a time, a marriage with so much potential for happiness, and have it end so abruptly—why, it was like crushing a chrysalis and depriving a beautiful butterfly of life! Already Lucy was beginning to forgive her dead husband for his infidelity. Something on his mind had been worrying him for some time, she had seen that, and it certainly wasn't the tavern slut. He had told Lucy he hadn't visited Pendleton for a year, and that bloated hussy certainly wasn't the sort of girl a man would have on his mind for twelve months. No, something much more important than that must have been disturbing him, and it seemed so unbearably cruel that now she would never find out what it had been; she would never be able to soothe him, love him, bear his children—a thing they had often talked about. No other man would ever blaze with Rory's fiery zest for life, nor awaken the searing flames of desire deep within her that he had awoken. These dancing, happy, carefree people—how she envied them! They looked as if they had never known loss or heartache. Yet how could one ever tell?

"Why so sad, Lucy?"

The pleasant male voice shattered her introspection. Men. Why wouldn't they ever leave her alone? Couldn't they see that she wasn't interested in them? That, for her, love had died along with Rory? She found herself looking into the green eyes of Adam Redhead, the man in charge of the Hardwicke horses. She couldn't bring herself to smile at him.

"Are you homesick because it's Christmas? You don't come from these parts, do you?"

She sighed. He seemed determined to engage her in conversation. She would have to make some semblance of friendliness. Later, when she was alone, she would have time enough for her memories.

"No. I come from Lancashire, but further west, Prebbledale way. That's where my parents live."

"D'you like it here at Rokely Hall? I'll wager Miss Rachel is a handful."

This was one topic on which Lucy could wax most eloquent. She proceeded to tell Adam about some of the things Rachel had said and done in the few days she had been working for her. When she finished, Adam looked at her in admiration.

"You must be a girl of spirit and determination, to put up with that. Did she give you that mark, the one on your cheekbone?"

Lucy put her hand up to her cheek and felt the hard, dry ridge of a scab. Of course! It was the place where Rachel's emerald ring had caught her. She had quite forgotten about it but, as she pressed it gingerly, it felt quite sore. She told Adam how she had incurred the wound and his brow furrowed with concern.

"That one girl could so mar another's beauty! She's probably jealous of you because you are so much more attractive than she is."

Was he being impertinent, or had he got too much drink inside him? From being open and friendly, Lucy withdrew a little and refused to reply.

Adam persisted. "Come and dance. That'll soon cheer you up and put you in the Christmas spirit."

Lucy declined, pleading the fact that she was far too hot in her thick dress, but still the man would not leave her alone. Maud caught her eye and winked at her. Drat the girl. Doubtless there would be gossip and innuendos the following day. She wasn't sure if she could stand it.

"Then, if you won't dance, have a Christmas drink with me. Here, give me your cup."

Without any compliance on Lucy's part, Adam seized her pottery mug, poured the remaining two inches of ale onto the floor, fished around inside his waistcoat and produced a small flask which he proceeded to open. He poured a trickle of amber liquid into Lucy's cup, then took a deep draught himself, wiped his lips with the back of his hand and replaced the flask in its hiding place about his person. He pushed the mug across the table towards Lucy.

"Go on. This'll warm the cockles o' your heart."

She felt she couldn't very well refuse him. He wasn't being unpleasant in the way Hardwicke and Emmett were unpleasant; he was just a nice-looking, ordinary man of twenty-six or so who was trying to bring her into the servants' community and make it easier for her to mix with them. She raised the cup to her lips and spluttered as the pungent spirit burned its way down her throat. It was neat brandy. She had only tasted brandy once before and that had been several years ago, when her father, in one of his drunken sprees, had offered her a nip and had laughed uproariously at her grimaces. She bravely swallowed the mouthful she had taken, and a few moments later found she was indeed feeling more relaxed and sociable, having begun to tap her foot to the piper's tune and smile at the whirling, staggering couples all around her.

"Now, how about that dance?" Adam invited, holding out his hand to her.

Lucy grasped it and was soon weaving in and out among the other couples, steered by Adam, who proved to be a fine dancer. She careered past Maud, who was now in the arms of Josiah, whose wife was in the throes of a most remarkable dance with young Tom, the under-gardener, which called for much whooping and kicking-up of feet. When the kitchen clock struck midnight, Hawkins, the butler, called for a toast to the King, and then another to their master, John Hardwicke, and all his family. On both occasions, Lucy downed more of the brandy and felt exceedingly floaty afterwards, as if she were moving around an inch or more above the floor. Abbie, one of the kitchen girls, had produced some mistletoe from somewhere and was going around holding it over couples' heads and exhorting them to kiss, which they all did with gusto. Then it was the turn of herself and Adam. His curly hair was plastered to his face with the sweat of his exertions and a broad smile wreathed his lips as his face bore down on Lucy's. She made no move to stop him. Indeed, she felt so exhilarated, so exultantly happy, that she responded to his kiss with far more enthusiasm than the occasion demanded and was suddenly aware of giggles and guffaws from all around as the other servants stopped whatever else they were doing to remark on the length of the kiss.

She realized that she was rather inebriated and would need to keep a tight control on herself, so she prised herself with difficulty from Adam's embrace, found a stool and sat down. Not everybody was behaving with as much propriety as herself. Old Dickon's twig-like fingers were clawing at Daisy's ample bosom, and two pairs of feet, one pair pointing upwards and the other down, could be glimpsed round the pantry door. Tom had Kitty, one of the dairymaids, spread along a bench, his hands vigorously exploring beneath her skirts, and even the sensible Maud had been pressed up against the wall and was allowing herself to be kissed and fondled by one of the stable lads. Lucy did not feel at all shocked at this spectacle. It just served to emphasize her feeling of not belonging. She could summon up no enthusiasm for such licentious behavior although she certainly did not condemn it in others. She just felt distanced from them all—and sad.

Adam stood next to her, his hand on her shoulder, his fingers entwined in her curls. She looked up at him and he bent his face down to hers, meaning to kiss her. The strange thing was that she *wanted* him to and it was this inexplicable urge that made her turn aside and announce, solemnly, that she wished to retire to her room as she had a headache coming on. A spasm of disappointment briefly contorted his features, then passed.

"But a few moments ago you were . . . you were dancing and laughing. What's wrong? Have I done something, or said anything, to upset you?"

"No," replied Lucy softly, sensing his bewilderment. "It's just that . . . well, I'm not used to strong liquor. I don't feel quite myself. Miss Rachel will chide me viciously tomorrow if I lack the energy to run round for her and do her bidding. You see . . ." She paused and smiled. She was about to impart a secret which she knew would set the whole household humming with gossip. She didn't care, for why should she feel any loyalty towards the girl who had treated her so badly? "You see," she continued, "Miss Rachel is husband-hunting—and her quarry is Lord Emmett."

There was no slipping off to bed for her now. The female servants clustered round her, demanding to know more, and there was much screeching, guffawing and slapping of thighs. But when they noticed how very pale and drawn Lucy had become and how she was having to resort to frequent blinks to keep her heavy eyelids open, they at last agreed to let her go and Maud accompanied her up the back stairs, having noticed that she was swaying so much that her legs would scarcely carry her. Lucy was grateful for the older girl's company as it prevented Adam from following her. However, she was not pleased to find, on entering the room, that Daisy was sprawled in a prostrate, snoring heap right in the middle of the bed, leaving Lucy a mere few inches' space to curl up in. Her

head was spinning round and Maud helped her undress, then took the stone bowl from the dresser
and placed it strategically close to the side of the
bed, having witnessed all too many times the effect
liquor could have on a person unused to much imbibing.

Lucy had no need of the bowl, nor did she spend
any time lying awake and cramped and cursing
Daisy, for a dream-sprinkled sleep overtook her
the moment her head touched the bolster. She
awoke next morning to a blinding headache and
the sound of Daisy coughing and groaning and be-
moaning her own excesses of the night before.

That day, Christmas Eve, Rachel was more of a
trial than ever. Harriet Hardwicke still refused to
have the scabby-nosed Maud anywhere near her,
so Lucy, feeling much under par, had to run from
one to the other. They were both in a great state,
Harriet because she felt sure the ball would be a
disaster, with few guests being able to attend owing
to the weather—snow still lay thickly on the
ground and the lanes had frozen over, causing
horses to skid and carriages to overturn—and
Rachel because Emmett had paid scant attention
to her during their visit to the squire the previous
evening and she was at a loss to know how best to
attract him. Lucy's patience was tried so hard by
Rachel's fractious behavior that she was almost
tempted to snap back at her tormentor, knowing
she would probably be dismissed instantly for such
impertinence, she managed with difficulty to keep

silent. At least Rachel wasn't in one of her violent, screaming tempers, for which Lucy, with her throbbing head, gave thanks.

At first Lucy worried that perhaps Hardwicke, with even more Christmas spirit inside his overweight belly than the previous night, might attempt to waylay her, but the ball passed without incident, the Hardwickes being much too busy entertaining their guests to dally with the servants. Lucy lost count of the number of times either Rachel or Harriet asked her to fetch this or do that, or escort one of their fatigued female guests to a retiring room. By the time the musicians had packed up their instruments, Lucy felt almost dead on her feet. Like the other maids, she was wearing her best uniform of black fustian with which she had been provided on her arrival. The fit was not perfect, because three of Rachel's previous maids, of varying sizes, had worn it for short periods before her, but she didn't in the least mind her servile disguise, unflattering though it was, as she had no desire to attract the attentions of any more men. She was already doing her best to avoid three—Emmett, Adam and, of course, Hardwicke.

It was the latter who was causing her the most unease. Lucy knew she ought to be thinking of some way of carrying out Philip's order but, the more she thought about it, the more she was forced to accept that there was only one way of obtaining the vital key and that was to take it while Hardwicke slept. The only way of ensuring that he slept heavily enough not to awake at the entry of an intruder into his bedchamber was to see that he consumed plenty of ale or wine. And the only way to make sure of that was to oversee its consumption herself. What that might entail Lucy realized only too well.

Christmas Day seemed to last for ever. There were several guests for the Christmas feast, friends and relatives of the Hardwickes, some of whom rode or drove over specially, having felted the hooves of their carriage horses to lessen the chances of an accident, and some of whom had stayed on after the ball.

All through the day, Lucy's thoughts were constantly with her mother and even the presentation of two surprise gifts—a tiny phial of lavender water from Maud and a blue satin garter from Daisy, who swore that she used to wear it herself when she was a girl, although now it would hardly pass round her puffy wrist—did little to lift her gloomy spirits. She imagined Philip striding up and down the draughty corridors of Darwin Manor wondering how near she was to the accomplishment of her task. Rachel was in a spitting, snarling mood, having failed to make progress with Emmett during the ball, and Lucy was forced to suffer having her hair pulled and being struck at with a hair brush as she sought to appease her ill-tempered mistress. She couldn't leave it much longer. Every time she laid eyes on Hardwicke, he had a glass or a tankard somewhere near his lips and Jamieson hovering nearby to provide constant liquid replenishment. The conviction grew on her that Christmas night would be an ideal occasion for . . . For what? With a sinking feeling, Lucy knew that the success of her mission would involve the kind of closeness to Hardwicke against which her very spirit cried out in outraged disgust. In other words, his seduction.

Early that morning Lucy had found an opportunity to steal into the library and peer behind the screen next to the fireplace. Hardwicke or another member of the household, by accident or prior knowledge, had operated the mechanism which closed the aperture in the panelling. Even if she needed to use her old escape route a second time, she doubted if she could remember exactly what she had done to release the hidden spring. It was this realization that had turned her against her previous idea of entering Hardwicke's bedchamber while he slept, seatching for the key, taking the document and tiptoeing back to her own room. There were too many people in the house now, too many bodies lying restless from over-indulgence in rich fare, too many ears overworking in the darkness, imaginations stirred by the alien creakings and stirrings of a house that wasn't their own. She could imagine the cry of "Thief!" that would be raised if she were spied creeping from Hardwicke's chamber. Or, if they didn't suspect her of being a thief, her morality would be in question and the incident relayed, in all probability, to Harriet Hardwicke. Then what would be her chances of stealing away from Rokely Hall under cover of darkness and conveying the deed to Philip?

Something occurred to Lucy that had not previously struck her. How was she to get back to Darwin Manor? It was nigh on twenty miles away, over a snow-covered moor piled with drifts and veiled hollows into which she might fall and freeze to death. She seethed with anger, the target being Philip. How clever he had been in explaining his plan, in instructing her in the lay-out of the interior of the hall—yet how remiss he had been in organizing the successful delivery of that prized treasure, the deed to his home!

As she ran the flat-iron over the bundle of petticoats that Rachel had thrust into her arms, demanding that they be returned instantly, completely freshened and smoothed, Lucy wondered if there was any way of getting a message to the Manor so that Matthew, or even Philip himself, could wait for her somewhere and convey her to safety. But that would mean naming an exact time, for she could hardly expect anybody to linger in the freezing cold. In any case, it would take several hours for her message to get there—that is, if she could find anyone to take it without arousing the suspicions of all and sundry. She could hardly steal a carriage or even a horse, from under the vigilant eye of Adam Redhead and his minions. The problem seemed insurmountable, yet she could not see how postponing her securing of the deed would make any difference. In any case, that particular worry seemed minor when compared to the sheer horror of what she would have to accomplish first.

"So, you little minx . . ." Hardwicke extended a

meaty hand and tweaked her ear. "Run away from me, would you? I'd a mind to find out where those stairs led to myself, but I'm getting too old for that caper. But I'm not too old for this, m'dear!" So saying, he drew Lucy towards him. She was still wearing her black fustian but had dabbed a few drops of Maud's lavender water on her throat and behind her ears. He sniffed appreciatively. "Mmm. Not a young girl's perfume, lavender, but a sight better than the smell o' the kitchen. Grrr!" Pretending to be a dog, he nuzzled and bit into Lucy's neck and she steeled herself not to scream. A few seconds later, he had unloosed her bodice and slipped the dress down over her hips, leaving her shivering in her shift.

She had deliberately placed herself in his way that evening, having found ways and means of remaining close to the study wherein Hardwicke was entertaining Emmett, the Squire and some other male guests. As soon as the sounds of roistering within began to die down and she guessed that goodnights were being said, she made sure she was passing the door just as it opened. As luck would have it, Jamieson was nowhere to be found and it was Lucy who received the order to deliver Hardwicke's hot rum to his bedchamber.

It was difficult to bring a smile to her features, but Lucy managed it. "Please, sir, forgive me for the other night. You took me by surprise and I was scared."

"A little virgin, I'll be bound," boomed Hardwicke, licking his fat lips for the umpteenth time.

"I like a girl who gives me a chase—but not too much, mind. I'm not as young as I used to be but—" his voice rose to a hearty crescendo—"I can still throw a passable leg over!"

Grabbing Lucy by the arm, he tossed her onto the bed and then lay down next to her. "Undress me, my pretty," he ordered.

As Lucy divested him of waistcoat, shirt, vest and, finally boots and britches, her stomach heaving at the sight of pendulous mounds of greyish flesh stippled with sparse hair, like a pig's, Philip's information about the key's hiding place came back to her. As she dropped each garment in turn onto the floor, she made a pretence of not liking to crush his brocade waistcoat and, while moving it, she felt swiftly inside the interior pocket. There was no key. Philip was wrong! To think she had got herself into this predicament for nothing! She had allowed no alcohol to enter her system this night, and her brain was as fast and fit as a racehorse on the field. If the key would not reveal itself to her, she would inveigle Hardwicke into telling her where it was.

Like wisps of smoke, an idea drifted into her mind, remained half-formed for a moment, then solidified into workable shape. Pursing her lips in a pretty, provocative pout, Lucy ran the tip of a fingernail across one of Hardwicke's shoulders, over his chest and down his stomach, stopping at the line of hair which reached downwards from his navel.

"You're a fine figure of a man, John Hardwicke," she murmured, marvelling at her ability to lie so convincingly.

He looked pleased, took hold of her hand and cupped it round that part of his male anatomy that disgusted her the most. She steeled herself to let it remain there. He squeezed her fingers encouragingly, indicating what he wanted her to do.

"I admire you," she fibbed. "You're such a *successful* man . . . How did you achieve—" she swept her glance around the room—"all this?"

"Oh, a bit of business here and there, m'dear," he replied, giving nothing away.

Lucy pursued her subject, her hand continuing to knead and tease his hardening flesh. Rory had taught her this method of satisfying a man. Pray God she could get it over with quickly so that Hardwicke would have no need to make use of her body. "What sort of business?" she inquired, in her most wheedling tones, hoping he would take the bait.

Silence was her answer. His eyes were closed and odd grunting sounds were coming from his lips, matching the rhythm of Lucy's caresses. Her ministrations were becoming too successful. She stilled her hand for a moment, only to have him take it and encourage her to continue stroking and squeezing. She felt her stomach rise and tasted acid bile in her mouth as his flesh stiffened and grew. Then he grasped her wrist to stay her movements.

"Not yet. We have all night. I don't wish to waste myself when I have your lovely body to enjoy . . ."

He sat up, the flesh on his belly shuddering and flopping. She closed her eyes then and steeled herself to go through the motions of love-making by remaining passive and unresponsive. Hardwicke, however, was a most demanding lover.

"Don't be coy, my sweet child. A girl with your color hair should be afire with passion!"

When Lucy still refused to respond, he gripped her by one shoulder, drew her towards him and sank his teeth viciously into her breast. She squirmed beneath him and he evinced his satisfaction in her liveliness. His sickly-sweet breath, carrying the scents of rum, decaying teeth and a poor digestion, panted in Lucy's face, making her feel close to vomiting. She turned her head aside to try and avoid the nauseous gale and he took this tossing motion as a sign of arousal.

"Child, you make me mad with lust," he grated, his yellow fangs bared, his hands plucking at her breasts, mauling them like a mindless child with a toy. "I'm going to take you, possess you, teach you what no callow lad could teach you! If you play your cards right, Lucy, you'll hold a special place in this household—as long as you come to me whenever I want you. You will, won't you, Lucy? Come to your master, be an obedient girl and give him love?"

As he said the word "love," Lucy thought she had never heard it so desecrated. He rolled it around his fat tongue, coated it with saliva and drooled it out, a travesty of the word she and Rory had instilled with so much depth of feeling, so much purity and strength of conviction. His hands were on her belly now, and he was awaiting an answer from her. Although she wanted to scream, *"No!"* and fight her way out of his obscene embrace, instead she gave him a lambent look, bit her lower lip coyly after the manner of a servant girl who had been offered the greatest favor her master could bestow, and softly murmured, "Yes, sir."

A look of triumph illuminated his jowly face. "Then, Lucy," he announced, placing his hand between her thighs and chafing her with bruising fingers, "when we are alone, you may call me, not 'sir,' but John. Only when we are alone, mind. We don't want the other servants getting jealous, do we?"

"No, sir—I mean, John." God, why wouldn't he stop scratching and prodding her? Why would he not be content merely with the touch of her hand? She cursed her ill-luck and Hardwicke's rampancy.

Sure of his welcome, he heaved his great bulk onto her and embraced her with rib-cracking strength. "No, no," Lucy moaned, her hips swivelling to try and elude penetration by his gross, swollen member that hung like a disfigurement from his loins. Oblivious to the genuine hatred and despair in her voice, attributing her words and gestures to a woman's natural coyness, he took a deep breath and jammed himself up against her, jarring every bone in her body. Something took possession of her then, maybe an instinct for survival, and she began to fight him, clawing his back, grazing his shoulders with her teeth, tossing her body this way and that beneath him. *Get off me! Get off, oh get OFF!* she screamed silently in her mind, summoning every ounce of her strength in an attempt to dislodge him. His pendulous stomach was squashed against her flat one, overflowing it grotesquely on either side where the surplus flesh hung down like dewlaps on a cow. The fat on his chest gave him breasts that were as full as a woman's, but unformed, mere satchels of blubber. She couldn't breathe, so compressed were her ribs beneath his bulk. She felt a grey mist forming around her and a terrible weakness stealing over all her limbs. In that moment, with a great heave of his vast hams, he penetrated her and the searing pain brought consciousness flooding back to her.

"Aah!" The cry burst from her lips as he battered his way through her internal muscles, which were cramped tight with hatred and fear. Tears sprang to her eyes and she thrashed about on the bed, panicking like a landed fish gasping for air.

"Oh, my sweet," he said, noticing her tears. "You give such a lovely ride, my dear."

I give you nothing, her thoughts replied. She clenched her teeth grimly and fought successful against the rising of her stomach, gulping down the excess saliva that preceded sickness. Pain radiated through her belly as he punched into her like a stallion, her body jerking involuntarily upwards as his uncontrolled movements thrust her off the bed. Again, she dug her nails into his flabby sides, tearing at them, leaving bloody crescents in the flesh. Far from deterring him, the perverted pleasure he gained from the pain of the wounds set his body shuddering until at last he spent himself within her. Then, still groaning and quivering, he rolled sweatily off her and reached for his tankard of rum. He gulped and passed the cup to Lucy who, although she loathed rum, took a sip to wash away the rank taste of Hardwicke's mouth.

"You're a lucky girl," he told her, picking up his discarded shirt to mop the sweat from his body. "You pleased your master." He chucked her under the chin and Lucy managed a weak, faltering smile. Wouldn't he sleep now? She hoped fervently that he would, but instead he started to kiss her anew. Misinterpreting the aghast expression that must have shown on her face, he laughed and remarked, proudly, "Yes, I am a bull, aren't I? Many mistresses before you have told me that they've never had a lover so lusty. But I'll give you time to recover, m'dear, though my seed is already stirring."

Now Lucy understood why Harriet had long forsaken her husband's bed. And as for Rachel's tales of her father's mistresses, for once, she believed the girl.

"You asked me about my wealth," continued Hardwicke expansively. "Well, little Lucy. I'm a man of two talents—and the other one is gambling."

CHAPTER EIGHT

Lucy held the brittle paper to her chilled flesh. In the guttering light of the candle she could scarcely read the closely written words, but the name "Darwin Manor" leapt off the rolled up page as if in answer to her unspoken question. Hardwicke shifted beneath the bedcovers and she stared at him anxiously, willing him to stay asleep. Then the regular rumbling snores recommenced and she breathed more easily.

Getting him to boast about his general good fortune had been simple, but she had found steering him into specific stories more problematical because he would keep saying, "You don't want to hear about that," and turning his attentions to her body instead. Eventually, though, she had managed to inject the topic of Darwin Manor into the conversation, saying that her former employer, Lady Clarence, had mentioned the fact that he owned two properties in Lancashire, Darwin Manor and Rokely Hall. She had always thought, she said, that the Darwin family owned the Manor themselves, so how had *he* come by it? He was reticent until she began flattering him and encouraging him and eventually he had recalled the night he won the deed from the elderly Earl. Lucy felt herself swamped by a feeling of outrage at the injustice, but nevertheless managed to find the words to praise his expertise at cards and added the fact that she had never set eyes on a deed before.

Hardwicke swallowed the bait. Rising from the bed, he had crossed the room, taken the key from the chest and unlocked the ornate bureau. As he pulled open a drawer Lucy stifled a gasp. So the drawer had not been locked after all! If only she had known, she could have spared herself the ghastly ordeal she had just been through! She could have taken the deed the night she had bolted up the concealed staircase and accidentally arrived in Hardwicke's bedroom. Oh, why had she not tried the key? She tortured herself with that thought, while trying to look suitably impressed by the document Hardwicke was flourishing beneath her nose. She started to take it, meaning to read it, then remembered that serving girls were not expected to be able to read and that it would be unwise to make Hardwicke think there was anything unusual about her. So, instead, she smiled blankly at it and made some remark to the effect that it was all a meaningless jumble to her.

Hardwicke replaced it in its drawer, tossed the key back inside the chest, clambered back into bed, swigged some more rum, announced his intentions of playing the rampant lover again—then suddenly, without warning, fell asleep. Lucy had to lie very quietly, gazing at him all the while, maintaining her uncomfortable position propped on one elbow for at least ten minutes before she was satisfied that he was really asleep.

Now she had the deed. In another few moments she would be dressed and ready to make the journey back to Darwin Manor, although she still had no idea how.

Her intention, as she started down the long drive, feeling conspicuously dark against the blinding whiteness of the snow, was to walk and walk, until she grew numb with cold, until she fell down and died maybe. For the cold would purify her again. Its searing knifeblade would cauterize the festering sores in her mind and body—the sound of Hardwicke's ugly words, the dull ache he had left in her womb, the bruises on her body, the terrible knowledge that she had been ravished by a man who thought of her only as a chattel, a mindless receptacle for his pleasure.

The clouds had been swept away by a bitter wind and the moon sailed high and frosty in an ebony sky, which was sprinkled with hard, merciless stars as sharp and cruel as glittering dagger points. A fox had passed the same way not long before, the prints of its pads not yet frozen. In spite of the cold that was already attacking her face, hands and feet, Lucy smiled to think of the creature hunting freely in the night. Then her smile faded as she was reminded of her own hunger. Although the emphasis all day had been on eating Christmas fare, she had been far too busy to do anything other than watch other people eat. She had visited the kitchen briefly and snatched a few scraps of turkey and goose left over from the Hardwickes' table, which had momentarily satisfied her, but the exertions of this night had left her ravenous and the cold only served to sharpen her appetite.

She knew Darwin Manor was somewhere to the right, for when Matthew had dropped her at the great iron gates, they had been on the left. No light was burning in the lodge and there was no dog to bark as Lucy slid the heavy iron bar back and swung the gate open just enough to permit her to exit. It was not until she had taken a good few steps down the slippery road that she felt alone, vulnerable and very scared. What if Hardwicke had been wakened by a bad dream and had found her absent? What would be his first reaction? To seek her in her room? And then, finding her missing, would not his first thought be to check his valuables to see if anything was gone? She calmed herself; who would dream that maid would steal a deed? Jewels, yes, and money, too; maybe even clothes—but never a piece of paper she would not even be able to read. Her second fear was that one of Hardwicke's guests might have a sudden impulse to leave at dead of night, and would pass her on the road. The snow might muffle the passage of a carriage and this thought caused her to turn her head constantly and peer into the whiteness behind her. Nothing stirred, except the wind soughing in the hedges and branches.

At times she trod the icy wheelmarks left by carriages, and at others she sank ankle-deep into crunchy snow, the surface of which was frozen just enough to prickle her ankles through her stockings. In spite of her stout shoes, her toes were soon so wet and numb that she could no longer feel them, and she recalled tales she'd been told of walkers in the snow who, on removing their socks after their return, had found that their toes came off too, snapping like icicles. Lucy had no desire to lose her toes so she kept trying to curl them and uncurl them inside her shoes, until numbing exhaustion prevented her. Soon, she was no longer conscious of moving at all. She seemed to glide, to drift like a ghost over the pallid landscape, weightless, ethereal. Soon she would dissolve and the wind would disperse her like smoke over the fields.

"Mother!"

Lucy suddenly saw Ann Swift's face a few inches in front of her own. She stretched out a hand, took a step forward and fell headlong into a drift that had piled up beneath the hedge. The uncomfortable invasion of snow down her neck and up her sleeves brought her to her senses. She had been seeing visions, the kind that visited one in a fever—except that Lucy knew she was suffering from the very opposite of a fever. If she gave in to the desire simply to lie in the softness of the snowdrift, wrap her cloak around her and go to sleep, she would freeze to death. One of her father's dogs had done that once—wandered from its kennel to be found buried in a drift the next day, a dog-shaped block of ice. No, she must carry on, warming herself if necessary with thoughts of Rory.

But annoyingly it was not Rory's face that kept on appearing in her mind, it was Philip Darwin's . . . and then, suddenly, this was replaced by the tousled hair, green eyes and cheerful grin of Adam Redhead. You stupid ninny, she chided herself; Adam is but a servant. But he knows about horses, reasoned the other voice in her brain, he's gentle and clever and sensitive. She must really be feverish now, she realized, because she could hear his voice clearly, calling her name.

"Lucy . . . Lucy . . ."

The repeated word—the word that meant *her* but was strangely devoid of connotation now, just a meaningless sound—echoed and rang as if the very trees were chanting it. She put a hand to her face, but both hand and cheek were so cold that she could feel nothing. Perhaps this was death, this losing of one's senses and identity, this confused wandering.

Aaaah! What was that? Something touched her shoulder, held it in a vice, shook it. She was a rabbit caught by a fox, too shocked to even squeal.

"I have nothing to give you," she whispered, too terrified even to turn round and face the mortal or phantom who was accosting her.

"That paper inside your bodice—is that nothing?"

It wasn't Hardwicke's voice, not that of his manservant, yet there was something familiar about it. Perhaps Hardwicke had not been asleep; maybe he had watched her through flickering eyelids, seen her glide to the bureau and remove the document. Or—Lucy hardly dared to put this frightening alternative into coherent thought—maybe someone had been inside the secret passage, watching through a chink in the secret door. In which case they might have seen not only the stealing of the deed but much more besides, the intimacies to which she had forced herself to submit and which she would want no one in the whole world to know about, ever!

"Look at me, Lucy."

It was gently spoken but it was, nevertheless, an order. Her spirit quailing, Lucy swivelled her eyes and encountered two candid green ones which gazed into hers as if seeing through to her soul.

"Adam! Wh-what are you doing here? How . . . how did you know?" Questions tumbled through her brain, each vying with the others for expression. She stood speechless, waiting for him to reply and, in those seconds which felt like hours, realized just how cold and miserable she was.

"I watched you."

Simple words, giving nothing away. How long had he been watching her, and for what reason? With as much delicacy as if he were handling priceless porcelain, he withdrew Lucy's left hand from inside her cloak, peeled off the sodden glove and proceeded to chafe it between his own large, warm hands. The pain was agonizing as feeling returned to her numb fingers. He repeated the process with her other hand and then, very gently, took her frozen face between his palms and pressed his lips

against each cheek in turn, blowing softly to bring
the life and color back into them. When this kind
action was completed, he did not release Lucy's
face straight away, but softly planted his glowing
lips on hers. She found herself responding to his
kiss, much to her surprise. He grew more ardent,
persuading her to part her lips and admit the entry
of his hot tongue. A fire was kindled deep down
inside her, sending heat coursing through her veins
as if she had drunk of a potent liquor. She could
feel that he was trembling in spite of his warm
clothing and indeed fine tremors were quivering in
her own limbs which were nothing to do with the
cold. No—this was wrong! She pulled away from
him and wrapped her cloak tightly around herself
again. She was still aware of the aches and bruises
caused by the hours she had spent with Hardwicke.
What was happening to her? Was there something
terribly wrong with her, in that men she hardly
knew had the power to engender such passionate
desire in her? Was she by nature a wanton, a slut
who would end her days in some low brothel, a
slave to her body's disproportionate demands?

"I'm sorry. Forgive me." Adam was standing
before her, his hands clasped, his head dejectedly
bowed. "I didn't mean . . . By God, what must
you think of me?"

Lucy had never heard a man sounding so
apologetic about having done something which
had, frankly, brought her pleasure. She stretched
out a hand, touched his for an instant, then returned it to her cloak.

"There's nothing to forgive. Just tell me why you

are here, and what you know."

"Let's walk. We'll freeze to death if we stand here."

Taking her arm, Adam marched her up the lane so briskly that her feet stood no chance of returning to their former numb state. His coat was roughly made from animal skins, sewn together with the fur inside, and a huge fur collar shielded his ears and face. A clump of fair curls had tumbled over his eyes and he tossed his head like a pony, to resettle his lion-colored mane.

"Just a bit further on we'll come to a gate, from which there is a track leading to a farmhouse. We'll take shelter there."

Lucy followed him obediently. Although she had no idea where he was taking her, she would be glad of warmth and shelter, and she longed for a hot drink and something to eat. Adam still hadn't satisfied her curiosity but they were walking at such a pace that she had started to feel a stitch in her side and she guessed that he was similarly out of breath.

They reached the solid door of the farmhouse. Smoke curled out of the chimney and a light was glowing through the window. As Adam pushed open the door for her to enter, she noticed a line of hoofprints which passed the door and seemed to lead in the direction of the outbuildings, but the welcoming wave of heat which caressed her body as she stepped over the threshold wiped all thought of them from her mind—until she saw the figure sprawled on a chair before the fire, highly polished boots propped on the fender. Although the head did not turn as she entered, that silky blond hair could belong to none other than—

Lucy gave an involuntary gasp. The man spun round and Philip Darwin's cool grey eyes surveyed her from head to toe.

"A brandy for the girl!"

"Certainly. I'll fetch it straight away."

Lucy was astonished to hear Adam accept Philip's peremptory order as if he were his servant. After a few moments he returned bearing a tray on which three glasses reposed, two of them brimming and one, which he handed to Lucy, containing a more modest amount of the amber fluid. Lucy gratefully downed it and gave thanks for the instantaneous warmth it produced in her body. The next moment she was mortified to hear her empty stomach emit a loud rumble. Philip laughed.

"When did you last eat?" he inquired.

"Not since yesterday—unless you count a few scraps that wouldn't have been enough to keep a dog alive!"

Her feeble joke was an attempt to lighten the rather tense atmosphere in the room, the neglected interior of which suggested that the house was seldom occupied. The air was thick with unvoiced questions and answers and Lucy's intuition detected a trace of unease, though whether this was purely between herself and Philip, between Philip and Adam, or between all three of them, she could not say. Adam disappeared into the kitchen and soon the sounds of rattling indicated that some kind of meal was being prepared. Between Lucy and Philip the tense silence persisted. She perched on a wooden stool, as close to the fire as she could get. The heat, combined with the lateness of the hour and fatigue from her exertions, made her feel drowsy but the sensation of Philip's eyes on her kept sleep at bay.

"You're thinner."

The barked observation sent her drooping head jerking upwards. She began to smile preparatory to making some harmless response, but his keen glance and thin-lipped look made her own features lapse back into solemnity. Why did he always have this effect on her? She could never relax in his presence. He made her feel supremely self-conscious and nervous so that she stumbled in her conversation and her awkwardness turned into resentment of his. Even during the weeks she had spent at Darwin Manor before leaving to begin her trials at Rokely Hall, she had felt that she needed to watch and calculate everything she said so that his incisive mind grasped the correct meaning of her words without reading any unintentional or unspoken undercurrents into them. Somehow, he gave the impression that, even as he spoke he was masterminding the whole conversation, plotting and planning several moves ahead. He must think very little of his fellow mortals, Lucy decided. Maybe that was why he had no friends, because he made people feel so small and incapable in comparison to himself. At least, that was how he made *her* feel. Yet she was still determined not to let him get the better of her. Now that she had his precious deed, she was free of him. This thought gave her confidence. Reaching inside her bodice and almost blushing beneath the strength of his penetrating gaze as she did so, she pulled out the rolled paper and handed it to him.

"My side of the bargain is completed," she told him quietly.

She noted the elegance of his fingers as he extended a hand and plucked the deed from her fingers. He did not say a word as he unrolled it and cast his eye over it as if to reassure himself that it was, in fact, the original and not a clever forgery. Then he turned to her, as unsmiling as ever, and announced, "Very well. I, too, will complete my side. You are free to go."

The realization took several seconds to dawn on Lucy but, when the truth finally sank in that she was no longer in bondage to any man or woman—neither horse traders, Philip Darwin himself, nor the tyrannical Rachel Hardwicke—joy broke out on her face. She could go home now and see her dear mother, whom she had missed so badly. Maybe she would go to London—she had always wanted to taste the excitement of the bustling capital. Perhaps she would even carry out the plan she had formed years before, of trying to trace the whereabouts of her brother Geoffrey. While these thoughts were playing through her mind, she had been staring unseeingly at Philip, a radiant gladness glowing in her features. But the pleasure and animation drained from her eyes and cheeks like wine from an upturned glass at Philip's sharp question, "Where will you go now?"

It was a question she had asked herself frequently before the peaceful, happy days at Darwin Manor had lulled her into a sense of false security. Would she ever see Martha again? Surely Philip didn't intend to open the door of the farmhouse that very night and watch as she walked out into the wild bleakness of the winter landscape in her pitifully inadequate clothes and not a ha'penny in her purse? She thought back to their bargain; there had been no mention of money between them, simply her liberty for the price of the deed. Yet, if there was any human kindness or gratitude in Philip's character, surely he would think of something to save her from a fate which would most likely see her perishing from cold and starvation?

A delicious aroma assailed her nostrils from the direction of the kitchen. She felt saliva gathering in her mouth at the thought of filling her stomach with food. She had regressed into a feral creature whose first instincts were to eat and survive. Philip Darwin was not going to stop her. If he ordered her to go now, before she had eaten, she would fight him tooth and nail. Fortunately, this resolve did not have to be put to the test, for a few moments later, Adam appeared bearing a steaming bowl of broth in which her avid eyes could spot big hunks of rabbit meat mixed with barley, herbs and vegetables.

"Poachers' broth," he told her, laughing and handing her a slice of coarse bread as an accompaniment to the repast.

She was halfway through the wholesome, satisfying meal before she looked up and inquired, "Am I the only one who is dining?"

Adam glanced at Philip, then down at his feet. Lucy's brow furrowed in puzzlement. Could they not answer even a question as simple as this? Her soup being more important just then, she returned to it, ladling it up in great spoonfuls and following each mouthful with a bite of the gritty bread. When there was nothing left but some small bones and an inedible crust, she heaved a deep sigh and felt her spirits returning to her. It was at this point that Philip uncoiled his long, lean body from the armchair and stood up with his back to the fire.

"I think an explanation is due to you," he stated, his face expressionless, his eyes half covered by his heavy, long-lashed lids. Lucy gazed up at him expectantly. There was a lot she wanted to know. "Adam here . . ." He waved a hand towards him and the head groom smiled disarmingly, reminding Lucy of the very first time she had been introduced to him in the kitchens of Rokely Hall. He still emanated the frankness and warmth which she found so appealing and she found herself recalling their passionate kiss in the lane. But this was not time for reminiscences, however pleasant or puzzling, and she hastily recalled herself to the present.

"Adam used to live and work in Darwin Manor. He's Martha and Matthew's son. We grew up together, he and I, until the Earl, my father, deemed it unfit for the youth of the aristocracy to mix with that of the serving classes, and separated us. Adam was sent over to Rokely Hall where he quickly rose to prominence in the stables—"

"But could he not have gained a better position in the house—as a steward, cellar master or even as

personal servant to Lord Hardwicke?" put in Lucy.
Adam answered her question for her.

"What? And be constantly in the company of
that dog fox and his vixen daughter? Far better to
be in the stables and out of reach of that bitch's
vicious tongue—and you know just how devilish
nasty Rachel can be!"

Lucy wasn't sure if that last remark was directed
at herself or Philip. Both of them had had considerable experience of Rachel in all her moods,
perhaps Philip more than herself.

"You weren't always in the stables, though, were
you, my friend?"

Although Philip's chuckling remark was an
aside, spoken in an undertone, Lucy nevertheless
looked wonderingly at Adam who, blushing, admitted that he had conducted a dalliance with
Rachel's maid-before-last, and it had been through
her that he had gained the information about
where Hardwicke kept the deed.

"Then she must have been acquainted with
Hardwicke's room!" As soon as she had blurted
out the remark, Lucy regretted it, seeing the mask
of displeasure that settled over Adam's usually
amiable features.

"Not more so than you yourself," observed Philip cuttingly.

Lucy hung her head in shame. She had hoped
she would not be questioned about the exact circumstances under which she came by the deed, but
it seemed Philip had a shrewd idea. Yet how dare
he even hint at criticism when it was to carry out

his bidding that she had been forced to endure Hardwicke's unutterably revolting attentions? Philip himself was solely responsible for the pain and horror she had suffered at the old man's hands.

"Adam has long been acquainted with my plans. I asked him to seek you out and watch you unobtrusively. When it seemed likely that you had the deed, which was the only reason why you were likely to leave the Hall in weather such as this, it was his job to lead you to me. And I must say that he carried out my orders to the letter," Philip continued.

Lucy couldn't stand the pleased look on Adam's face, like a dog that had been patted and praised by its master. On the two occasions when he had kissed her, he had seemed a man of spirit and initiative. Was he really a mere lackey of Philip's or was he playing some devious game, in the hope of advancement, perhaps, if there were to be an increase in Philip's fortunes? For, if Philip could afford to employ his childhood playmate, then there would be no need for Adam to spend one second longer at Rokely Hall. Suddenly, the whole atmosphere in the unkempt room seemed to rise up and oppress her. There was too much that she did not understand. She felt as if they had both, in their own ways, been using her as a pawn in some master plan of which only a small portion had been revealed to her. Raising her head high, she plucked her cloak from the back of the chair where it had been placed to dry and told Philip, with as much dignity as she could muster, "Seeing that you have no further use for me, I shall be going." Then she snatched open the door and launched herself out into the cutting wind and all-masking whiteness.

Almost immediately Adam came bounding after her.

"Where d'you think you're going? If you've got nowhere, then come back to Rokely Hall with me. I'll see that nobody suspects you of the theft. I'll find a way of looking after you, I promise."

"Back to Rokely Hall?" Lucy's voice was hollow with bitterness. Was this the "freedom" she had suffered for, the freedom to return to slavery in the service of Rachel or some other like her, or to the sweet trap of the arms of yet another man for whom she had neither yearned nor planned? She noted the hopeful expression in Adam's eyes and the truth struck her. The man was in love with her. She was not flattered by the observation, just rather sad—for him. She remembered his efforts to cheer her up at the servants' party, his tender ministrations to her freezing hands and face in the lane and the passionate kiss that had warmed her more than ten cloaks would have done. Perhaps, had she been a different kind of girl, she could have loved Adam in return. She despised herself for feeling somehow superior to him, a feeling which had not been present in her until she had watched his behavior towards Philip. That man! Whatever problem she had, the root always seemed to be Philip Darwin. How she hated him! If only he could be stripped of his cruelty, coldness and arrogance and invested with some of Adam's warmth and tenderness, why, then a man might stand before her who was worthy of her love, a man possessed of a mixture of strength and sensitivity, proud but just. But Adam was demanding an answer.

"Well? What do you say?"

"No, Adam. I could never return to that . . . that prison. I appreciate your offer, Adam Redhead, but I'm not a servant. I was not raised as one and I have no intention of spending the rest of my life as one."

A crestfallen look was starting to appear on Adam's freckled features. Would it be too unkind, she wondered, to add what she had been about to confess—that she was not in love with him and could not envisage herself as his wife? A peremptory voice cut in, taking the difficult decision out of her hands.

"Did I not tell you that Lucy is Martin Swift's daughter?"

Adam's mouth fell open and a look of respect entered his eyes. Lucy's father was a legend to anyone who worked with horses, as Adam did, and Philip's remark had done more to distance her from Adam than anything she could have said. She could tell that he was putting her on a pedestal, alongside Philip, and although it was a relief not to have to turn down his proposal, the knowledge of how much he had aroused her physically before she had discovered his innate talent for servitude made her feel irritated with him. She felt he was intelligent and resourceful enough to find a way round any kind of awkward or dangerous situation, yet here he was, mutely allowing Philip to take the lead. Philip grasped Lucy firmly by the hand and led her back into the farmhouse. Adam marched obediently after them and Lucy was afraid to look round in case she saw any trace of disappointment on his face.

"No, do not remove your cloak," ordered Philip, seeing Lucy's hand straying towards the clasp. "We are not lingering here. I have a horse outside and will take you back to Darwin Manor before an outcry is raised and your footsteps are traced to this spot. Adam will return to the Hall now. And if he is questioned, he will claim that he was out gathering firewood as the kitchen store was getting low, noticed your footprints, tracked you this far, but found nothing but the hoofprints of a horse and concluded that you had been met by somebody. They will not question any further. Adam is a trusted employee and anyone would vouch for his honesty."

Adam left to tramp the two miles back to the Hall and as the door closed on him, Lucy felt a faint twinge of regret but she had no time to wonder why, for Philip was already dousing the fire and blowing out the candles. In a few moments' time they would be heading up the hill in the opposite direction to Adam's lonely journey.

CHAPTER NINE

"Down by the Sabden Brook
He strayed both late and early.
So strange and wild his look,
His hair was black and curly . . ."

Lucy broke off her song and put down the lute on which she had been accompanying herself. She had found the instrument lying covered in dust and cobwebs in the Manor's long-disused music room and had asked Philip's permission to retune its strings and restore the neglected instrument to playing condition. Her mother, who had been a passable musician before her marriage to Martin Swift had drained her of any form of creative pleasure, had schooled Lucy in the lute, guitar and piano and had been gratified to see her daughter develop into a performer of some accomplishment. Her skills had grown as rusty as the lute strings through lack of practice over the last few months, but now that she had ample time for playing she found she could not concentrate. Every note she

played, every word she sang, sounded shallow,
hollow and devoid of emotion. She felt locked up
inside her own head, incapable of expressing her
feelings—or even of understanding what those feelings were.

"You can stay until the weather improves," Philip had told her.

Martha had welcomed Lucy back with open
arms and life continued just as it had been before
Christmas, on the surface at least..But something
had subtly changed. She was not a prisoner any
more, being kept at the Manor against her will.
Now she was an invited guest and her host was as
gallant and charming as he could be.

Now that he had no further claim over her, Philip treated her almost as a sister. He seemed much
happier now that the deed was back in his hands.
Hardwicke had paid him a visit—luckily Philip had
spotted him coming up the drive and had had time
to warn Lucy to hide in her room—and when the
fat, red-faced man had departed, utterly convinced
that Philip was as much at a loss as to the whereabouts of the deed as he was himself, Philip had
knocked at her door to tell her that it was safe to
re-emerge and they had both laughed and capered
like children, drunk with the success of their
scheme. The only thing Lucy feared was that Hardwicke had undoubtedly spread her description
abroad and she would be in constant danger of
being recognized unless she left the area completely, for the simultaneous disappearance of both
maid and document was too much of a coincidence
and Hardwicke was convinced that Lucy was the

thief. Quite apart from that, so he had confided to Philip, Rachel was making his life a misery by moaning constantly that she would never find another maid as good as Lucy. It gave Lucy a moment of secret pleasure to think that she could succeed at anything she turned her hand to—with one exception. There was nothing she could do which would enable her to stay at Darwin Manor, particularly now that the weather had improved.

The snowstorms had lasted throughout January, but with the first days of February, the ice had melted, the sky had cleared and the snowdrops had pushed their belated way through the sodden ground. Any day now she was going to have to be on her way. She didn't want the embarrassment of waiting until Philip told her to leave. It would have to be her own decison and, without money, her only recourse was to return home. Back to her father's violence and drunkenness, back to his unsuitable and unacceptable marriage plans. However, she had grown a lot stronger and more resilient since leaving home. Maybe now she could stand up to her father and defy him not with childish protests but with reasoned, adult argument. Martin, for all his faults, was not an ogre like John Hardwicke.

So, over the weeks Lucy had convinced herself that the path home was the only one she could tread, to arrive as the prodigal daughter and, she hoped, to be welcomed back without too many questions being asked. But she wasn't looking forward to leaving. Part of her reluctance was, she knew, a distaste at having to admit her own defeat and tell her parents that she was returning just as she had left, without a crock of gold or a rich husband to show for her five months of absence. She would never be able to tell them that, for a short space of time, she *had* had a husband, a man of whom they, from their superior social position, would have disapproved. She could never possibly tell them of the circumstances surrounding that strange marriage. They would never understand how she, their daughter, could have loved the wild, wandering man with the strange visions and poetic words. That would always have to remain her secret. She cried for him less often now, and had even, when thinking cynically of men in general—her father, Philip, Adam and Hardwicke—numbered Rory among them on account of his infidelity. Yet she had as good as killed him . . . She would never forgive herself for that, nor forget. If only she hadn't taken the horse that morning. If only she hadn't returned when she did and caught Rory with that girl. Perhaps, if she hadn't known of his rendezvous, they might have sorted out their problem, whatever it was, and might still be living together now, in blissful happiness. But life was full of "If onlys." Now it was "if only I could stay a bit longer at Darwin Manor . . ."

She strode impatiently to the window and peered out. It was a sparkling day with a clear blue sky and a pale sun as fresh and delicate as the underside of a primrose's petals. Lucy's heart should have rejoiced as she gazed out over the rolling parklands of Darwin Manor, yet the premature beauty of the new year was lost on her. She could see no happiness in her future, nothing to look forward to. What delights faced her at home? What joy was there in watching her mother age, her father drinking even harder? She would help her mother about the house, go visiting, and entertain in a very small, limited way, aid her father in any way he deemed fitting for a daughter. And eventually, though she could hardly bear to think about it, they would die and she would be left alone in the house, to grow old herself without even the consolation of a husband and family around her. For she would never marry again, she knew that. All men were flawed: Rory by his womanizing, her father by his drinking, Adam by his servile streak, Philip by his . . .

Oh, Philip! Lucy simply couldn't express her opinion of Philip, even to herself. It would not form into coherent words. He still disturbed her, made her uncomfortable, yet he could make her laugh, too—and at times she had caught him looking at her in a way that reminded her rather too clearly of the time when he almost raped her in the stable. He was unlike anyone she had ever met before, at times so aloof and arrogant, but at others so friendly and open. He had announced his intention of going back to the cavalry soon and that was yet another reason why she should say her farewells and leave.

As if summoned by her thoughts of him, Philip suddenly came into view, wandering round the corner of the house in the general direction of the lake. He had a brindled hound by his side, and as Lucy watched, he bent and fondled the animal's ears.

Lucy caught her breath. There was something very intimate about what she was witnessing. Unaware that he was being watched, completely off his guard, Philip was showing a warmth of affection towards the animal that she would never have guessed was in his nature. He stooped, picked up a twig and hurled it as far as he could. The barking animal hurtled after it, brought it back and laid it at Philip's feet. Then it rolled over onto its back, tongue lolling out, letting Philip tickle and caress its soft, pinkish-brown belly. His mouth moved as he spoke to it and Lucy felt her heart move, too. They made an attractive picture, the tall, slim, striking-looking young man with the silky yellow hair and the playful, adoring dog. Philip's fingers, stroking, rubbing, teasing. . . Was that how they caressed a woman's flesh, brushing the hair back behind the ears, running down the spine, sweeping over the body with such assurance and expertise?

Lucy stood mesmerized, delicious tingles afflicting the more sensitive areas of her body. Then she realized what she was doing. No, *no!* She couldn't, she *mustn't* think of Philip that way. What was wrong with her? She brushed her forehead with her hand. It was cool, yet the rest of her body felt suffused with a burning heat. What kind of a fever was it that heated the blood without mounting to the brain and producing the usual symptoms of icy shivers and a red-hot forehead? There must be *something* wrong with her. Her body seemed to be refusing to obey the orders of her brain. There was a languorous heaviness in her limbs and disturbances in all her intimate parts, the way she used to feel when Rory touched her and she knew he wanted her. But there was nobody in her room, caressing her and murmuring promises of love. All she had done was take an accidental look at Philip Darwin fondling a dog.

She left the window and sank onto the bed, trying to think of anything that might calm her and banish the aching, unwanted pangs of longing from her body. She was shocked by her physical arousal. The old worry that had first afflicted her after she'd given herself so readily to Rory, that had bothered her again after she had allowed Hardwicke to make love to her in order to steal the deed, and that had then returned when she found herself responding so readily to Adam's kisses, began to plague her again. Women were not meant to enjoy such sensations. Her own mother had told her that, in a rare moment of candor once when Lucy had inquired how her sister Helen could bear to allow her husband to share her bed. Her mother's words came back to her in full.

"A woman allows a man to bed her only in order to produce heirs. Once the bedding has been successful, any reasonable man will leave his wife alone and seek *that* kind of pleasure elsewhere, with *that* kind of woman."

"What kind of woman?" Lucy had wanted to beg. Was *she* "that" kind of woman? What was wrong with the human species, if only men were allowed to enjoy the intimate pleasures of marriage? What was wrong with her, in that she enjoyed it? Could she be a rare hybrid, a creature with the body of a woman but the thoughts and

lusts of a man? And could men see that she was . . .
"that" kind of a woman? Was this why she had
found herself in so many dangerous sexual situations, starting with the unbidden entry of her
brother-in-law into her bedchamber?

The terrible throbbings and yearnings were beginning to abate now. Lucy had herself under control again, though she was no less worried about
herself. She found herself praying that these forbidden desires would never again afflict her, and as
she prayed she thought of all those holy people, the
monks and priests and nuns. Did they ever feel like
this? And if they did, what did they do about it? Of
course, they used the power of prayer, just as she
was doing. If God could keep them from sinful
thoughts and longings, surely he could do the same
for her? Then she reflected that God probably had
much more important things to do, like stopping
people murdering each other, than stopping a
woman longing for a man.

But which man? It wasn't Rory who was featur-
ing in her thoughts now; she could have understood her feelings if she had been reminiscing
about his lovemaking. It wasn't even Adam who
had inspired these unwelcome symptoms of desire.
Again, if a lusty thought about Adam had entered
her head, she would have been able to work out the
reason, which was that Adam had admittedly
aroused her with his kisses. But Philip Darwin . . .
The only time he had ever kissed or touched her
had been in fury and revenge—except for that one
half-forgotten occasion when he had reached out
and touched her hair as she sat next to him while he

traced a map of Rokely Hall on the table top. Her
body was not a thinking organ in its own right. It
could not possibly know more about Philip than
her memory had recorded. She despised her
breasts, her loins, her trembling limbs for their unruly, insubordinate behavior.

When she and Philip dined that evening, Lucy
could hardly bring herself to look at him in case it
all started happening again. However, he was in a
morose and uncommunicative mood, with a sullen,
down-pulled twist to the corners of his mouth
which defied all her efforts to reverse them in a
smile. Leaving him to gaze thoughtfully into the
logs, she sought the company of Martha, who was
teaching her how to spin.

Fortified with home-made dandelion wine,
Martha began chattering about Adam and about
how she wished he could come back and work at
Darwin Manor instead of having to work for that
perfectly dreadful Hardwicke family. All at once
she broke off her flow of conversation, fixed Lucy
with a direct and meaningful gaze and announced,
"He asked after you, did our Adam, last time he
was here visitin'."

"You mean . . . Adam comes here?" The
thought had never crossed Lucy's mind. Of course
he must visit them. He was their son after all, and
Rokely Hall was but a few hours ride there and
back.

"Last Thursday he came. It was his day off.
'How's Miss Lucy?' he asked me. I said as you were
farin' well and he says to make sure I give you his
. . . regards."

Martha's slight hesitation conveyed to Lucy that perhaps his message had been something more than "regards." Love? She could never imagine herself marrying Adam, yet those kisses of his . . . And many was the time that she had found herself regarding Martha almost as a mother. It was strange how, before being introduced to Adam, she had not known that their surname was Redhead, having known them simply as Martha and Matthew. Did they, perhaps, view her as a possible daughter-in-law? They knew who her father was and the fact that the Swifts owned a pleasant house, a few acres of land and, doubtless, a certain amount of money, too. Their son would do very well for himself if he married her. After all, Martha knew about what had passed between herself and Rory. No doubt she now thought of Lucy as slightly tainted merchandise who would find it difficult to make a match among her social equals. In any case, who *were* the Swifts' social equals? A horse dealer, no matter how expert and successful, was still a horse dealer; and, as such, only slightly above the domestic servant class. She recalled her original reluctance to tell Martha the fact that she and Rory were actually married. Well, now she would tell her and this would place her in a different light. They would see that she was a girl who knew her own mind and would not hold with other people making plans for her behind her back.

Martha listened attentively to Lucy's tale, but with a growing look of concern on her wrinkled face. When Lucy had finished, rather than looking at her with the respectful expression she had expected, the small woman leant towards Lucy, placed a hand on hers and said, sympathetically, "I'm sorry, my dear, but you shouldn't have believed him. That was not a lawful marriage."

Lucy's head reeled. What twaddle was the woman talking? She turned on her angrily, a protest on the tip of her tongue, but Martha's restraining hand and unwavering, sympathetic gaze reduced her planned attack to a mere chilly, "What do you mean?"

"I know this must come as a shock to you, child, but has nobody ever told you that, in order for a marriage to be legal, two witnesses must be present?"

"But there was Smithy and . . ." Of course. Pat didn't count. He was the one who was actually performing the ceremony. Martha was right. She and Rory had never been married at all. And those happy weeks during which she had shared his bed —why, she had been acting no better than that wench in the tavern! Shame stained her cheeks crimson. She hung her head and stared into her lap, watching her fingers twist nervously around each other. Then, on a sudden impulse, she snatched Rory's necklace from round her neck, snapping the thin, cheap chain, and flung it into the fire. She regretted her action almost immediately and dashed towards the hearth, but Martha had anticipated her and, seizing a fire iron, hooked out the trinket on its broken chain. It was warped and twisted by the heat of the flames and the chain was blackened to a sooty thread. In its ruined, misshapen state, it seemed to symbolize Lucy's wrecked dreams and lost love. She took the tiny, spoiled thing and laid it in the palm of her hand, where it made dirty smudges. The symbolism was too overpowering for Lucy's vivid imagination to handle and she felt giant sobs come welling up from the pit of her very soul and threw herself upon Martha in a storm of sorrow.

"There, there, child. Shush, now, it'll be all right. Don't you fret yourself, 'tis all over now. He's gone, he won't come back, and what matters is that you thought you were married; that means you did no wrong."

"Do you really believe that, Martha?" asked Lucy through her tears.

The old woman nodded and continued to rock her like a baby, so that her sobs began to ebb like a passing rainstorm, leaving a strange calmness in their wake. The weeping had cleared Lucy's mind. Now she knew what had been worrying Rory so much. She could understand perfectly now how Rory, for all his impulsiveness and waywardness, must have found guilt lying heavily on his heart, knowing that he had cheated her. If he could have plucked up the courage to explain, how would she have reacted? Obviously he had expected her to be furious and heartbroken, to flounce off after denouncing him as an unfeeling, lying exploiter of innocent young girls. Yes, she would have felt this way, but not for ever. First and foremost had been her shining, wholehearted love for him, which nothing could have changed. As soon as he had expressed his desire to marry her a second time, and legally, she would have said yes and clung to him, knowing that the truest, most important thing of all was the fact that he wanted to spend the rest of his life with her as her lawful husband. Poor Rory. How upset and confused he must have been. Maybe he thought she had already guessed and that was why he had sought solace in another's body, thinking the situation was beyond hope.

Did she resent him for the way in which he had taken her in? She examined her feelings and concluded that she didn't. All she felt was sympathy, coupled with a strange sense of relief. The realization that Rory must have been suffering from a guilty conscience removed some of the burden from Lucy's soul. It was his own folly that had killed Rory, just as much as her precipitous actions.

Although she did not realize it until many months later, this moment marked a turning point in Lucy's life, the end of her period of mourning for her lost love. Whenever she thought of him in future years, it was to be with sympathy and gentle sorrow; the tearing, agonizing longing for him had gone for ever.

The next day dawned as bright as the last. At eleven, after she had breakfasted in her room, Philip sent a message that he was preparing horses for the two of them and that they were to take a ride up in the hills. Lucy's spirits bubbled with anticipation. She missed the daily riding she used to do at home in all weathers and her restless, active nature demanded regular exercise.

Without recourse to the mounting block, she

sprang in agile fashion into the saddle, clad once again in her borrowed riding habit.

"How well you look today," remarked Philip as they set out down the long, straight drive.

Lucy found herself surveying him and discovered that, in his tight white britches, highly polished boots, brocade doublet and black velvet cape, he cut a very handsome figure, added to which his grey eyes sparkled with animation and a slight flush of exertion from sitting his trotting mount accentuated the fineness of his complexion and the height of his jutting cheekbones. She felt her heart miss a beat as she looked at him, and she goaded her horse into a canter so that Philip was momentarily left behind. He overtook her in a galloping flurry and the two of them raced neck and neck towards the high, wrought-iron gates, reining in their mounts at the very last moment, in a slither of hooves.

They were still laughing and bandying words as they ascended the winding track leading to the top of the ridge which overlooked the valley. A keen wind set her gelding's hide and ears twitching as they toiled up the last stretch of pebbly pathway and paused on the top of the hill. Behind them stretched the patchwork of the valley which coiled for many meandering miles, connecting a dozen hamlets and villages and banded with the silver, snaking river. Ahead lay countless acres of nothingness, open moorland, growing more and more hilly until the hills became mountains and the valleys turned into the great lakes of Cumberland and Westmorland. To their left, half a mile away perhaps, was a hump which rose some fifty feet into the air, like the back of a giant animal, crested with a spinney of dark, gaunt trees. As she looked at it, Lucy felt a sudden shudder and sensed magic in the air, old, pagan magic which had existed centuries before Darwin Manor had been built.

Philip's laughing invitation of "Come on!" as he spurred his mount into a canter across the stony ground dispelled the mysterious, evocative mood and Lucy set off after him, keeping a sharp watch on the ground ahead lest her mount should stumble on a loose stone or slip on a patch of muddy earth.

Their route led them across a series of hillocks and dips until Philip at last slowed down in a sheltered, grassy grove. A cluster of gnarled mountain ashes, twisted and bent by the winter nor'easters, presided over the head of a clear mountain stream that fell in a miniature waterfall from the rockface, bubbled merrily through the grove and splashed among the next outcrop of rocks, no doubt continuing in this energetic fashion until it joined with the river that ran through the distant valley.

Philip dismounted and tossed the reins over a tree stump. "Look!" he said, gesturing towards some feature at ground level which Lucy could not see without dismounting herself. When she did so, she found that the object at which Philip was pointing was apparently nothing more than a heap of stones close to the foot of the tiny waterfall. She glanced at him in puzzlement, and then back at the stones. It seemed rather strange that such a variety

of stones, some obviously not native to this particular part of the countryside, should have collected
just at that spot. Something seemed to sparkle in a
shaft of sunlight and Lucy looked closer. It was
fragment of green glass from an old bottle. There
was a flash of blue, and one of red—more glass.
She looked back at Philip, wonderingly. His face
creased into a grin.

"I used to come here when I was a boy," he explained. "I tried to build a dam once, to trap the
water and form a swimming pool, but the force of
it carried away my stones every time. This is all
that was left. I often come up here. I can pretend I
am young again and all my problems just fall away
and disappear, like the water dropping from the
rocks."

Lucy was moved by his statement. Suddenly, as
she looked at Philip, she could see the small,
golden-haired lad in knickerbockers and stout
shoes, scrambling about over the stones, or sitting
beneath the ash trees pretending to be some character out of a game—a mountaineer perhaps, having just scaled the summit of the highest mountain
in the world, or a fugitive king fighting to regain
his lost kingdom. Philip kept a lot of his deep inner
self well hidden but, when he revealed it in fleeting
glimpses such as this, it touched something in
Lucy's heart.

A hush had descended on them. Here in the
hollow, the howling and singing of the wind in the
rocks could no longer be heard. The distant piping
of a chaffinch, the babbling of the stream, these
were the only traces of reality in what had become

an enchanted place where neither time nor reason existed. Surely . . . *surely* Philip would kiss her now?

But he didn't, and Lucy was suddenly conscious of the restless, ceaseless movement of the horses' teeth snatching at the short grassblades, the slow swishing of their tails and the lingering disappointment in her heart.

That night, the feelings she dreaded revisited Lucy. She tossed and turned feverishly in her bed, trying to force her mind onto other, less disturbing subjects but, try as she might, thoughts of Rachel, her childhood, and all the other subjects she grasped at and fought to hold steady in her mind simply evaporated. In their place came visions of Philip stroking the dog, Philip standing in the grove, Philip laughing, bent over the neck of a speeding horse or looking at her with that sudden, speculative, appraising expression. The vivid images crowded in and obsessed her, giving her no rest but filling her with aching yearnings and uncomfortable stirrings in her blood. Why did he affect her this way when she didn't even like him? Why should a glance from him make her head swim as if she'd drunk a whole glass of brandy? Every time she was in his presence, she tingled with awareness of him as if a million tiny needles were pricking her all over. It was not fear, she realized, that made her so nervous and self-conscious when he spoke to her; it was her admiration for him making her want to say and do only what would raise her, rather than lower her, in his estimation.

As she lay there thinking about him, a sinful compulsion began to take control of her mind. She had no idea what time of night it was—two o'clock, perhaps, maybe even three—but she knew Philip would be in his bedchamber, reading maybe, or perhaps even in bed, his yellow locks spread across the white linen pillowcase, his face flushed pink from sleep, his sinewy body warm and relaxed beneath the covers. She wanted to light a candle, creep down the long corridors in the shadowy darkness, find his room, silently open the door and offer herself to his embrace. She imagined his expression as he opened his grey eyes—those eyes whose color could change from smokey warmth to steely hardness in an instant—and saw her standing there, her tousled chestnut curls tumbling over the shoulders of her white cambric nightgown with its tiny, feminine pleats and lace trimmings. Surely his heart—and body—would be moved at the sight? He would not—*could* not—reject her.

The compulsion grew stronger. She *had* to go to him, even though she barely knew her way to his room and though she knew she would freeze in the draughty corridors. She couldn't dress, or even throw a shawl or cloak over her nightgown. It would ruin the effect of spontaneous innocence that she wanted to create.

The embers in her hearth were still glowing. Lucy thrust a candle into their midst and held it there until the wick sprouted a tiny flame. Then she left her room, shuddering as the chill night air penetrated her thin layer of clothing. Stealthily, silent as a moth in flight, she glided down the dark cor-

ridor which linked her room to the others on that
floor, shielding her candle with one hand lest a sudden draught extinguish its brave little flame. There
was an empty room next to hers, then a small store-
room which held the household's spare linen. Opposite were two more empty rooms, then the corridor took a turn to the left, opening into a hallway
at the top of the stairs. Several huge, framed
portraits of relatives and ancestors of the Darwins
frowned sternly down from their gilded frames and
an ornate French clock, a relic of the Darwins'
more affluent days, glinted elegantly from a corner
table.

Two master bedrooms opened off this hallway,
and Philip's . . . She seemed to remember that
Martha had told her it was the one on the left. No
chink of light filtered out from around the door.
He was obviously fast asleep. Lucy's heart beat
quickly as she silently moved the handle, keeping
the candle behind her so that the sudden glow of
light would not wake him up. She could make out
the silhouettes of the carved oak panel at the foot
of the bed and a heavy, imposing chest of drawers
beneath the window, but in order to see Philip himself she would have to move the candle so that its
light shone directly onto the pillow. Gradually she
illuminated the room, moving the flame an inch at
a time so that the pool of light it cast slowly en-
croached on the darkness. When the border of the
candle's glow touched the pillow, Lucy stifled a
gasp—there was no head resting there. The bed
was totally empty and looked as if it had not been
slept in at all.

Crestfallen, she closed the door and stepped out once more into the hallway. Maybe she had misunderstood Martha's instructions. Perhaps she had meant the room on the left as one ascended the staircase, rather than as one looked down it. She repeated her actions on the other side of the hall, opening the door slowly and gently and lighting the room gradually. But once again there was no sign of occupation.

By now Lucy was shaking from cold and fear and the bravado she had felt was beginning to leave her. Perhaps she should simply return to her own bedchamber and count herself lucky that she had been saved from humiliating herself by an act of fate, the fact that Philip had not yet felt the need for slumber. Perhaps he was in the study or the library, still poring over a book, oblivious to the time of night. But the compulsion to see him and make her longings plain to him swept over her once more in a raging, fevered surge that sent the blood thudding through her veins and lent her a restless energy that she would not normally have possessed at that hour. Down the stairs she tiptoed, only to find the study door ajar and the room in darkness. The library similarly yielded no occupant. She thought of the huge ballroom with its ghostly atmosphere and shuddered. Even if Philip was in there, which she doubted, nothing would take her through the door into that empty, echoing space with the drapes that wafted in the eddying draughts like the billowing skirts of spectral dancers. And she knew that the faulty catch on the door had a strange way of locking unbidden visitors in. There

were other doors, but where they led she did not
know, and she had no desire to explore them in the
middle of the night. Apart from the servants' quarters where Martha, Matthew and the cook, deaf,
crabby Meg who was so old that she scarcely had
the strength to lift the larger cooking pots, were
taking their rest, the whole ground floor of the
rambling Manor seemed deserted. Even the
brindled hound had not lifted its head and barked.
It was stretched on a mat at the foot of the main
stairs, regarding Lucy through one half-open eye.
The eye closed and the dog heaved a deep sigh and
proceeded to ignore her. Lucy paused, stroked its
soft fur, then remembered having watched Philip
do the same thing. The burning urge to find him
possessed her once more and she began to climb
the stairs, up one sweeping flight, the marble like
ice beneath her bare feet, onto the first landing,
then, on an impulse, to the landing above.

Here, the layout was almost precisely the same.
A hallway, a couple of spindly tables bearing orna-
ments, more large, sombre paintings, the subjects
of which seemed to glare accusingly at the
candlelight that was disturbing their nocturnal re-
pose, and a series of closed doors. Maybe she had
completely misunderstood Martha. Perhaps it was
on this floor that Philip slept and not the one
below. As she raised her candle, debating what to
do, an area of shadow in one corner suddenly as-
sumed the shape of a man. Lucy stood transfixed,
unable to scream, her vocal chords paralysed by
fear. The man appeared to be heavily built and
dressed in something which gleamed dully in the

weak, flickering light and, where his eyes should be, he appeared to be wearing some kind of slitted mask like an executioner. He made no move towards her and she suddenly realized that he could not. The lurker in the shadows was nothing but a rusting, empty suit of armour.

The relief she felt lent her courage and without further hesitation she walked unfalteringly towards the door on the left and pushed it open. The candle's guttering light sought the head nestling into the pillows, and found it. The name she was about to whisper died on her lips as Lucy found herself staring into two red-rimmed, horribly distended eyeballs, yellowed like old parchment, in the center of which were two milky blue discs which hypnotized her with their avid stare.

A crack opened beneath a nose on which the papery skin clung thinly to the bone that gleamed below, and a dry voice, like wind soughing through the old, dead husks in a granary, rasped faintly, "Eleanor?" Then the eyes bulged frighteningly and the living cadaver sat up, its livid flesh tinged red in the candlelight as if it were already upon the funeral pyre. The crack opened to a cavern and a sound burst from it as if a demon had gained possession of its soul. *"ELEANO-O-O-R!"*

CHAPTER TEN

"Philip . . . Oh Philip, I am so terribly . . . I didn't mean . . . I—I . . ." Lucy's words, spoken in a voice that was leaden with tears, were incoherent and were torn from her in spasmodic gasps. Philip looked ashen as he paced the floor, the green velvet jacket that was slung round his shoulders looking most incongruous over his nightshirt.

"You frightened him to death, that's what happened! He thought you were his dead wife, come to claim his soul at last. And I'm not surprised the old man was misled. If you had wandered into my bechamber dressed like that, I would have taken you for a ghost, for sure. But, in God's name, woman, what were you doing in his room? Sleepwalking? Or looking for another deed to steal? Why didn't you kill Hardwicke while you were about it? Instead, that swine is still alive and poisoning the face of the earth with his cheating and whoring, while my poor father . . ." He whirled round to face Lucy, his eyes flashing like slivers of silver, his lips taut with fury.

"Philip—no, don't hit me, *please*." Her whimper appeared to infuriate him still more as he stood over her, his hands on his hips, his hair thrown back from his stark, white face. "I—I just got lost. I couldn't sleep . . . I ached all over and thought that, if I could only walk a bit, ease my muscles—"

"A walk? Dressed like that, with no shoes? In February? You must be mad! Or else there is some sinister meaning to all this which I have yet to hear about."

"No-no, nothing s-sinister. I was . . . I just . . ."

"What were you doing at the top of the house? You knew my father's room was there and I warned you never to trespass. I told you the extent of his madness. Did you *want* to kill him?"

"No. Of course not." Lucy's words were scarcely audible. This was worse than anything else that could have happened, worse even than entering Philip's room and having had him reject her. To—to *kill* his father! She had not known that he had cared for the old man so. Now, not only was she held in the deepest possible suspicion, but he would never again look on her with that light of warm interest in his eyes. What's more, she knew, beyond the shadow of a doubt, that she would be asked to leave as soon as the sun was up.

The implication was in Philip's words, which were an order rather than a suggestion: "You had better go to your room."

Without casting him a backwards glance, she stumbled to the door of Philip's bedchamber, the one opposite the elderly Earl's and, almost missing her footing on the stairs, so blinded was she by her tears, she fumbled her way to the solace of her room, sobbing brokenly. She would never forget the way that skeletal body had levitated from the pillows, the way the clawing fingers had reached towards her, the insane look in the hideous eyes. It had been his dying shout mingled with her screams that had roused Philip and sent him dashing into the room brandishing a sword, expecting to have to beat off robbers, or else Hardwicke come looking for his deed.

When he had seen Lucy standing there in her nightshift, a dripping candle wavering in one hand, he had given an exclamation and had then brushed hastily past her and gathered up his father in his arms. He was too late. The old man's spirit had already fled to rejoin his beloved wife's in some trysting place for faithful souls. All that was left was a brittle shell, which death had drained dry. Lucy had slunk, trembling, out of the room, to allow Philip some privacy for mourning his dead. But almost immediately he had left the Earl to chase after her, and had bundled her into his own room, where the tirade of questions and accusations had started.

She lay huddled on her bed, her knees drawn up into her stomach as if to protect her against the outside world. Her right hand, stretched above her head, spasmodically gripped and released a handful of goosefeather pillow as the spasms of sobbing overtook her. For it to end like this, before it had even begun, before she had had a chance to tell Philip of her growing love for him! It seemed so unjust. She was doomed, fated. Like a sailor who shot an albatross was doomed to sail the seas forever until, bereft of water, food or companionship, life itself deserted him, so was she doomed to wander the earth from place to place, keeping neither friend, lover, nor roof over her head, until . . . until what? Until she died on the moors and her bleached bones were found, years hence, with nothing to identify them as being the mortal remains of Lucy Swift? Or until her wanton, uncontrollable desires led her to perish of some unmentionable disease in a city gutter? She would throw herself on the mercy of the reverend sisters of some convent and become a nun. That was the only thing that would save her from a whole string of stillborn love affairs.

But, even as the idea came to her, Lucy knew she was fitted by neither religious upbringing nor temperament to become a docile nun, with all her wild, volatile feelings sublimated to the love of God. As her sobs degenerated into weary gasps, and her body started to sink into an exhausted sleep, she knew that it was her immutable destiny to go home, back to Prebbledale and the grey stone farmhouse, back to her thankful mother and the calculating mind of her devious father.

Lucy had never been so wrong about her own future. Martha, dressed in black as befitted a household servant in mourning, woke her with a summons to join the new Earl in the library directly. She had completely forgotten that Philip would naturally inherit the title. How should she address him now? "Sir?" "My lord?" Obviously the casual "Philip" of the previous months would no longer do at all. For a time they nad pretended to be friends and equals, but now he was elevated to a rank way above her own. She could no longer meet and speak with him as openly and carelessly as before, even if the tragedy of the previous night had never taken place. It didn't matter now, she thought bitterly. The Earl is dead, long live the Earl, and may she be given some assistance to get speedily home.

However, Philip had his own plans—and they were far beyond the wildest bounds of Lucy's imagination to conjecture. As she walked into the library slowly and respectfully, wearing the homespun dress that Martha had given her and carrying her own old dress wrapped in a bundle, all ready for a hasty and no doubt ignominious departure, Philip, from his seat at his father's magnificent mahogany desk, barked, "And where, pray, are you going, madam?"

"N-nowhere," stammered a dumbfounded Lucy, remembering to add, "Sir."

"I may be Earl of Darwin now, but there is no need to address me like a snivelling serving maid addressing her master. We are partners, you and I, in crime, if nothing else."

The way he stressed the word "crime" made Lucy look at him fearfully. Had it all come back to this? Did he view her now in exactly the same way as he had viewed her when she first arrived at his door to deliver a useless mare? As a felon and a miscreant? His next words substantiated her worst fears.

"There is more than one crime I could get you hanged for now."

"No!" The word burst from Lucy's lips. He had no right to resurrect this old threat. She had already paid for her first crime . . . more than paid for it, if having had her body abused by Hardwicke could be counted as evidence in her favor. The only crime of which she stood guilty now was the crime of having succumbed to her longing for a particular man, the one who now sat in judgement on her.

"Be seated, Lucy." His calm, imperious tone both terrified and infuriated her. It would be so easy just to tell him her real reason for wandering the house so late at night. So easy—yet so utterly impossible. She would never let Philip Darwin know how close she had come to crawling into his bed like a common slut.

Obediently, she perched on the very edge of a hard wooden chair, still clutching her bundle. Philip's keen gaze cut into hers, his eyes hard and opaque as flint.

"Never has one wrongdoer been given so many chances to redeem herself."

Whatever it was, she couldn't do it. She would run off and go home first. How could she perform any task for him now, knowing that all she would receive at the end of it would be, not his gratitude and pleasure, but a cold dismissal and the knowledge that he felt nothing for her but distrust and withering contempt? Yet she knew she *had* to do it, whatever it was, because of the terrible hold he still had over her, now more than ever. What judge could ever assume that she, a girl of no means, had entered an elderly Earl's bedchamber at dead of night for any purpose other than that of crime? As for murder, an astute judge could no doubt ascribe a variety of motives to her presence, dressed in white and bearing a single candle, in the chamber of a man known to be haunted by visions of his dead wife. Philip had her cornered and, once again, she hated him for it. Yet the undeniable power that emanated from his stern being set something deep inside her quivering like a jelly. She loathed him, detested him, but she still wanted him, too; it was something she found impossible to understand in her confused mind.

"What I want you to do for me now is far less difficult than the last task you carried out for me, even though, God knows, the crime you committed is far greater."

Lucy bit back the retort on her lips. She was not going to tell him the truth about her nocturnal ramblings. Let him think whatever he wished.

"This time the most difficult part of the task will be performed by myself."

She looked up in astonishment. Whatever did he mean? What was the catch?

"For heaven's sake, girl, drop that bundle. You look like a gypsy selling clothes-pegs."

The insult stung her and she placed the rolled-up gown she was carrying on the faded library carpet with deliberate, insolent slowness. If she could not protest at his treatment of her in words, then she would do it with actions.

Philip appeared not to notice. "My father's death was a shock to me in more ways than one. After Matthew and I had laid him out, I spent the rest of the night going through his papers and private boxes and I received more than one very unpleasant shock. I remember telling you about my father's gambling habits, how he was so foolish that he let that damn rogue Hardwicke rob him of all we possessed: the Manor, which you know about, of course, our fortune and—" his voice softened with respect—"my mother's jewels." Lucy nodded. Philip continued: "I knew some of the jewels had gone, stolen by that . . . that *vermin* over at Rokely Hall, but I never guessed that my father had let them all go, even my mother's ring."

He paused and stared thoughtfully down at the papers that were spread over the table. The pause grew into an acutely uncomfortable silence which made Lucy wish fervently that she could escape from the room by simply melting invisibly into the atmosphere. Maybe here, as in Hardwicke's library, there was a secret door by the fireplace. Lucy turned her glance speculatively towards the oak panelling, but Philip's voice recalled her wandering thoughts.

"Saturday next. That is the night of the great ball at Bidstone House which Lord and Lady Bellingdon are giving on the occasion of their younger daughter Pamela's birthday."

Lucy felt her mouth grow dry. Surely Philip would not expect her to go to the ball? Why, she had nothing to wear except one of Lady Eleanor's extremely outmoded gowns. Besides, the Hard-wickes could not fail to recognize her.

As if reading her mind, Philip announced, "Nat-urally, the Hardwickes will be attending, especially since our dear Lord Emmett is in Manchester on business and will doubtless allow Rachel to feast her grasping little eyes on his esteemed and manly personage."

Despite the turmoil her thoughts were in, Lucy found she had to stifle a giggle at the thought of the unpleasant twosome the couple made, Rachel with her pale eyes, stringy hair and flat body and the preening, lisping, effeminate Emmett, about as at-tractive as an earthworm.

Philip, however, did not betray a trace of humor, even if he felt it. He went on: "Hardwicke will in-form Adam of the time they mean to depart, so that he can ready the horses for the journey. Adam will have this information in the morning and will then send a messenger here. That will be the signal for you to set out on a fast horse for Rokely Hall. I know what an excellent rider you are, so you can take Redshanks, my bay. How good is your memo-ry?"

He shot the question at her so fast that Lucy found herself spluttering. "Well, I . . . it depends what you mean. I—"

"Can you remember how to mix that unguent that your—"his voice adopted a sneering tone that set her bristling with anger and guilt—"expert *friends* used when they wished a horse to act lame for a while?"

"I . . . I think so." The mixing of the ointment

had to be exceedingly precise, as did the timing. Apply too little, or mix it too weak, and the animal would merely stumble slightly, then recover. Mix it too strong and the creature would fall to its knees, unable to rise until the effects of the paralysing drug had worn off. What could Philip have in mind?

"Excellent. Today is Thursday. You have two days in which to gather together the ingredients and mix your potion. Then, my little witch, you will fly on your broomstick over to the stables of Rokely Hall and apply a good, strong dose to the hooves of two of the carriage horses. I think the ointment takes about an hour to penetrate the muscles and become fully effective?"

"Yes. That is correct." How did Philip know this fact? Perhaps he had truly studied the activities of her late companions more closely than she had imagined. "How am I to enter the stables un-observed?" she inquired, feeling that it was, in truth, a most risky business and fearing for her skin, if not her life, if Hardwicke or Rachel should observe her.

"It is all arranged. It will be almost dark by the time you reach the Hall. Approach over the fields by a way which I will describe to you. A line of trees will shield you from the rear windows of the Hall. I have arranged with Adam for the gate lead-ing to the stableyard to be unlocked. He will be in the coach-house, engaging the coachmen and grooms in conversation. He will keep them there as long as he can but I would reckon you have no more than ten minutes in which to enter the loose boxes, pick out the correct horses, apply your fiendish mixture to two of them and get clear of the stableyard."

"Why two? Surely one lame horse would be sufficient? In any case, what is your purpose? Simply to prevent the Hardwickes from attending the ball?"

She knew Philip's plan had to be on a grander scale than mere spiteful pettiness, but she was so curious to hear whatever else he had in mind that she couldn't wait for him to spell it out in his own time. She wanted to know now, even if she had to appear dense and foolish in order to spur him on.

"No, no, you silly little goose. What good would that be to me? I couldn't give a hang if Rachel finally manages to lure Emmett into proposing; it's just the kind of thing she would do in order to up-stage her neighbor at her own birthday party. And equally well, what care I if Hardwicke spends the whole night whoring with some silk-clad slattern? I just don't want them to do it with my mother's jewels on their pox-ridden bodies. Surely my plan is clear to you now?"

Lucy thought that it was, but she had no desire to hazard a guess. She wanted Philip to explain it himself, because she was so enjoying his colorful vehemence in describing the Hardwickes and their habits, so she continued to gaze at him in silence, her eyes wide, inviting him to continue. Listening to him talking like this, she could almost forget that she was once more a prisoner, subject to his orders and bereft of his love.

"The ball begins at eight. Bidstone House is one

hour's fast drive from Rokely Hall. As Rachel is bound to make them late with her grumbling and her preening, my guess is that they will take the shorter but more hazardous moorland road rather than the less direct one through the valley and round the hill. I asked you to apply your physic to two horses because I could not take the risk of your picking the one horse in the entire world which was unaffected by your medicine."

"But will they not think that something suspicious is afoot if two of their best horses go lame at the very same moment?" Lucy's doubts about the scheme were increasing with every moment that passed.

"They will not have time, I assure you. They will have something far more important than collapsing horses to occupy their minds—the appearance of a fearsome, armed highwayman!"

"You mean *you* are going to rob them of your jewels? You, an Earl become a common thief?"

Philip gave a hollow chuckle with little humor in it. "I shall only be reclaiming what is my rightful inheritance. As for turning thief—it seems a very easy thing to do, which rests lightly on the conscience."

The way he looked at Lucy through half-closed lids, a calculating expression on his face, made her cringe inside. Whatever he thought, she was not a natural born thief. It did not come easily to her, as he was implying. She hated it. She feared the risk of discovery and the chance that she might forget her instructions and make some mistake. And yet there was a certain thrill about cloak-and-dagger activities which appealed to some wild streak in her, the same streak that had caused her to fall in love with Rory—and now, regrettably, with Philip, too.

"But when the horses recover . . . what then?"

"Matthew is a countryman born and bred. His predictions about the weather never fail. He says it will be misty on the moors these next few nights, and I believe him. When I appear, I shall be intoning some jiggery-pokery which they will take for a spell. Then, when I have left with my booty and the horses have miraculously recovered, they cannot fail but to believe that they met with a magician who cast some enchantment which caused their horses to stagger and fall at the very spot where he materialized."

A silence fell between them. Lucy shuffled her feet nervously, her mind filled with a thousand reasons why this latest of Philip's plans was too dangerous to undertake, for him if not for her. At length she summoned up her courage and spoke.

"Surely your position with Hardwicke is dangerous enough already? He must have boasted to his cronies about having won this house from your father. How will you explain your now having the deed to it, if challenged? And the jewels. Countless people will have seen Rachel and her mother wearing them, and I cannot believe that Hardwicke and his family will not tell of their theft by this highwayman. You will be in possession of stolen property—you could be hanged yourself!"

The irony of her statement was not lost on Philip, who smiled wryly before he replied, "I think not, Lucy Swift. You see, for all his faults, Hardwicke is a cautious man. I doubt that anyone has been told of the loss of my house. For him to have bragged of that would have scared off the other local prey of his gaming. No; he would have kept silent about the house, taking possession of it on my father's death, but with a pretence that he had purchased it from me. To have admitted that he had won it at cards would have been too alarming for his future dupes. As to my mother's jewels, I shall certainly have to avoid showing them off; I may even have to sell them abroad to raise money to keep the estate going anyway.

"But remember that Hardwicke is hated in the county, and beyond, too. Most of the families about here have lost small fortunes to him, and were he to challenge me and accuse me of theft, and were I to denounce him as a cheat and a swindler, it would be I who would be supported. You see, people do not like to admit their gaming losses, Lucy. If Hardwicke accused me of theft, he would have to admit precisely how much he had won from my father. Others would begin to realize that it was not they alone who had lost all to the wretch, and my own counter-accusation of cheating at cards would ring true.

"My belief is that Hardwicke will keep silent about his losses and look for other ways to seek his revenge on me. That I look forward to eagerly as another opportunity to better him!"

Lucy had to admit to herself, albeit grudgingly, that the plan seemed flawless. If only she could be there to see the expression on Rachel's face as the horses fell, halting the others and tangling the traces and necessitating that the whole Hardwicke family leave the coach and stand in the mud and mist in all their finery! She felt sorry for Rachel's mother, that sad, ineffectual woman whom she had no desire to harm. Philip was correct, though. The jewels were his by right and had been unfairly won from his father. She could only applaud his imaginative efforts to retrieve the Darwin inheritance. There was one thing, however, that she could not tell him, for fear that not only her future freedom but her very life would be in jeopardy, and that was the fact that she had never actually mixed the numbing potion herself but had only watched Smithy gathering herbs, boiling their essences and adding a white powder which he had purchased from an apothecary. There was only one thing she could do and that was to confide in Martha and Matthew and enlist their aid.

As soon as Philip had dismissed her and she had left the library with a misery in her heart which she tried her best to ignore, she went down the passageway leading to the kitchens where she knew she would find Martha helping the doddery old cook. When she started to explain her problem to the red-faced maid, whose brow was dripping with perspiration as she stirred a pot which hung over the roaring fire, Martha dismissed her with a wave of her hand.

"No use talking to me o' these things. Matthew's the one. He's out yonder somewhere sweeping the path or summat. He'll know what you want."

Somewhat surprisingly, Matthew *did* know exactly what Lucy wanted—and why. It was obvious that Adam kept nothing from them, no matter how secret, and Lucy caught herself wondering if perhaps, trustworthy though she knew them to be and much as she liked them, they knew more than was good for them to know. But who was she to suggest that a son should not confide in his own parents? In any case, she felt she trusted Martha and Matthew more than she did Adam. It was a wonder he didn't harbor a deep-seated grudge against Philip for forcing him to work at Rokely Hall. And yet, surely he could have taken a job elsewhere? He did not have to work at the Hall. Maybe he stayed there purely out of loyalty to Philip, in order to aid him with his plans. After all, if Philip succeeded, and wealth and property were to be his once more, would not Adam benefit also?

Matthew informed Lucy that she should leave it to him. He even offered to mix up the potion for her, but a slight niggle of distrust prompted her to thank him but inform him that just obtaining the ingredients would be sufficient. She would do the rest. She hoped he would not think that her father, the most reputable of horse experts, dabbled in such underhand and illegal practices.

She saw Philip only very briefly the following day as he was busy making arrangements for his father's burial which was to take place the following Sunday. Messages had to be sent out to relatives and old family friends and the Manor was to expect several somber and sympathetic visitors on the day of the funeral. He still found time, however, to run through the next day's arrangements in a manner which made her feel rather like a child having a lesson drummed into its skull by an over-strict teacher. She felt pathetically grateful to him for smiling at her in a kind fashion at the end of her repetition of his orders, then hated herself for feeling that way. What had happened to her pride, her self-esteem? Had they totally deserted her and left her at the mercy of a sardonic, cold-hearted man with humorless grey eyes, who only had to crook his little finger to induce her to obey his every whim? Really, she despaired of herself. She might want him, but she would never win him. Why could her benumbed brain not understand this fact? The moment her next ordeal was over, she would leave and be free of the ill-luck which had dogged her ever since she had set foot in the Manor.

Galloping at break-neck speed over the moorland path in the dangerous dimness of dusk was a joy indeed. A wild notion came into Lucy's head simply to keep on riding, right past Rokely Hall and out to whatever lay beyond—new surroundings, people who knew neither her nor her history and didn't care, being content to accept her as she was. Yet, attractive as the idea was, it would mean never seeing Philip again, and that she could not bear. Better to help him carry out his plan, which was almost like a glorified version of the games he used to play on the hillside when he was a small boy, and hope that maybe, just maybe, something would make him change his attitude towards her, bring back that warm light into his eye when he looked at her. She didn't seriously believe that, if she were to run off, he would accuse her of having murdered his father, but she did have a slight, niggling fear that, if he wanted, he was more than capable of doing so. It might not be wise to disobey him. In any case, how could she? She had no desire to run from him. She loved him, and every length her horse travelled away from Darwin Manor, the more she found herself longing to see him speeding after her.

But no figure approached in the twilight. There was nothing but still trees, rocks and gathering gloom. Ahead, in a hollow between two rocky ridges, she could see the clump of dark evergreens that marked the site of Rokely Hall.

Lucy kept to her instructions and slowly walked her horse past the line of sturdy oaks that separated the formal gardens from the surrounding land. The gate leading into the stableyard was wide open, as Philip had predicted. The messenger from Adam had reported that the greys were to be used that night, four magnificent, powerful animals which, fortunately, shared adjacent stabling. Lucy slid the bolt on the door of the first stall and the startled animal whickered softly in surprise as she stood beside it, running an expert hand down its flank before picking up a hoof and daubing it liberally with her foul-smelling ointment. The well-trained gelding made no fuss as Lucy treated each hoof in turn. Then, giving its long, dappled nose a stroke, she vacated its stable and entered the next. The second horse, however, was of a decidedly different temperament. It snorted and shied at the presence of a stranger and Lucy could not corner it to reach its hooves as it was so busy skittering from one end of the loosebox to the other. She let herself out only just in time, before the affronted beast took a nip out of her shoulder. The third carriage horse, however, allowed Lucy to do anything she wished and rewarded her with a slimy lick from its gigantic tongue which left a line of equine spittle right down one cheek.

Wiping herself dry with one sleeve, she was just stealing off to the shadow of the trees where she had left Philip's bay tethered to a branch when she heard a door opening and the sound of men's voices spilling out in the clear night air. One of them was unmistakably Adam's. Due to the re-calcitrance of the second horse, her task had taken several minutes longer than she had intended. How was she to get away unseen, now that the stable staff were milling around the yard, throwing open the gates of the coach-house, rushing around with newly polished saddlery? She was worried that the pungent smell of the unguent might still be linger-ing round inside the loose-boxes. Nobody with a sharp nose could fail to wonder at the odor and she prayed that the strong smell of the animals and their droppings would cover up the alien traces.

At last came a moment when no one was in sight. Lucy crept out of the stableyard, swung herself into the saddle and began urging her horse into a slow sidle beneath the massive, leafless trees. Suddenly her horse shied, snorting in terror, as a shadow detached itself from the rest and came to an arm-waving halt before her. Lucy almost lost her seat and had to struggle for control of the frightened animal. As soon as she had calmed it down with a pat and a soothing word, she brought it to a halt beside the figure who had caused the trouble. It was Adam.

"I kept the men talking as long as I could. You should be half a mile away by now. What happened?" he inquired.

She explained and when she had finished, he took hold of her horse's bridle, placed a hand on her knee in far too familiar a fashion, and whispered in a low, urgent voice, "Philip should never have sent a girl on an errand of this nature, especially you. You know that I care for you, and about what happens to you. How did he persuade you to come over to the Hall and put yourself in danger like this? What is his hold over you?"

When Lucy refused to answer, not wishing to incriminate either herself or Philip in any way, he continued, in the same tense, hurried whisper, "No matter. I can see that you are prepared to do anything for him. Though what Philip has done to deserve . . ." His voice tailed off. "Hasten now," he said. Stepping back, he gave her mount a hefty slap which sent it charging off in the direction of the field beyond the trees.

Lucy hung on grimly, cursing Adam for what seemed an action of mere spite and jealousy. By the time she was safely out of sight of Rokely Hall and had nothing but open hillside between herself and Darwin Manor, she had come to several more conclusions about Adam Redhead . . . and she did not like their implications in the slightest. She could understand one man being jealous of another over a woman, but there seemed to be more than jealousy involved. Far from acting the subservient slave to Philip, Adam was not only criticizing his former master, but displaying signs of positive enmity which boded ill for any plans of Philip's in which Adam was involved. Philip must be blind to trust him. Adam's allusion to some hold Philip seemed to have over her surely meant that neither Philip, nor Matthew, nor Martha had told Adam of Philip's suspicions regarding herself and the old Earl's death. Maybe Matthew and Martha were in ignorance, too. Perhaps this was one thing Philip had kept to himself. But—and this gave her a few uneasy qualms—there had been something in Adam's voice as he spoke the words, "What is his hold over you?", which implied the possibility of Philip's having a hold of some sort over Adam, too: the way he had stressed "you" so slightly that it took a sharp pair of ears like her own to pick up the significance. Or was he merely referring to the love affair which he imagined the two of them to be having? Perhaps the phrase had been mere sarcasm, and by Philip's "hold" over her, he meant a handsome face and a lusty pair of thighs, and was sick with envy at the thought.

If only he knew the truth! Yet if he did, he would be bound to try to pay court to her—and she would be bound to reject his advances once again. Better to leave him thinking that Philip and she were in love. It was at least half true.

CHAPTER ELEVEN

Matthew had been right. Philip took up his vantage point on a hill overlooking the moorland road in a chilly swirl of mist that grew thicker by the second. It was too dark to check the time by his father's heavy, gold pocket watch but he guessed it must be somewhere in the region of a quarter past seven. Any time within the next half hour he might hear the Hardwickes' coach come rumbling up the steep track, hear the voice of the coachman and the crack of his whip as he urged on the toiling horses, while Rachel screamed from inside the rattling vehicle, "Hurry up there, coachman, we're going to be late!"

His horse moved restlessly beneath him, seeking an escape from the damp, bitter wind, and Philip's hands were numb on the reins by the time his lonely vigil was rewarded by the sound of an approaching carriage. He spied the yellow flare of the lamps, illuminating the hindquarters of the horses . . . But something was wrong. Instead of the four greys he had been led to believe would pull

268

the carriage that night, there were only two, plus
two chestnuts. What had gone wrong with his
plan? The silly bitch must have mixed the ointment
wrongly, causing the other two greys to fall lame
before leaving the stables! A rich stream of curses
left Philip's lips. He could not believe that such a
simple strategy could possibly have failed. Here
were the Hardwickes, a mere quarter of a mile
away, with his jewels, boxed up inside the coach, so
close, so nearly within his grasp and yet so impossible to retrieve. When would he get another
opportunity as perfect as this one?

He shrank back, merging into the shadows of a
clump of trees as the Hardwicke's equipage drew
level with him, fifteen feet below. The driver's whip
lashed out and curled round the flank of one of the
rear horses which put on a sudden spurt so that, for
a moment, the carriage jerked diagonally across
the path before resuming its rhythmic forward
trundle up the stony track. A streamer of mist
curled around the hillside and blanketed the road.
It was impossible for Philip's eyes to penetrate the
dank opacity, but he knew that, by the time the
patchy mist cleared, the Hardwickes would be out
of sight around the next hill. He patted his horse's
neck and gave the impatient animal the signal to
walk. Horse and rider picked their way carefully
over the rocky ground and had just descended onto
the level surface of the road when a tremendous
crash and a barrage of hoarse shouts and curses,
mingled with piercing female screams, caused them
to stop in their tracks. The ears of Philip's mount

flickered to and fro and Philip himself strained to catch the sounds through the darkness and deduce their cause.

Quickly, he guided his horse off the road again and plunged up the hillside. The veil of mist shredded and parted before him and there, stationary, a short way ahead of him, was the Hardwicke's carriage, two puzzled coachmen arguing over the body of one of the leading greys which was sprawled on its belly, unable to rise. The whites of its eyes were rolling in a terrifying manner and its flanks were shuddering with the effort of trying to regain control over its paralysed legs. Philip mentally took back all the imprecations he had hurled at Lucy. His prayers had been answered after all.

Without a moment's consideration of whether or not Hardwicke or his attendants might be armed, he drew his pistol from his belt and, with a shout of, "Ho, there!", urged his horse towards them at a fast canter.

Harriet Hardwicke pressed her hand to her chest and seemed about to faint at the sight of the armed, masked man who was wrenching open the carriage door. The color drained out of John Hardwicke's ruddy-hued face as he splutteringly protested that they were carrying no money or valuables. Philip gestured with the barrel of the pistol towards the necklaces and earrings that the two women were wearing. Harriet snatched off her earrings, lacerating one ear lobe in her haste to hand the delicate amethysts to the dangerous-looking villain who was standing there in such menacing silence. Then, without any urging, she handed over the ruby necklace and rings. Without a word, Philip pocketed the jewels, then turned to Rachel who was regarding him with a look of icy, imperious disdain. He moved the mouth of the pistol close to her neck, but still she refused to hand over the gems, with which she had proposed to dazzle Lord Emmett that evening, to a common highwayman. Philip was forced to speak to her.

"Unfasten those trinkets you're wearing and give 'em to me."

He spoke in a rough, grating tone, to disguise his voice as much as possible. Rachel's eyes were fixed on him in such a penetrating stare that he felt she was stripping him of his mask and would announced to her parents at any moment that the audacious robber was none other than her former betrothed.

"Do you want me to kill you, pretty lady?" Philip inquired harshly, jabbing the end of the pistol barrel into her neck, just below the ear, in which dangled a flashing emerald surrounded by small diamonds.

"Do as he says, daughter. This blackguard will only shoot you if you don't." The remark emanated from Hardwicke, who was crouching in cowardly fashion in the far corner of the carriage's interior, ignoring the moans of his wife who was slumped next to him, a lace handkerchief held to her mouth.

"Then shoot me, scoundrel," invited Rachel, regarding him coolly and insolently.

His pistol still fixed against her neck, Philip
raised his left hand and brought the full force of its
leather-gloved might crashing down onto Rachel's
right cheek. She screamed and clapped her own
hand over the fiery fingermarks that scored scarlet
streaks across her sallow skin. With one tug, Philip
wrenched the necklace from round her musk-
scented neck, stuffed it into his pocket to join the
rest of his booty, then, with twin tweaks, plucked
each earring in turn from her ears. Rachel was
wearing white kid gloves, beneath which Philip
could detect the bulging outlines of the jewels she
wore on her fingers.

"Your rings," he ordered, pressing the gun still
harder against her neck. "It would give me great
pleasure to shoot you—all of you," he added, cock-
ing the trigger with a click which made Harriet
squeal and press her hands over her eyes.

Philip's slap had shaken Rachel's nerve and she
made no delay in drawing off her gloves and tugging the rings from her square, mannish fingers.
She handed them to him, pouring them in a jin-
gling heap into the palm of his hand. Scarcely letting his gaze leave Hardwicke and Rachel for an
instant—their maid had swooned the instant he
had entered the carriage and Harriet was only
semi-conscious—he selected one, a large emerald
on a gold band, the mount of which was fashioned
like two hands meeting around the stone, then let
the rest trickle through his fingers like so many
fairground trinkets onto the carriage's dark floor.
He removed the gun and Rachel immediately sank

to her knees and began scrabbling about, retrieving them. Philip noted with satisfaction that the marks he had left on her cheek were beginning to turn into purple bruises, which would doubtless ruin her chances of receiving a proposal that evening.

Bidding the company a cheery "Adieu!" he slammed the door of the carriage closed behind him. The coachmen were nowhere to be seen. He made to mount his waiting horse, then noticed that the grey carriage horse was beginning to make a wobbly ascent from its prone position. Remembering his promise to Lucy to mutter spells and incantations, he raised both arms high in the air as he imagined a true sorcerer would do and, in a loud voice, intoned the first nonsense words that came into his mind.

A sudden ear-splitting report from behind him took Philip by surprise. He hurled himself sideways just as a bullet whistled past, grazing his shoulder in its passage. Thoughts pelted through his brain at thrice the normal speed. As soon as he hit the ground he kept on rolling, clutching his shoulder so that his would-be assassin—one of the coachmen, no doubt—would think him seriously wounded. Wincing as his body collided with dozens of sharp rocks and projections, he directed himself towards a thick cluster of gorse bushes and, shielding his face against their myriad thorns, burrowed into the center of their thick stalks, where he found himself in a natural hollow, with the prickly twigs spreading above him and around him in a protective shield.

He could hear distant shouts, and the scrunching

of feet over the hard, pebbly ground. He held his breath as a pair of boots strode over to the very base of the clump of bushes where he had taken refuge. The boots paused awhile, then turned and began to move slowly away, and Philip noticed with great interest that affixed to the gleaming leather were a pair of very distinctive silver spurs. Cavalry spurs, they looked like, although it was impossible to tell for certain in the darkness. As soundlessly as he could, Philip squirmed forward on his belly, wriggling like a snake around the thick, twisted gorse stems. His eyes had not deceived him. They *were* cavalry spurs. If he were not mistaken, they were the very pair which he had given, three years earlier, to Adam Redhead.

Lucy paced up and down, unable to rest. For the third time, she made a circuit of the rooms she had come to know so well, the library, the study, the long, elegant drawing-room, the banqueting hall, even the deserted ballroom, with Philip's hound trotting docilely by her side. Finally she sank exhaustedly into a chair in the drawing-room and rang the bell for Martha or Matthew to bring her some food and drink to sustain her during her long vigil. "Dear dog," she said, fondling the hound's silky ears. "You're not happy without your master, are you?" The animal gave her a mournful glance from its liquid brown eyes in reply. "Where is he, then?" she murmured, rubbing the short hair at the back of its neck. "Do you think you could find him?" The animal shifted half an inch closer to her, as if for comfort. Sighing, Lucy removed her caressing hand and informed the animal, "No, I'm not very happy, either."

The dog sank down with its heavy head on its forelegs and gazed morosely into the fire. Lucy envied that ability to relax, that capacity for waiting, and wished she had some of the animal's patience. The door opened and Matthew came in bearing a mug of hot posset, some delicious freshly baked bread and an assortment of cheeses and cold meats. He placed them on a small table at the side of her chair, then asked meaningfully, "Master not home yet?"

"No, Matthew. I have no idea where he could have got to."

Did Matthew know about the "robbery?" How much had Philip—or Adam—told him? The same uneasy feeling which had affected her after her meeting with Adam that evening stole over her again. Matthew knew something; she was sure of it. He was implying that something might have gone wrong with Philip's plan. Yet, at the same time, he was not giving anything away. Could he and Martha suspect Adam's loyalty to Philip? If this was the case, why had they not intimated their suspicions to Philip himself? Of course, they were Adam's parents. Their loyalty towards their son came first. Yet she could tell that Matthew was worried and unhappy. He lingered in the room as if trying to make up his mind whether or not to tell her something. Then, abruptly, he walked out, leaving Lucy staring unseeingly at the steaming cup of untasted liquid in her hands.

The uncomfortable, prickling sensation in her bones warned her that Philip was in some kind of danger. Either that, or his scheme would fail owing to something as simple as Adam having persuaded the Hardwickes to take the longer, safer route to Bidstone House after all. She had no reason to suspect that Adam wished to harm Philip physically in any way. Maybe she was building it all up in her imagination and Adam was still Philip's trustworthy servant, in which case she was doing him a grave injustice. Yet she knew that Adam loved her, and that, when in love, people were capable of doing strange, out-of-character things. She herself was guilty of several extraordinary aberrations from her normal behavior. What else could her easy acceptance of her "marriage" to Rory have been? Her commonsense told her that there was no point in going out searching for Philip, but on the other hand she knew that, if another two hours passed without his return, she would not be able to prevent herself from saddling a horse, lighting a lantern and scaling the hill track which Philip had taken earlier.

The clock on the marble mantelshelf chimed ten. Where *was* he? Had he himself been apprehended by a genuine robber up on the moors, who had stripped him of his jewels and horse and left him to walk the tedious distance back to Darwin Manor on foot? Or had Hardwicke or one of his attendants been armed, in which case Philip might be lying dead or injured on the lonely hillside? She could not bear the suspense. Swallowing a mouth-

ful of her now tepid drink, she placed the cup
beside the untouched food, left the warm room and
set out for the side door leading into the
stableyard, with Philip's dog bounding joyfully at
her heels.

There were now only three horses living in a
stable which had once held twenty or more:
Philip's young, fast bay, a chestnut and a docile
hack on which Martha rode to market. Philip had
long ago returned the useless mare which Lucy had
brought him to a local horse fair, where it had
brought a far lower sum than the unpaid fifty
guineas which he had used as bait to trap the horse
traders. She paused and stroked the velvety nose of
the friendly piebald hack, then a fusillade of barks
sent her whirling round—to see Philip riding into
the yard.

Lucy's first instinct was to run to him, but dis-
cretion sent her shrinking into the shadows.
Watching him secretly like this gave her a strange,
excited feeling such as she had felt the day she had
observed him playing with the dog. There seemed
to be something slightly stiff about his movements
as he dismounted from the saddle—or perhaps it
was just tiredness. He led the chestnut hunter into
its stall and unsaddled it himself, rubbed it down
with a cloth and fed and watered it, while Lucy
cowered in an empty stall, hoping the dog would
not seek her out and advertise her presence. She
was lucky. The faithful animal preferred the company of its master and did not once come whining
around her hiding place.

Having attended to the horse, Philip approached

the Manor by the same side door which Lucy had used. She gave him a few minutes to get safely inside and out of sight of the door, then followed. She wondered if he were already looking for her and decided that, if that should be the case, she would tell him that she had been in the music room, where surely he would never think of looking at past ten at night. She re-eneetered the deserted drawing-room, where her discarded meal was still lying. Philip's return had released her appetite and she took a slice of the wholesome bread, buttered it and placed a piece of delicious cold ham on it, which she was halfway through eating when Philip's sudden arrival in the room interrupted her.

She looked up in surprise as, without a word, his face totally expressionless, he deposited a pile of glittering gems in her lap. She exclaimed in delight as the firelight worked magic on their faceted surfaces and brought out the rich, warm glow of old gold, and the delicate sheen of silver.

"So, your hold-up was successful. Long live highwayman Philip, the peril of Pendleton Moors!" Lucy's gay words were greeted by a brief smile, which flickered across his face and faded almost instantly.

"Yes, I have the jewels," he replied briefly. "Not without a great deal of worrying and wondering if you had let me down when you visited Rokely Hall."

"I? Let you down? How could I? Matthew brought me all the correct ingredients and I mixed that ointment perfectly."

"Ah. Matthew." A look of interested speculation crossed Philip's strained features, but he did not venture to explain the reason for his exclamation. "I was waiting on the hillside above the road," he continued. "The Hardwickes' carriage came along on schedule, but with only two greys pulling it. The other two were chestnuts. I deduced that you had mixed the potion wrongly and that the two horses you had, shall we say, 'interfered with' had collapsed too soon and had had to be replaced."

"No, I—" Lucy was not given a chance to justify herself. Philip, standing before her with his back to the fire, seeking to drive out the night chills from his bruised and aching bones, insisted on carrying on with his story of that night's endeavors. He was not the relaxed, friendly man he had been for the past few weeks, but more like the Philip of old, cold, distant and inscrutable.

"The carriage passed me and I was about to relinquish my plans and come home instead when one of the greys fell. In the resulting turmoil, I was able to persuade Harriet and Rachel to hand back my possessions."

"Do you think there is any possibility that you could have been recognized by them?" Lucy inquired, fascinated by Philip's account, yet puzzled by his lack of enthusiasm regarding the regaining of his prized heirlooms.

"None. I wore a mask and disguised my voice well. I have no doubt but that they took me for the very creature I was trying to be, a highwayman."

Although they did not know it, both Lucy's mind and Philip's were obsessed with a single name: Adam Redhead. Philip did not tell Lucy of the shot that had missed its mark, nor of the way in which he had been forced to hide until the marksman had given up his search for the wounded or dead body. He especially did not tell Lucy of the reason for believing that the man who fired the shot was Adam, nor of his suspicions regarding Adam's motivations for the crime. And Lucy, in turn, refrained from telling Philip of her unsettling conversation with Adam earlier that evening, and the unease she had felt on talking to Matthew. Her reluctance stemmed not from a desire to protect Adam in any way, but from the fact that on no account did she want Philip to know of Adam's confessions of love for her. She knew Philip was not the sort of man to be spurred on by the knowledge that he had a rival. She wanted him to feel that the way was clear for him to love her, if such a thing were possible. He was certainly not displaying any particular affection towards her at the moment.

"I had the satisfaction of striking a blow."

The relish with which he related this unexpected piece of information dragged Lucy out of her uncomfortable reverie.

"Oh?" she inquired. "Against whom?"

Philip's face split in a wide grin and for a second some warmth shone through, like the sun piercing thick clouds. "Rachel. I thought you would be pleased to know."

Lucy's delight at hearing that the cruel, haughty girl had received a blow in payment for all those she herself had meted out to innocent victims in the past gave her a satisfaction that was tempered by her disappointment in Philip's attitude towards her. Surely now he could afford to relax and show some kind of generosity of spirit? He was the Earl now, he had his deed back, and his jewels. She thought the least he could have done was to have called for some wine. A minor celebration was definitely in order. But Philip's chill, rigid air persisted.

"I would like you to choose something in payment for having helped restore my house and my jewels to me," he announced, indicating the items still reposing in Lucy's lap. "If you see nothing there which takes your eye, I have some of my mother's less valuable, but perhaps prettier baubles upstairs. I shall bring them. They may be more to your taste."

"But Philip!" Lucy looked at him in amazement. She had never expected him to make her such a handsome gift. "These jewels are so exquisite, so grand. When would I ever find the occasion to wear something so splendid?" The fine stones were worthy only of being seen at Court, not within the lowly confines of the parish of Prebbledale which is where she now knew beyond the shadow of a doubt that she was bound. Her duties here were over, it was obvious.

"Then sell it. Buy yourself some new dresses," snapped Philip impatiently.

Lucy recoiled at his words and his tone. Why

had he suddenly turned against her like this? Did he honestly believe that she had caused his father's death? He was waiting for her to make her choice. One item stood out from the tangled mass of jewellery in her lap and that was the large, curiously designed emerald ring that she had last seen adorning Rachel's hand. She picked it up and held it out.

"With your permission, I should like to take this ring."

"*No.*" Philip's eyes flashed with unaccustomed fire as he focused on the object in Lucy's hand. He took it from her, then, seeing the disappointment in her face, explained apologetically, "I am sorry. I had momentarily forgotten that ring was there. It means something very special to our family and I am afraid that I cannot let it go. You can have anything else, but not that ring."

There was nothing else she really wanted. Something about the ring had captured her imagination; the other jewels, even the fiery-hearted rubies, seemed lacklustre and uninteresting by comparison. In the end, she picked out a pair of delicately wrought amethyst and silver earrings. She knew they would not fetch as much as gold and diamonds if she were to try to sell them, but neither would they raise very much comment if she were to wear them; they would serve as a reminder always of the months she had spent at Darwin Manor, and of the man she loved but whose love she could not gain in return.

Philip approved of her second choice and gathered up the rest of the jewels, bidding her a curt goodnight as he took them up to his room where no doubt he would lock them away with the deed and what few other valuables he possessed.

Lucy was left sitting disconsolately by the dying fire. Apart from those dreadful few days before she had come to terms with Rory's death, she had never felt so low and dispirited in her whole life. She cursed Fate for having allowed her to be seen by Philip in the worst of circumstances. She had come to him as a cheat and a thief, and was leaving as a suspected murderer. Add to that her borrowed, ill-fitting clothes and there was not much to admire and love about her, either inside or out. By now Philip must be desperate to see the back of this awkward guest who had long outstayed her welcome. Yet what about all the help she had given him? He would never have regained either the deed or the jewels if it had not been for the aid which she, and only she, had been in the unique position to give him. For him, she had suffered the cruel gibes and blows which Rachel had hurled at her, the outrageous mauling at the hands of John Hardwicke which still made her feel physically sick and disgusted whenever she thought about it, torments of fear, near death in the cold on the night she left, and Adam's embarrassing proposal, to say nothing of the danger she had endured that very day.

Surely Philip was aware of everything she had gone through on his behalf? Or was he really so cold and self-centered that he could use anybody to fulfill his purpose and then discard them without a second thought?

She remembered that hot, almost lusting look
which had come into his eyes on that very first afternoon when, wearing his mother's beautiful silk
dress, she had joined him in the banqueting hall.
She had seen that look again on an odd occasion
since then, such as that moment when they had
been standing by the waterfall and Lucy had been
certain that he wanted to kiss her but was holding
himself back for some reason. Yet maybe she was
totally wrong. Maybe the only kind of "wanting"
Philip was capable of was the sort she had almost
experienced at his hands when he had dragged her
into the stable after she had delivered the mare.
Perhaps he had no finer feelings at all . . . And yet
her intuition told her that there was a great deal of
tenderness and sensitivity in his character that, for
some reason known best to himself, he preferred to
conceal. He was an enigma to her. She refused to
give up and slink back to the Swifts' farm and the
dreary future she knew would be hers until she was
absolutely certain that no vestige of affection for
her dwelt in Philip's heart. Her pulses raced as she
realized what she must do. She had failed in her
last attempt to visit him in his room, but this time
there was no dying, hallucinating old man to stop
her. She had nothing to lose, so there was nothing
of which to be afraid.

Lucy's hands were trembling as she stood in her
bedchamber lacing herself into that same exquisite
pink dress which had evinced such an admiring
look from Philip when he had first seen her in it.

Dressing in such a complicated garment without the aid of a maid was difficult, but she did not wish anyone to know what was in her mind. How shaming it would be if she were discovered tiptoeing up the stairs to his room when she was supposed to be tucked up in bed in the nightgown which Martha had laid neatly out on the bed for her. She brushed her chestnut curls until they shone, then tightened the tiny clasps of the amethyst earrings on her ears. Her neck felt far too naked without an ornament round it, as the neckline of the dress plunged so deeply. The necklace Rory had given her was too badly damaged to be wearable. She would have to go to Philip as she was and he would have to understand that she had no jewels apart from the earrings he had given her. Besides, she needed him to want her for herself, not for her surface appearance.

The thought of being close to Philip, of yielding herself up to him, filled her with quiverings of anticipatory desire. Once again, she recognized those now familiar feelings in her body, the sensations she dreaded and yet, on this occasion at least, welcomed. She wanted to show herself to Philip as a passionate woman, to respond to his caresses with the wild abandon that was natural to her, not with decorous sighs and maidenly protests.

Taking just one candle with which to light her way, Lucy stole out of her room and down the passageway, quailing at the loud rustling made by her skirts and hoping the sound would not alert any listening ears. When she reached the second land-

ing, she paused. Suddenly, the audacity of her actions struck her. Was she not cheapening herself in
Philip's eyes by carrying out her bold plan, and behaving no better than the slut who had seduced
Rory in the inn? No, she was not going to seduce
Philip, rather put both of them in a position where
he could, if he wished, seduce her. She would tempt
him with her mere presence in his room, but nothing else.

Her heart hammering like the hooves of a speeding horse, she reached for the door handle and very
slowly turned it. A lamp was lit inside the room.
Philip was seated at a desk, reading. He looked up
in open-mouthed astonishment as the swish of
Lucy's dress advertised her presence. She felt a hot
blush break out all over her face and neck as she
stood there in a dress which was a blatant invitation to any hot-blooded man. Philip scraped his
chair back and got to his feet, gazing at her in a
silence which was heavy with unspoken thoughts
and wishes. He took a small step towards her and
she licked her lips nervously and felt a sudden desire to run pell-mell from the room. Why, oh why
had she subjected herself to this embarrassment?
She felt like a fairground freak being gawped at by
curious but uncaring eyes.

No, do not weaken. Be brave, she told herself. *He
is not sure why you are here. You must tell him, or
show him*. But what could she say? All at once she
found herself in sympathy with every man who had
ever been in love and, through tradition, had been
faced with saying the first word, making the first

move, and risking heartbreak and rejection. Yet, no matter how much she wanted to, she could not tell Philip Darwin that she loved him. But if she could not tell him . . .

Her feet carried her forward on a wave of reckless courage. She was face to face with him, feeling that her body and soul lay naked in his unwavering gaze. She stretched out one trembling hand and brushed the silken sleeve of his shirt—but the instant she touched him he sprang away from her and leapt towards the window, where he stood gazing blankly out at the dark night which shrouded the Manor.

Lucy waited, her feet and tongue paralyzed. Surely he would say something? Would he not even speak her name, ask her the reason for her unexpected visit? He did not move, just stood with his back to her, ignoring her. A rush of tears sprang up from deep within her. Stifling a sob, she turned and fled from his room, just as she had fled from it such a short time before. And, as then, she retraced the same dark route back to her bedchamber, stumbling and weeping as she had done on that previous occasion, but now feeling that her world had truly ended. That last time she had preserved a shred of hope that maybe, when she had expiated her so-called crime, she would regain a favored position in his eyes. Now she knew she meant nothing at all to him—if, indeed, she ever had.

Not only Philip, but the whole of Darwin Manor was rejecting her, telling her she did not belong to its world but should return to her own lowlier one.

She had aspired too high. How could she ever have dreamt that an Earl could feel anything more than either friendship or base lust for the daughter of a horse dealer? She had found her match in Rory, she knew that now. For all her pretensions to being a lady, her ability to read and write, to sew and draw, to grace social events with pretty talk and play simple melodies on a piano or guitar, nothing could alter the fact that she was a girl of no breeding, not fit to make a match with a gentleman of quality. Philip was too polite to point it out to her, that was obvious, but now she knew her station. Why else had he forced her to play such menial roles in the working out of his schemes? Because he thought her fit to play the part, not only of Rachel's serving maid, but also of Hardwicke's whore. Ugh! A shudder of pure self-loathing gripped her body and almost made her want to vomit. He had used her, and now he was finding it embarrassing to dismiss her. Well, she would spare him the trouble of saying the words. By the time the next day dawned, she would be gone.

CHAPTER TWELVE

The pink silk dress, now an object of Lucy's burning hatred, lay on the bed in a careless heap, its pleats and folds creased and disordered. Lucy sighed to herself as she knotted the last lace on the old, stained dress which she had worn the day of her arrival at Darwin Manor. She wished to leave the house with no more than she had brought when she came—with the sole addition of the earrings which she knew she would be unlikely to be able to keep in her possession for long, unless Prebbledale was much nearer than she had imagined.

She was about to douse the lamp and find her solitary way out to the stables when she remembered Martha. The motherly old woman had been so kind to her that Lucy could not possibly disappear for ever without bidding her goodbye, even though it was now nearly midnight. She rang the bell to summon her, and when the bustling little woman finally entered the room, wearing a nightgown and shawl, Lucy silenced the questions which were on her lips by announcing, "As you can see, Martha, I am leaving. I regret not being able to take the lovely dress you gave me, but unfortunately I find it bears too many reminders of episodes I would prefer to forget." She looked at Martha's glum face, and felt herself softening. "I'll never forget you, Martha, and your kindness. And Matthew, too. I wish . . . I wish I could stay, but unfortunately . . ."

What could she tell her that would convince the woman that she was doing the right thing? Martha took the opportunity of Lucy's silence to ask the question she was obviously bursting to ask.

"And where, pray, might you be going?"

Smiling wistfully at her and hoping the signs of her recent weeping did not show, Lucy spoke the one word, "Home." Then she added, "Please tell Matthew I shall take the chestnut but I will see that it is returned as soon as possible."

Martha's eyes held hers for a moment in a searching gaze. Then, giving her arm a squeeze as if to say, "Be brave, girl, everything will turn out all right," she left the room.

There was no moon that night but the stars were out in a clear sky. Lucy was not sure in which direction Prebbledale lay, but something told her she should take the hill road. Really, she decided, it did not matter how far away her home lay, thirty miles or a hundred, so long as, by dawn, she had put as much distance as possible between herself and Darwin Manor—and the temptation represented by Philip himself.

Letting her horse pick its own way up the pebbly track, she allowed her mind to wander and found that, in her imagination, she was in Philip's bedchamber, eavesdropping invisibly on his thoughts. Almost immediately, she stopped herself doing it. These were not Philip's thoughts, but her own make-believe. She would never know the way he really felt about her. What point was there in speculating?

Maybe he had never bothered to think about her at all, except in terms of the things he wanted her to do for him. If only she could stop aching for him like someone who had been separated from her lover! There had never been anything between her and Philip. Why could she not wake up and realize that it was all in her own head? Why did memories keep returning and torturing her, reflections of their friendlier, happier moments, recollections of the humorous remarks he had made which had caused her to laugh, and, in particular, memories of that day by the waterfall, and the evening when he had reached out and touched her hair?

She was mortified to find her thoughts straying to that morning in the stable when he had displayed such violent passion towards her and had only been prevented from raping her by the untimely arrival of Rachel. If only he had displayed one ounce of that same passion earlier that evening! And, if Rachel had not arrived when she did, might not one taste of her body have led him to desire another? No. She must shut out these thoughts, ban them from her mind. That chapter of her life concerning Darwin Manor and all that passed therein was over. She had to forget, for the sake of her own sanity.

"*What* sanity? Am I not already completely mad to be thinking about Philip this way?" she muttered with a hollow chuckle, not realizing she had

spoken aloud until she noticed her horse flicking it
ears. All sanity had deserted her. She *was* mad–
mad for a man who cared not one jot about her o
her future happiness.

She reached a crossroads on the lonely path. I
was too dark to read the signpost, so she let he
horse plod on, not caring where it was taking her
letting the reins lie loosely in her curled fingers.

Suddenly, without warning, the whole worl
seemed to tip up. The signpost described a somer
sault before her eyes and she found herself flyin
through space, to land on her side with a jolt tha
knocked all the breath out of her. Her horse, whos
rearing had been the cause of her dizzying fligh
and undignified landing, was standing panting b
the side of the road. Lucy could see no reason fo
the steady, well-mannered chestnut's un
precedented behavior but, as she lay gasping
trying to get her breath back and work out wher
or not she had sustained any injury, the though
came to her that crossroads were notorious amon;
the superstitious as being haunted places wher
witches met and hanged men reappeared. Animal
were gifted with the second sight. Perhaps he
mount had seen or sensed something which her les
sensitive human senses had failed to recognize . .

Her arms seemed to work all right. She move
her feet and ankles, then her legs. They, too
seemed whole. As she sat up, she felt a stab of pai
in the shoulder on which she had landed, and brief
ly closed her eyes as she gave it a rueful rub. Whe
she next opened them, she screamed aloud in terro
and alarm, for a dark-clad man was standing in th

road, looking down at her.

She scrambled to her feet but stood no chance of running away for, with two swift strides, the man was at her side, gripping her arm. As he drew closer, she recognized the familiar features of Adam Redhead.

"You! It was *you* who made my horse rear and throw me. Why did you not make me aware of your presence instead of appearing like a ghost?" Fear and shock had made her angry, as relief flooded her being. Perhaps Adam could set her on the right road for Prebbledale and home.

"You were not riding sidesaddle like a woman. With your cloak wrapped around you and your collar turned up like that, you could have been anybody, perhaps even a highwayman. In the better weather, when there is more traffic about on these hill roads, highwaymen are a frequent hazard." He smiled at her and she began to relax. At least Adam cared for her and would not allow any harm to come to her.

"Then, if this spot is dangerous, what are you doing here alone, so late at night?" she inquired.

A guarded look came into Adam's eyes. "I . . . I have somebody to meet," he explained, not very satisfactorily, his eyes scanning the darkness all around them. Then, hauling his gaze back to Lucy's dishevelled, muddy figure, he asked, with a sudden tone of concern in his voice, "I forgot. You may be hurt and it will be my fault. Are you all right?"

"I think so," replied Lucy, trying to laugh. "No bones seem broken."

"I am glad. Now perhaps you can tell me where *you* are bound at such an hour. Who was the unthinking person who allowed a young, pretty, defenseless woman to stray alone on the moors at night?"

"I suppose you could accuse Philip Darwin of that breach of etiquette," said Lucy lightly, and regretted her words the instant she saw the vicious expression that drew back Adam's lips in a feral snarl.

"That arrogant, callous toad!" he exclaimed venemously. "I hate that man more than I hate the Devil himself!"

Lucy felt the blood draining from her face and she stared at him aghast. This was not the soft-voiced, willing valet who had deferred to Philip in such a servile manner, the man she had scorned for seeming weak and feeble-spirited. This was a creature driven by bitter hatred, the reason for which she could not begin to guess.

"It was he I was looking for, that cheating cur of a brother of mine. I meant to kill him, but he escaped me. I know he is here somewhere. Just one movement, one rustle in the bushes and I will have him!"

Lucy's eye lighted on the carved handle of a pistol protruding from Adam's pocket and felt a stab of terror. She did not understand. He said he hated Philip, and in the next breath he was talking about his brother. Yet Philip had told her that Adam was an only child. A slow, unwelcome suspicion began to dawn in her mind. The fair, silky hair of exactly the same shade, although Adam's was a mass of wild curls whereas Philip's was straight; a slight similarity about the nose and the set of the jaw. Could it . . . ? Could they . . . ? She did not even have time to ask herself the question. Adam's lips closed on hers with crushing force and her bruised shoulder ached in protest as he clutched her to him so tightly that the breath almost left her body for the second time that evening. Unlike the gentle kiss in the snowy lane, this one was determined and merciless, stabbing her lips with hard teeth, wrenching her jaws apart to admit his searching, choking tongue.

Lucy fought against him, trying to push him off, but some demonic strength possessed him and the more she struggled, the more he tightened his grip until a red mist swam before her eyes and she felt herself becoming limp in his grasp like a half-strangled animal. Feeling her resistance weakening, he pushed her onto her back in a clump of dead bracken that crackled beneath her as she fell.

"He's taken everything that is mine, the house, the jewels . . . We made a deal, but he has no more right to them than I. Why should he live a fine life in the Manor, when *I*, the son of Lady Eleanor, am forced to slave for the Hardwickes, waste my noble blood in servitude?"

His hand was struggling with Lucy's dress, pushing beneath it. His weight was pinning her down. She could not escape. His hand had found her breast now and was squeezing it, and his hoarse breath was rasping close to her ear, while his eyes were wide and white-ringed like a madman's.

"'Jewels, money, let them hang. Let *him* hang! I

shall kill him, sooner or later. And then I shall have the Manor—and you as my lady!"

His hands began to work their way over Lucy's body with a furious speed. She drew up her knees to try and throw him off her, while her hands clawed at his face and tore at his hair. She screamed, beat at him with her fists, kicked out with her feet, and suddenly his attack slacked as if the struggle had exhausted him and drained the strength from his limbs. With one push, Lucy was free and Adam lying unmoving by her side. Had he had some sort of fit? She had heard of this sort of thing happening to people who were unbalanced and who overspent their strength. But there was no time to lose—he could recover at any second. Scrambling to her feet, Lucy set off down the hill to where she had last seen her horse . . . and had gone but two steps before she came up against something solid and unmoving, but unquestionably alive—the silent, terrifying bulk of a cloaked and masked man.

The scream died on her lips as a hand was clapped across her mouth. Now she could see plainly what had befallen Adam. A heavy tree-branch lay beside his head and his light-colored hair was stained dark with blood.

"Your money and your jewels, pretty lady," demanded the man, in a thick country accent which held the trace of a sneer. "Come on now, me lovely lass. Your jewels and your gold—or you'll wish I'd never saved ye from that lusty scoundrel over yonder."

Lucy thought quickly. She had no money, only

her amethyst earrings to hand to the highwayman
—but what would she do without them? This thief,
he must have known hard, penniless times in his
life, or else why would he have taken up this way of
life? Thinking she could plead with him and
awaken his sympathy, Lucy pulled back her cloak
to reveal the old, ragged dress beneath. "Please
sir," she pleaded, "if you have any pity in your
heart, spare a poor girl. See my clothes? I have no
money, no valuables at all, not even a home to go
to." The latter was almost the truth; her father's
small-holding certainly did not feel like home. "I
thank you for what you did to save me," Lucy
added, still hoping to appeal to his better nature, if
he possessed one. "But now, having preserved my
life and my virtue, could you not simply release me
and let me go my way?"

He laughed, a low cruel chuckle which froze the
blood in her veins, then thrust his hand into the
small pocket inside her cloak. When he withdrew
it, her two earrings were dangling from his fingers,
the silver gleaming in the dim glimmer of starlight.

"So you wouldst lie to me, would ye, you un-
grateful little bitch?"

"No! Please . . . I am sorry . . . I didn't mean to
conceal anything from you." Now he had discovered she was lying, what fate would lie in store for
her? Whatever it turned out to be, she would accept
it calmly and philosophically. She had been
through too much already. Her fighting spirit had
flown. She felt weak, exhausted, beaten. Maybe
this was no more than she deserved, a lonely, degrading death, half-raped by a madman, robbed

and stabbed by a highwayman. She had brought it on herself, just two days earlier, when she had lain sobbing on her bed and had imagined the sight of her own bleached bones lying on the moor. She had inflicted a death-wish upon herself and there was nothing she could do to prevent it happening.

"I . . . I n-need those j-jewels," she stammered, through chattering teeth. "They're . . . they're the only thing I have. I am on a long journey. I shall s-starve if I c-cannot sell them."

Her words appeared to make no impact on the surly figure who had her wrists imprisoned in his strong hands.

"Please . . . You have my only possessions now. Will you not l-let me go?"

"Yes, me little spring filly. When I've 'ad me fill o' those pretty lips o' yorn!"

Her lips, already bruised and torn from Adam's brutal attack were covered by a pair which were warm and surprisingly gentle. *But,* she thought, *any minute now and it will be like Adam all over again* . . .

She closed her eyes to blot out the hideous sight of the leather mask that shielded most of the man's face from her view, and tried to apply her trick of being able to shut off her senses and withdraw from her surroundings. But the feeling of cold metal against the fingers of her left hand made her gasp and jump. The man must have drawn a knife from his belt. Was he about to threaten her into submitting to him? Or was this, after all the dangerous situations she had been through, the most final of all, the one she would not survive? She could almost feel the blade now, slipping between her ribs, filling her with agony so that her thoughts, her memories, all the things that made her the individual human being she was, came draining out with her blood. Perhaps, if she were to remain very, very still and not annoy him . . .

There was that sensation of ice-cold metal again. He was not moving as if to cut her, however, but was pressing something against her hand. It could not be a knife, there were no sharp edges. Now he was fumbling with one of her fingers, doing something to it, trying to force something against it, over it. Was it some kind of instrument of torture, a thumbscrew perhaps? Her hand was suddenly freed and she snatched it up to her eyes . . .

The tight, restricting object around the third finger of her left hand was a large, ornate ring. In the darkness, she could just make out a design of clasped hands around a many-faceted stone.

As she opened her mouth to cry his name, Philip removed his mask. Lucy could not speak, she could not think, all she could do was look, feast her eyes on the embodiment of her longings, while her fingers moved, testing the unaccustomed weight of the unfamiliar ring. Had he followed her simply to give it to her, because he knew she coveted it? Or had he suspected that Adam might be up here at the crossroads? Then Adam's words came back to her. He had arranged to meet his brother, he said—but he and Philip *could* not be brothers. It did not make sense. A sudden groan reminded her that Adam was still in the vicinity, and obviously still alive.

"Here, help me." Philip was kneeling by Adam's side, calling to her.

He was busily tying Adam's wrists behind his back, before the stunned man could recover enough to make a dash for freedom, and he motioned to Lucy to secure Adam's ankles, offering her a piece of halter rope which he had obviously brought out of the stables with him. Finally, Philip fashioned a gag from his leather mask and, with the cheery observation of, "Don't want him shouting his head off and waking the whole valley up, do we?", he slung Adam's body over his shoulder as if he had been a bag of potatoes, then lifted him across the back of his bay horse, securing his helpless body to the saddle with some extra lengths of rope.

Lucy's chestnut was some way down the hillside, cropping at the bracken. Philip called its name and the obedient animal cantered up to him and stood rubbing its head against the front of his cloak.

"You'll have to carry two, I'm afraid," Philip informed it. Bidding Lucy mount first, he swung himself lightly up behind her and they set off down the path, leading the bay with its awkwardly balanced human load behind them.

"What will you do with him?" Lucy asked, nodding her head towards Adam's inert body.

"He tried to shoot me this evening."

"Oh, no!" gasped Lucy, leaning back and feeling the protective strength of Philip's body behind her. So her earlier suspicions had been correct. Philip *could* have been lying dead on the hillside at precisely the time she was looking at the clock and worrying about him. The chestnut stumbled under its double load and Philip twitched the reins to pull its head up, and tightened his embrace on Lucy in the process.

"Are you going to . . . Will he be hanged?"

"How can I deliver him up for justice when his only crime was attempting to shoot a highwayman who was holding up his employers' coach?"

"Oh." Lucy fell silent. She had not thought of that. Philip was truly in a very awkward and embarrassing position. Then the question that had been uppermost in her mind came back to her, as they turned a bend in the track and she spied the dark patch of trees that shielded Darwin Manor from the winter winds. "Is he really your brother?"

Philip heaved a deep sigh, as if she had touched on a subject which brought him great pain and suffering.

"My half-brother, I suppose you could call him."

"But . . . Martha and Matthew . . ."

"They are not his parents. But we shared the same mother."

Lucy let a shocked gasp escape her lips. A philandering father, especially an Earl, she could understand—but for a gentle, beautiful, and, by all accounts, delicate woman to give birth to a bastard! She could not believe it.

"I realize that it sounds like a sordid story, but it is a sad one, too, if you will permit me to tell it."

They still had a mile or so to ride before they reached the Manor gates, and Lucy was only too eager to listen to this tale which she knew would explain so much about Philip, about Adam, about the strange, haunted atmosphere of Darwin Manor.

"You have seen the painting of my mother that hangs in the banqueting hall?" Lucy nodded. "All the men adored her, particularly my father. I was born and father, partly out of respect and partly I think out of fear of damaging her fragile health, refused to share her bed for quite some time. My mother was very fond of music and dancing. When I was three months old, she insisted that a ball should be held, where she could show me off to her friends and celebrate my birth. However, something went wrong. Rather than fêting my birth, my mother found herself celebrating the conception of my half-brother."

"Do you know who Adam's father was?" asked Lucy, full of sympathy for all of them, the beautiful, wayward mother, the jilted, loving father, Philip, the lonely boy deprived of a mother, and even poor, obsessed Adam.

"I believe he was a young army officer, the cousin of one of the titled guests who brought him along as he happened to be home on leave after a campaign. Shortly after his . . . dalliance, he went back abroad, and was killed in a skirmish. My mother was not in love with him. In fact, she was full of remorse, and begged my father for forgiveness. He, with his pride hurt so badly, refused to give it. My mother moved to the top floor of the house and she and my father did not speak to each other until after Adam's birth, when it was obvious that she was dying. Seeing her so ill, my father at last forgave her, but it was too late. He never forgave himself for his unyielding attitude towards her. It preyed on his mind. He refused to remarry after her death and became totally possessed with her memory."

"So it was Adam's birth that killed her. What became of him?"

"My father would have nothing to do with Adam. He refused to adopt him or acknowledge him in any way, so Martha and Matthew, being childless themselves, brought him up as their own son. One day when I was seven or eight, I forget exactly when, I let slip in a boastful moment that, if only my mother had not been so wicked, he would have had a share in the Manor and all our possessions. My father, you see, had made the mistake of telling me the truth when I was really too young to understand the significance of it.

"From that moment onwards, our easy friendship turned into a kind of rivalry. Then, when we grew older, Adam developed a kind of fawning admiration for me which I could not bear. My father and I decided it would be best if he were sent away from the Manor. The position in Rokely Hall became vacant, Adam was fond of horses, and so it was all arranged. He continued to treat Martha and Matthew as if they were his true parents, because he knew that, without them, he would have been cast out by my father to fend for himself.

"When I decided to take up a commission in the cavalry, Adam begged to be allowed to accompany me. I refused and I think that it was at this point that his heart really hardened against me and he

became determined to usurp my position at the
Manor."

"But . . . did you not suspect his change of
heart?"

Philip lapsed into silence and did not answer
Lucy's puzzled enquiry. His silence persisted for
the rest of their journey, throwing Lucy back on
her own worried thoughts. Why was Philip bringing her back to the Manor? What was to become of
Adam—and of herself, for that matter? And why
had Philip made her the gift of the ring? Guilty
conscience at the way he had treated her? Why,
too, had he seemed not a bit surprised to see her up
on the moor, and for what reason had he dressed
himself as a highwayman in order to meet Adam?
These and a dozen more questions occupied her
thoughts until their horses' hooves rang on the
cobblestones of the stableyard.

"Wait here," Philip ordered her. "I will fetch
Matthew and Martha to take care of Adam."

Lucy felt very nervous about being left alone
with Adam who, bound and gagged as he was, was
making strenuous efforts to free himself of his
bonds. She could not look at him, remembering the
startling change in his personality from gentle
wooer to raging demon. He was making grunting
sounds, like a wild animal, and she was terrified in
case he should suddenly escape from the ropes that
held him and try to kill Philip or herself. The appearance of Matthew, followed by Philip and
Martha, put an end to her fears. Seeing them,
Adam appeared to calm down. He was untied from
the saddle and helped down. His ankles were un-

bound, enabling him to walk, although Matthew and Philip kept a tight, restraining hold on his arms.

As soon as they were alone, Martha turned to Lucy and inquired, in a nervous whisper, "Has he told you?"

"You mean, told me about Adam?" asked Lucy in turn.

"Yes."

"A little. I know he is not your son, and that he was jealous of Philip."

"He loves you, you know. I think that's what finally turned his mind."

Lucy looked at Martha with a horrified expression. To think that those feelings went so deep that they had finally tipped the balance between envy and revenge—murder, even! And all the while Lucy's own thoughts had been concentrated totally on Philip. No wonder Adam hated him. To him, Philip must seem like a malicious enemy, standing in the way of everything he desired for himself. Adam was not blind. He must have noted the expression on Lucy's face and the tone of her voice when she talked about Philip. And that worst jealousy of all, jealousy in love, had set his brain boiling with murderous intent.

She suddenly became aware that Martha was weeping. Great, silent tears were sliding down her wrinkled face and Lucy put a comforting arm around her, just as Martha had, in the past, done for her.

"They'll hang him or put him in Bedlam. Poor lad, he's just not right in the head. All those years

I cared for him, since he was a little 'un. We loved him, Matthew and I."

"There, there. Come on," murmured Lucy consolingly. "I'm sure Philip will not insist on anything so drastic."

"But Adam tried to *murder* him!"

Martha broke down in fresh sobs and there was nothing Lucy could do but wait quietly until Matthew returned and led his weeping wife into the house. It was very cold and Lucy stamped her feet to try and warm herself up. She did not know what to do, whether to follow the two servants back into the house, or wait until Philip reappeared and settled her fate for her.

She retreated into the main stable building, where the body heat of the horses and the bulky bales of straw provided some protection from the chill night air. As she stood there, idly stroking the bent ears of Philip's bay, the horse's owner strode into the building, a lantern held high in the air.

"Oh, there you are. I was wondering where you had got to. I thought maybe you had slipped off again, like you did earlier this evening."

There was a slightly challenging tone in his voice which made Lucy raise her chin defiantly.

"You looked for me, then?"

"Yes, I came looking for you. Your room was empty and Martha, after a great deal of prompting, I may add, told me that you had gone. I must say that I had my own suspicions as to where—and somehow your home didn't enter into them."

"But I—"

Philip's voice interjected: "It so happened that I

knew who else was out roaming the hilltops this very evening."

Lucy's mouth dropped open and she flew hotly to her own defense.

"You didn't think for a moment that I . . . ? That Adam and I . . . ?"

"Look at it my way, Lucy Swift." His voice was firm and did not betray any clue as to what light he was now regarding her in, friend, waif or traitor. His gaze was level, his face expressionless. Her legs felt weak and she sank down onto a hay bale. "That night Adam brought you to the farmhouse. You left and he followed you out. I was right behind the door. I heard his offer and I did not hear you turn him down. Not in the way a disinterested woman would slap down an unwanted wooer. Oh yes, you put up a modest showing, full of maidenly protests. You did not wish to return to the Hall, you did not wish to pass your life as a serving maid. But I did not hear you tell Adam that you could not go with him because you did not love him, or were in love with somebody else."

During this speech Philip's eyes had begun to flash with animation. His level tone had deserted him and an odd suspicion formed in Lucy's head. He sounded almost like a jealous lover—but no, it was impossible. Still, she kept him under acute observation as he continued his speech.

"I thought nothing more of your . . . *alliance,* until the strange business with the horses. That is when I decided that you and Adam were in league to foil my plan. You had told him which horses had received your treatment, he had made sure that

two others were substituted to pull the coach, and
Adam's plan was then to kill me, claiming ignorance of my identity. He would then collect a
sizeable reward from the Hardwickes for having
beaten off the robber and saved their lives and their
jewellery, and he would return to Darwin Manor,
hoping that he would have the nearest claim to the
property, and could inherit both it and the title and
make you his wife."

Lucy burst out laughing at this absurd suggestion. Her laughter turned into near hysteria and
she fought to regain control of herself. Finally,
wiping the tears of mirth from her eyes, she looked
up at Philip who was regarding her with some ir-
ritation.

"And what is so funny, pray? Can you not see
how it all seemed to fit into place?"

"B-but . . ." Lucy's voice was still tremulous
with laughter. "If you really suspect me of such a
plot, why are you telling me all this? I should be
wherever Adam is, tied up like he is, awaiting trial
by a judge and jury."

"My darling Lucy, I had only to eavesdrop on
your surprise meeting with Adam on the moor and
witness the way he treated you to know there was
no liaison between you. And when I saw him attack you, I wanted to kill him. It would have been
so easy! But then I would have had blood on my
hands which I would have been forced to explain.
And when it came out that he was my half-
brother . . . Well, judges never quite know how to
deal with family matters. I would not like to guess
how it might have gone for me."

"Why did you come after me in a highwayman's outfit? And why did you not reveal who you were straight away, instead of playing out that ridiculous act? I must admit, though, your accent was most convincing!"

"Eeeee, thank 'ee kindly, ma'am!"

They both burst out laughing, quite spontaneously. In the glimmering light shed by the lantern, Philip looked years younger than he had seemed earlier that evening. The strained, tense lines had melted from his face and he looked quite boyish, although there was still a slight air of unease about him that Lucy could find no reason for.

Suddenly, the laughter was gone from his face. Sitting down beside Lucy, he hung the lantern on a hook on the wall behind them, and laid his hand on her arm. Instantly, she felt her muscles tense, and an excited thrill run through her. So her feelings for Philip still persisted, after all her attempts to eradicate them!

"I shall tell you why I was dressed as a highwayman. Firstly, because that was how Adam expected me to look. He had not seen me steal away, long after his shot had been fired, and after the Hardwickes' carriage had gone on its way. He still thought I might be lying somewhere, wounded. My plan, if I did not find you first, that is, was to leap out and surprise him."

"And what were you intending to do with me? Shoot me?" She gave him a sidelong glance and saw him bite his lip, as if trying to force himself to say something he did not altogether wish to say.

"No, Lucy. Not shoot you." His grip tightened

on her arm and two of his fingers strayed to her wrist and began to stroke it, absently at first, but then meaningfully, sending agonizing shivers of desire for him coursing through her veins. "I was going to give you a fright and kidnap you, and not reveal until later that your abductor was myself."

"Why ever not? Do you think I would have been upset or displeased?"

"I did not know. I hardly dared expect that you would have welcomed it—that you cared for me, or felt anything for me."

Lucy could not believe she was hearing the words he was speaking. His expression was full of doubt and hope. He was waiting, for a word, a gesture, an expression of encouragement.

"Philip, if you only knew . . ." How could she tell him of all those hours of torment she had been through, wanting him, loving him? She still could not say the words she wanted to say, so she asked instead, "Whatever made you think I did not care for you?"

His reaction was instantaneous. Words of guilt and remorse burst from his lips as if he had been storing them up for weeks.

"After the way I treated you in the stable when we first met? And the things I made you do for me? How do you imagine I felt? Like the most unworthy, low creature that ever lived! I denied my feelings for you, I hid them, but I could not let you go. You do not honestly think that I thought you had murdered my father, do you? It was all I could think of to keep you with me a little longer, so that I could see you and be near you. I felt that after

that terrible experience in his room when he died,
you might go running off, and I could not bear it.
I might have seemed callous and cruel, Lucy, but
. . . I am terribly slow to realize things about people. It took me years to recognize the truth about
Adam. Martha and Matthew could see it, but I was
blind. And I was even blinder about you, Lucy. It
took me so long to realize that . . . that I love you."

There was a strange singing noise in Lucy's ears,
and a weightless, uplifting feeling in her body, as if
she were about to float right up to the ceiling. As
Philip lowered his lips to hers, Lucy raised hers to
meet him. Their mouths mingled, their kiss grew
more passionate. Lucy raised her arms to encircle
his strong, firm body, and encountered the new
ring on her finger.

"Philip?" she murmured. "This ring. Why would
you not give it to me when I first wanted it?"

He reluctantly drew his lips from the soft
warmth of Lucy's neck and replied, "It is a family
custom of ours that the emerald ring is worn only
by the wife of the Earl of Darwin."

"Then why have you given it to me?"

Lucy felt she already knew what he was going to
say, but could not possibly believe that he would
say it. His voice spoke the very words her heart
yearned to hear him say. Yet even as he spoke
them, she wondered if, maybe, she were not a witch
who had placed the thought in his head and written
the lines he was to speak. With a feeling of unreali-
ty, she heard him say, "Because I want you for my
wife. If you want to be, that is . . ."

Her heart was too full to allow her to speak. She

planted her lips on his, moistened them with her tongue, then opened her mouth to him, drawing him down to her, allowing his hands to roam freely over her body. At first he responded passionately, then broke off, looking around him and murmured worriedly, "Not here. We must go back to the—"

"Why not here?" Lucy gazed at him, knowing her love for him was shining out of her eyes.

"Because—oh God, Lucy Swift! I've wanted you for so long!"

"Then why wait any longer?"

His answer was to take her in his arms and push her firmly back against the hay bale. His lips closed on hers, his hands swept her body, awakening vibrant surges of desire that radiated from her loins to the outermost reaches of her body, like the intense, scorching rays of an August sun. She felt his body quivering with a need that corresponded to hers.

"You're right, my darling," he murmured, as his seeking hands slowly smoothed her skirts away from the trembling warmth of her thighs. "Why wait any longer?"

The earth rocked and explosions of ecstasy sent shooting stars bursting through her brain as he moved his body over hers.

More Fiction Bestsellers From Ace Books!